A Typical Family Wedding

LIZ DAVIES

CHAPTER 1

'You *did*?' Beverley clapped her hands with joy. She had sensed that a proposal might be on the cards, and she'd had a feeling last night was going to be it.

She had been about to fill the kettle for her morning cup of tea when Ron came downstairs, but all thoughts of breakfast fled as she absorbed the wonderful news.

Ron nodded, bending down to ruffle Pepe's ears. The poodle absolutely adored him, and the dog closed his eyes in ecstasy and tilted his head to the side.

'I take it Annabelle said yes?' Beverley thought she had better check, even though Ron was grinning fit to burst.

He nodded again, clearly too overwhelmed to speak.

Beverley helped him out. 'Did you take her somewhere nice? What sort of ring did you get her? Ooh, I hope you did it properly and went down on one knee!'

'If you'd let me get a word in edgeways— Oof!'

"

Beverley launched herself at him, her eyes filling with tears, and she sniffled into his shirt as his arms came around her. 'Have you set a date?'

'Not yet. We'd like to get married within the next six months, though. There's no point in delaying it.'

'I'll need a new hat,' she sobbed.

'Not if you don't want to wear one. It's not compulsory,' he said.

Beverley drew back in disbelief. 'Of course I will! *Helen* will be wearing one.'

'Ah.' He nodded his understanding.

Wiping her eyes on the sleeve of her dressing gown, she added, 'I bet it won't be one of those fascinating things, either. It'll be a proper hat.' She wrinkled her nose. 'And knowing her, it'll be bigger than anyone else's. Think satellite dish and you'll get the picture.'

She could envisage it now, and it wouldn't be beyond the realms of possibility for that damned woman to want to upstage the bride. Mind you, May, the bride's mother who also happened to be Beverley's sister, would probably have a good go at that, too. May had never been backward in coming forward.

'Will Helen *want* to come?' Ron wondered doubtfully.

Beverley snorted. 'She definitely will. That woman won't want to miss a chance to dress up and lord it over the rest of us mere mortals.'

'So you don't think she'll be there purely to help us celebrate our marriage?'

'Don't be daft.' Beverley had a wicked thought. 'You don't *have* to invite her if you don't want her there. It's not as though you and her are best buddies.'

'I suspect Annabelle might feel obliged.'

'I don't see why. She hardly knows the woman,' Beverley retorted.

'She knows Kate, and we did all go on holiday together last summer.'

'If it had been up to Helen, you wouldn't have been allowed to come,' she reminded him.

Ron gave her a squeeze. 'But it wasn't up to her, was it? It was up to you.' The man who she had come to regard as a son, kissed the top of her head and she hugged him fiercely. 'Did I ever thank you?' he asked.

'What for?'

'If it hadn't been for you insisting on me coming along, I wouldn't have met Annabelle.'

Beverley simpered. Ron was right in that respect, and she felt rather smug to think that their romance was down to her.

Releasing her, Ron said, 'I'd better be off. Got an appointment with a collie who has barking issues.'

Pepe gave him a baleful stare, as though he knew Ron was about to give another dog the attention which he deemed to be rightfully his.

'What about breakfast? You can't go out on an empty stomach,' Beverley protested.

'I'm not hungry,' he replied.

He was probably too excited, she thought. 'At least have a cup of tea.'

'I'll grab a coffee on the way. What are you getting up to today?' Ron asked, heading to the door and patting his coat pocket to check he had his keys.

'This and that.' Beverley's reply was airy but vague. She didn't have anything much to do, apart from the usual chores of washing up her breakfast things and running the vacuum cleaner around.

Abruptly she realised that when Ron and Annabelle moved in together her world would probably shrink, and a wave of sadness threatened to spoil her mood. She would miss him dreadfully, although she would never tell him so. Unlike her arch-enemy Helen, Beverley wasn't one for guilt-tripping, and she would do nothing to taint Ron's happiness.

Following him to the front door, she stood on tiptoe to give him a peck on the cheek. 'I'm so happy for you. You and Annabelle make a lovely couple,' she declared, and Ron grinned, joy shining out of him.

Beverley closed the door after he'd gone and leant against it. She was happy for him, but she couldn't shake the feeling she was losing him. She had come to regard him as a son since he'd moved in with her over a year ago, and the old proverb that a son is a son until he takes a wife and a daughter is a daughter all her life, popped into her mind.

She snorted. Tosh! Ron would never neglect her just because he had got married. He wasn't that sort of a man. That he looked on her as a mother (he had lost his own several years ago) was a source of endless wonder to her, and in her heart Beverley knew that wouldn't change.

'Uncle Ron is getting married,' she told Pepe, who was eying her with concern – although Beverley was under no illusion that his concern most likely stemmed from the fear he might miss his walk if his mistress didn't stop moping about and get a move on.

He whined and pawed at the door.

'I'll take you for a walk in a minute,' she told him. 'Stop nagging. I've got to have a wash and get dressed first.' She might even put some lippy on. It seemed a lippy kind of day.

'I don't suit hats,' she mused aloud, as she went into the bathroom, weddings and headwear still on her mind. 'I bet Helen does.' Pepe followed close behind. She knew he didn't understand a word she said (she wasn't that daft) but since he was a puppy she had got into the habit of talking to him. She guessed she'd be talking to him an awful lot more once Ron moved out.

Beverley peered at her reflection. The face gazing back at her looked rather miserable, so she tried on a bright smile for size. It felt wrong.

'May looks good in a hat. Tell me the truth, Pepe: if you didn't already know, would you think we were sisters?'

Pepe stared up at her.

'I didn't think so.' She turned away from the mirror. 'My sister reminds me of Helen sometimes. She can be a stuck-up, snotty cow, too. And before you get on your high horse, I bet if you could speak you would call her names, because she doesn't like you one little bit. And neither does Helen. Never trust someone who doesn't like dogs, that's what I say.'

She opened a drawer in the cupboard next to the wash hand basin, took out her make-up bag and rifled through it, looking for a lipstick that didn't clash with her lilac hair.

She quickly gave up.

Beverley didn't possess much make-up and what she did own was old and past its use-by date. A bit like her.

It was the thought of Helen in all her perfectly made-up and manicured perfection that had led Beverley to consider putting some slap on today. It wasn't something she normally did, but her daughter's mother-in-law brought out the worst in her. She hadn't taken to the woman the first time she'd clapped eyes on her, and she hadn't changed her mind over the years.

The feeling was mutual. Helen couldn't stand the sight of Beverley, either.

'Bugger it,' she announced. 'Who's going to care if I'm wearing lipstick or not? I know I shan't.'

Pepe wagged his tail in agreement.

'You love your mama just the way she is, don't you?' she crooned, bending down to scoop the dog up and rain kisses on his furry black head. 'Who is mama's bestest boy?' she murmured, as the poodle wriggled in her arms.

She put him down and he darted out of the bathroom. Seconds later he was back with a bright red leather lead in his mouth, his intention unmistakable. Pepe wanted to go for a walk, and whatever Pepe wanted, Pepe usually got.

With an indulgent smile, Beverley hurried to get dressed, the lipstick forgotten. She had more important things on her mind – like a wedding to look forward to.

***

'No beach today,' Beverley said firmly, as the dog pulled on his lead. 'It's too blowy. We'll go to the park instead. You like the park, don't you? It's got lots of lovely smells for you to sniff.'

She tugged at Pepe's collar, wondering whether she should have made him wear his coat.

He hated it, but it kept him warm and dry, and considering the February sky was overcast with scudding clouds and a hint of rain in the air, she should have insisted he wore it.

Never mind, they wouldn't be out long. Just long enough for him to pee on a few bushes and stretch his legs. She often thought that owning a dog was a two-edged sword. On the one hand, it did get her out of the house. But on the other, if she didn't feel like going out, she had no choice – she had to go out regardless.

Beverley had yet to make up her mind whether this was a 'glad I'm out' kind of walk, or an 'I'd prefer to be on the sofa' one.

Still, she knew enough to realise that when you got to her age if you didn't use it, you would lose it, so going out for a walk once a day was good for her. It kept her active and gave her exercise that she wouldn't otherwise have had.

Look at Helen: she played golf most days, and for a woman in her seventies she was agile and fit. Slim, too, but Beverley didn't want to poke that particular hornet's nest of resentment and envy right now. She had given the damned woman enough headspace as it was for one day, without adding weight-envy.

Mind you, May was also a beanpole. And what irked Beverley was that her sister didn't even try. It came naturally to her – just as being pudgy came naturally to Beverley.

She picked up the pace, even though a quick stomp around the park wouldn't do much to shift her extra poundage. She'd have to do more than a bit of park-stomping to get rid of her excess baggage if she intended to lose weight before the wedding.

Suddenly Beverley stopped dead, jerking Pepe to an abrupt halt. The look he gave her was resentful.

'Sorry, my gorgeous boy, but I've had a thought. I'm going to be the *mother-of-the-groom*. Oh, my!' She did a little hoppity skip, then stopped when she realised she had an audience.

A scruffy brown terrier was standing a few feet away, observing her solemnly.

'What are you looking at?' she demanded, then cast around for its owner.

The dog didn't appear to have anyone with it.

'Are you out on your own?' she asked, bending over and holding out her hand for it to sniff.

The dog stared at her, its tail wagging uncertainly, but it made no move to approach.

'Pepe, go say hello,' she urged, slackening her grip on the lead to give the poodle more room to manoeuvre.

Pepe sat down.

Beverley nudged him with her toe. 'Don't be stubborn,' she hissed, out of the corner of her mouth. 'For once in your life, will you do as you're told?'

Pepe ignored her. He was also ignoring the other dog, so she tried not to take it personally. Pepe was a law unto himself.

Muttering something about Ron needing to do some more work with him, Beverley lowered herself creakily onto her haunches, hoping she would be able to get back up again.

'Come on, poppet, come to Aunty Beverley.' She held out her hand once more, then had an idea and delved into her coat pocket. 'Strawberry bon bon?'

The terrier pricked up its ears, its gaze fixed on the sugary pink sweet in her palm.

It took a cautious step closer, but before it took another, Pepe whirled around and snatched the sweet out of her hand.

'Pepe! Manners!' she exclaimed. 'You naughty boy!'

The poodle ignored the rebuke, his jaws working furiously as he chewed the sticky toffee. A dusting of pink icing sugar coated his nose, and his chewing became more frantic as he pawed at his muzzle.

'That'll teach you to be so greedy,' Beverley crowed. 'Serves you right if you've got toffee stuck to your teeth.'

It was a good distraction though, and she hurriedly pulled out another bon bon while her naughty pooch was occupied.

'Come here, poppet,' she crooned to the terrier, holding the sweet out.

Not wanting this treat to be snatched from under its very nose, the dog dashed up to her and gobbled it up.

Beverley used the opportunity to grab it by the scruff of the neck and check to see whether it was wearing a collar.

'Oi! Get your hands off my dog!'

Beverley froze for a second, then slowly looked up to see an old gent shuffling hurriedly along the path.

When she said *old*, facially he was probably around her age, but he didn't appear to be faring as well when it came to mobility. The walking stick he was holding could double as a handy weapon though, and he was brandishing it vigorously on every third step as he approached.

She released the dog, and the terrier immediately trotted over to him. The man came to a halt, thankfully just beyond striking distance, although he still looked rather irate.

'I thought it was on its own,' Beverley retorted, her voice as stiff as her knees as she struggled to get to her feet.

'Well, she's not, so mind your own business.'

'A stray dog *is* my business.'

'I just told you – she's not a stray. She belongs to me.'

'You were nowhere in sight.'

'I *was*! I was over there.' The old gent pointed his stick along the path he had just hobbled down.

'I didn't see you.'

'You should get yourself some glasses if your eyesight is that bad.'

Beverley drew herself up to her full height of five-foot-three. 'There's nothing wrong with my eyesight.'

'There clearly is, if you couldn't see me. What am I – *invisible?*'

'I wish you were,' Beverley muttered.

With one leg stuck awkwardly out in front of him, the man bent down to clip a lead onto the terrier's collar.

At that very moment Pepe decided he wanted to investigate the other dog after all and lunged towards it, taking Beverley off guard.

Yanked forward, she was almost pulled off her feet and she stumbled into the old chap. Before she could regain her balance (and her dignity) the terrier darted behind her owner with Pepe hot on its tail, and a weird dance ensued as the terrier, with nowhere else to go, circled her master.

Pepe followed suit, his lead tangling in the other dog's, and the unthinkable happened.

As if in slow motion, Beverley felt herself falling.

Her hand shot out instinctively, her fingers grabbing hold of the first thing they came into contact with, which happened to be the old man's coat, and she took him down with her.

The pair of them landed in a heap of limbs, leads, and waggy tails.

Beverley lay there stunned and winded, praying fervently that she hadn't broken a hip.

It took her a moment to gather herself and when she did, she realised she was lying on her side with her face inches from this annoying man's nose. His eyes were open, and he was staring back at her sightlessly.

Beverley suppressed a shriek of alarm.

He was dead. She'd *killed* him: or rather, Pepe had. *Oh, hell.*

She shifted position, trying to squirm away from the corpse. As though to urge her to get up, a cold nose booped her ear and a wet tongue gave it a sloppy lick. Pepe whined, and she wondered whether he realised what he had done.

'I'm going to have you arrested,' the dead fella said, and Beverley let out a blood-curdling scream.

'Arggh!' the chap yelled back. 'Are you trying to kill me?' He pushed himself into a sitting position and glared at her. 'You nearly gave me a heart attack.'

'*Me* give *you* a heart attack? I thought you were *dead.*' She struggled to sit up, gingerly checking each of her limbs in turn.

'If I was dead, it would be your fault. You and that dog of yours. It's a menace. I should report you.'

'My Pepe wouldn't hurt a fly,' she retorted haughtily. 'Anyway, this would never have happened if your dog had been on the lead in the first place.'

'She *was* on the lead when your dog attacked her,' the old curmudgeon snapped, heaving himself upright with a grunt and a groan.

'But she wasn't to start with, was she?' Beverley managed to get her feet underneath her, but her knees didn't seem to want to cooperate. Maybe she should sit here for a while. The tarmacked path wasn't too cold, and thankfully there hadn't been any rain for a couple of days so it was quite dry. And she was seeing the park from Pepe's perspective, so that was a novel experience.

'Get up. You're making the place look untidy,' the old guy grumbled.

'I can't.'

'What do you mean, *you can't?*'

'Are you deaf as well as daft? I mean, I can't.'

'I've got a gammy leg and I managed it.'

'Bully for you.'

'You can't sit there all day.'

'Who says?'

'I do.' He huffed grumpily. 'Here.'

He held out a hand and Beverley eyed it with suspicion for a moment, before taking it. He was right. She couldn't stay here much longer – the cold was already seeping into her bones. And for a Saturday morning the park was remarkably empty. Not another soul was in sight. No one to come to her aid except for the ornery old git who had put her in this position in the first place.

As she grasped his hand, he leant back as though he was about to lift a tonne weight and she was sorely tempted to drag him down again. But for once, common sense prevailed as she allowed herself to be heaved upright.

More grunts accompanied this mammoth task, and not just from him. Maybe she should take up armchair yoga? She hadn't realised she had become so inflexible.

She stood there, panting with the effort, testing herself for any injuries.

'Are you all right?' he asked.

She nodded. 'Are you?'

'Yes. No thanks to you. Or your dog.'

Both Pepe and the terrier were quite content to stand quietly, observing the antics of their owners with bemused expressions on their furry faces.

'Don't start,' she warned the chap. 'I'm not in the mood. If you want to have a go at me, you're going to have to wait until I've had a proper sit down and a cuppa.'

'If anyone needs a sit down and a cup of tea, it's me.'

'Oh, shut up.'

'You can't tell me to shut up,' he blustered.

'I just did.'

He glared at her furiously and Beverley glared back.

The stand-off seemed to go on interminably, but it probably didn't last more than a couple of seconds. He was the one who broke it. Beverley was determined that she wouldn't give in first.

'I'm going to have a cup of tea,' he muttered grouchily. 'You can come with me if you want. Or not. It's up to you. I don't care what you do.'

'I'll come.' Beverley made up her mind quickly. 'It will have to be somewhere that takes dogs,' she warned, in case he had forgotten he had one with him.

'It does.' He began to walk away.

Beverley gingerly put one foot in front of the other, decided that her legs were in working order, and followed smartly, hurrying to fall into step. For a man with a gammy leg, he certainly didn't hang about.

'Where are we going?' she asked.

'My house.'

She paused for a heartbeat, wondering if that was wise. He could be a serial killer for all she knew.

Bugger it: she hadn't had this much excitement for ages. She'd take her chances. Anyway, he might be taller than her but she had a weight advantage. And she didn't have a gammy leg. She reckoned she could outrun him.

'Is it far?' she asked.

'Just around the corner.'

'Will your wife be there?'

'She's dead.'

'I'm sorry.' Beverley held her tongue for a couple of steps, then she asked, 'Did you do away with her?'

His barked laugh startled her. 'No, I did not.'

'Are you going to do away with *me*?'

'Don't tempt me.'

'Are you a mad axe murderer?'

He tutted. 'No, but I'm beginning to see the appeal…'

CHAPTER 2

Was this woman never going to shut up? And what *was* she blathering on about? Axe murderer, indeed! If he was going to murder anyone, he would choose a less messy method.

Andrew was beginning to wish he hadn't invited her back to his place. He didn't know what had possessed him. The only thing he could think of was that he must be suffering from a concussion, despite not having bumped his head.

He snorted. Who was he kidding! He was well aware that the reason he had suggested grabbing a cup of tea was because he was too much of a gentleman to walk away. She had gone down with one hell of a bang, and he had been surprised and extremely relieved that she didn't appear to be injured.

His stiff knee was playing up, he felt a bit shaky, and he was desperate for a sit down, but he hadn't been able to bring himself to leave her.

He was regretting his chivalry now, though. The woman had verbal diarrhoea. She hadn't stopped talking, and all of it was nonsense.

'What's your name?' she asked, taking a mobile phone out of her bag. It was the first sensible thing she'd said since he'd clapped eyes on her.

'Andrew.'

'A. N. D. R. E. W.,' she spelt out slowly, her finger pecking at the screen like a cross sparrow.

'What are you doing?'

'Texting Ron to let him know about you, in case he has to phone the police.'

Andrew halted. 'Pardon?'

'You know, in case I go into your house and never come out again.'

'Believe me, you'll *definitely* come out again,' he growled, even if he had to drag her out by her purple hair. 'You don't have to come with me.'

'Oh, but I want to.'

'Why?'

'I'm Beverley, by the way.' She thrust out a hand. 'Nice to meet you.'

Andrew wished he could say the same, but he shook it anyway. 'Why?' he repeated.

She shuffled awkwardly, refusing to meet his steely gaze. 'I… um… need the loo. Can we get a move on?'

He rolled his eyes, a habit he had picked up from his late wife, God rest her soul. Andrew started walking again – or should he say *limping*.

Beverley asked, 'Is it far? I know you said you live just around the corner, but *which* corner?'

'This one here.' They were now out of the park and were on a wide tree-lined road made up of semi-detached houses that had been built in the 1930s. 'It's the third one along.' When he reached his gate, he gestured towards his front door. 'Are you sure you want to come in? I might have given you a false name.'

'I'm going to have to, else I might have an accident.'

Andrew grimaced. Quickly he unlocked the door. 'Downstairs loo, second on the left,' he said.

Beverley thrust her dog's lead into his hand, shot past him at a rate of knots, dived into the cloakroom and slammed the door firmly shut.

Then she began humming. Loudly.

Bemused, he shook his head and shrugged off his coat, hanging it on a hook in the recess under the stairs. 'Are you two going to behave?' he asked the dogs.

Twinkle stared up at him in adoration, ignoring the intruder in her house. Andrew wasn't fooled. The adoration was in expectation of the chew treat he always gave his dog after a walk.

Beverley's dog was wandering around, tail up, nose down, as he sniffed.

'Let's get you a chew each, then I'll put the kettle on,' he said to them.

Since Vivienne died, he had found himself talking to his dog more and more, until now, three and a half years later, it wasn't unusual for him to hold a full-blown conversation with her. Andrew swore blind that Twinkle understood every word.

He heard the toilet flush and the sound of the tap running as he retrieved a couple of chews from Twinkle's cupboard.

Twinkle was already sitting at his feet, waiting patiently, her tail sweeping across the lino, her attention never leaving his face. The poodle was still busy sniffing his way around the kitchen exploring every nook and cranny.

'Can your dog have a treat?' Andrew asked as Beverley appeared in the doorway. 'Twinkle is having one.'

'Pepe? would you like a treat?' The poodle ignored her.

He ignored Andrew too, until Andrew offered Twinkle her chew. Twinkle snatched it, as though she was worried the other dog might steal it.

Pepe booped Andrew's hand.

'Here you go. One for you, too.' The poodle took it delicately, then retreated to his mistress's side.

'Sit down, take your coat off,' Andrew said. 'Tea or Coffee?'

'Tea, please. Not too strong. A splash of milk and three sugars.' She removed her coat and slung it on the back of one of the kitchen chairs, before sitting down.

Andrew winced. That was Vivienne's seat. No one else ever sat in it. He should have said something, but it was too late now.

'Biscuit?' he offered instead.

'What have you got?'

'Um… custard creams, digestives, jammy dodgers? Or I might have some shortbread left over from Christmas.'

'Won't they be stale by now?'

'The packet's not been opened.'

'That's OK, then. I'll have one of those.' A pause. 'Please. And thank you,' she added.

He was relieved to see that she had found her manners, however when he offered her a biscuit and she took three, he decided that she was greedy as well as talkative. Not the best combination.

And when she gave one of the biscuits to her dog, he nearly spluttered into his tea.

'If I had known you were going to waste it on your dog, I wouldn't have offered you one.'

Beverley's expression was indignant. 'Pepe is part of my family, so why shouldn't he have a biscuit?'

'It's not good for him.'

'What are you, the biscuit police?' She dunked one of the shortbreads into her tea.

'I'm just saying. Human food isn't good for dogs.'

'You sound just like Ron,' she grumbled, her mouth full.

That was the second time she had mentioned the name Ron, and Andrew guessed the man must be her husband. 'He's right. Some human food is poisonous to dogs. Like chocolate, for instance.'

'I know that. I'm not stupid. And I don't feed him human food all the time. But he is partial to roast chicken and vegetables.'

'Aren't we all.' Andrew's reply was heartfelt. He only ever had a roast dinner when he visited his daughter's house, and because she lived in Peterborough he didn't get to see her as often as he would like.

It was too much of a faff to cook a roast for himself. Too many pans. And the gravy wasn't the same. Mind you, no one could make gravy like his Vivienne. It had been so good, he used to mop it up with a slice of bread.

'Live here on your own, do you?' Beverley asked. Her eyes were darting about, taking everything in. They lingered on the photo in the windowsill of him and Vivienne on their fortieth wedding anniversary, then moved on to one of Judith, Duncan and the boys. It was one of his favourites.

'Yes,' he replied. 'My wife died three years ago. It'll be four years this August.'

'Sorry. Getting old is a bummer, isn't it? Losing people you love. Our generation is dwindling faster than nuts on a bird feeder.'

Andrew blinked. What a weird analogy. It was true, though. Every week brought news of another acquaintance having popped his or her clogs.

Beverley's expression brightened. 'Mine left me.'

'Your… who… what?'

'My husband. He left me years ago. Looking back, I can see that I was well rid of him, although I didn't think so at the time.'

'I thought *Ron* was your husband?'

'Whatever gave you that idea? Ron's my…' She hesitated, and he wondered whether she was about to say *lover*. She struck him as the type to embrace life and all it had to offer, and he pitied the poor bloke, despite Beverley being an attractive woman. Good cheekbones. Nice skin. And a sparkle in her eye that he didn't want to think about too deeply.

But those clothes and that hair...

He shuddered. Colourful was the kindest way to describe it.

Clashing, would be more truthful.

Someone ought to tell her that purple hair didn't go with an orange jumper. Or the blue patterned skirt with green and red flowers. She looked like she had been caught in an explosion in a paint factory. Although, he had to admit that she did brighten up his kitchen.

And for someone to not wear black in February was a pleasant change. Or beige: he was referring to himself here. He was the king of beige and brown. Carrying on with the bird theme that his guest had started (he was a keen garden-twitcher and usually fed his feathered friends throughout the winter), it was as though Beverley was the brightly coloured male bird, and he was the much drabber female.

'Ron is like a son to me,' she was saying. 'I'm going to miss him dreadfully when he's gone. Six months, they said.'

'Oh, God, I'm so sorry.' The poor woman. She must be going through hell. No wonder her mind was all over the place. The elderly couple three doors up had recently lost their son in a car accident, and Andrew didn't think they would ever recover from it.

Beverley beamed. 'I'm not sorry. Or rather, I *am*, because it'll be hard living on my own again, but I've never seen him so happy, so I can't begrudge him that.'

'He's *happy*?'

'Wouldn't you be?' She was giving him a strange look. 'Otherwise, why bother? Unless you're royalty and it's a marriage of convenience.'

'Pardon?' The woman was talking in riddles. Or… bugger! She might be suffering from *dementia*. He should have realised, and he immediately felt incredibly sad for her. Then he wondered whether it was safe for her to be out on her own.

'Like they did in the old days,' she continued, oblivious. 'Kings and queens wouldn't marry for love, but for land and alliances. Ron and Annabelle aren't like that, of course.' She chuckled. 'They haven't got the money or the blue blood. But they have found love. I've never seen a couple as happy as those two. Not even Kate was this lovey-dovey, and she was besotted when she married Brett. Kate's my daughter, by the way. Oh, I do hope they have a big wedding!'

'Who? Kate?'

'No, *Ron*. Keep up.'

'Ron's getting *married*?'

'I just said so, didn't I? In the next six months, he told me, but they haven't set the date yet. I suppose it depends on where they want to tie the knot. All the good places are booked up a year in advance. I know, because my neighbour's granddaughter had to book her venue eighteen months ahead. In my day, we didn't bother with long engagements like that. Mind you, we couldn't afford fancy venues, either. It was the local chapel and a do in the working men's club afterwards.'

Andrew felt as though he had been flattened by a rainbow-coloured steamroller. 'Ah... uh... congratulations. Married, eh? Lovely. New hat?' His Vivienne had always insisted on a new hat if there was a wedding in the offing. She used to love a nice wedding.

Beverley snorted. 'A whole new outfit, not just the hat. Something smart and classy, because no doubt bloody Helen will be invited.'

'Bloody Helen?' Who were all these people she was rabbiting on about?

'My daughter's mother-in-law. I've never met such a stuck-up woman in my life. She thinks she's something special.' Beverley leant forward. 'She's one of those ladies *wot lunches*. And she plays golf, too. Think twin sets and pearls, and you'll get the idea.'

'You're like chalk and cheese, then?'

'Yeah. I'm the cheese – nicely matured. She's the chalk – brittle and leaves a nasty taste in your mouth.' She smacked her lips and pulled a face.

'You've eaten *chalk*?'

'Not eaten it exactly: tasted it. Yuck.'

'Why would you taste chalk?'

'Why wouldn't you? Taste everything life has to offer; that's my motto.'

'Is it?' he replied faintly.

She sobered. 'It used to be. Maybe not so much these days. Not got the knees for it.'

Neither did Andrew.

'They think me a right miserable old biddy,' she said.

'Who does?'

'My grandkids. Maybe they're right. I do tend to moan a lot. Mainly about the weather, the state of the economy, and the youth of today.'

'If you can't moan about that, then what can you moan about?' Andrew replied gallantly. He could empathise – he did his fair share of moaning about those exact same things.

'And Christmas. I hate it,' she said.

'I'm not too keen on it, either. Not since Vivienne passed. It's not the same somehow.'

'It's a lot of fuss and expense just for one day, which is usually spent with people you only end up arguing with.' She pulled a face again, and he wondered whether her opinion was formed from experience.

'A bit like a wedding?' His tone was dry.

Beverley shot him a surprised look, then burst out laughing. 'Exactly like a wedding!' she cried. 'I don't much like those either, but I am looking forward to this one.'

'Despite Helen?'

'Despite Helen,' she agreed sourly. Then she brightened. 'Maybe she won't be invited,' she said, before her face fell once more. 'Who am I trying to kid? She probably will be. After all, she was there at the beginning when Ron and Annabelle first met. If it had been up to Helen though, Ron would never have been allowed to come on that holiday.'

'Fancy another cuppa? Then you can tell me all about it.' Andrew, for all his doubts about the sanity of the woman sitting in his kitchen, was intrigued. Beverley was like a breath of fresh air, and suddenly life seemed to have a little more colour.

***

'Let me get this straight,' Andrew said half an hour later, trying to make sense of the very long, extremely detailed and incredibly convoluted story Beverley had just told him. He counted the relevant points out on his fingers. 'Kate buggered off by herself for Christmas because you and Helen were staying with her and her family for the festive season and you ladies don't get on—'

'Not just because of that, although I must admit neither Helen nor I were on our best behaviour. The kids were also being awful, and Brett was as much use as a chocolate fireguard.'

'Right… Brett's her husband, yes? Helen is his mother.' It was hard to keep all these people straight in his mind. 'Anyway, Kate ran away. Ron, who was homeless at the time, knew Kate because he used to sleep in the doorway of the charity shop she worked in. He and Kate used to chat, and Brett only tracked her down because Ron gave him a clue about where she might have gone.' Andrew paused. 'It can't have been easy for Ron, living on the streets.'

'I'm sure it wasn't. Kate did what she could to help.'

Andrew picked up the thread of the story again. 'When Brett found her and bought her home, he invited Ron to Christmas lunch to say thank you, and that was when you met him and took him in.'

'He's not a stray dog, you know! I didn't *take him in*.' She made quotation marks with her fingers. 'I invited him to stay with me for a couple of weeks to teach Pepe some manners because Ron used to be a dog handler in his previous life.'

'Ah, yes… Pepe peeing on Brett's leg incident. And the pooping on Kate's bedroom carpet debacle. And did you mention something about Pepe eating a whole leg of roast lamb?' Andrew eyed the poodle with renewed respect: the dog was a small curly-coated hooligan.

'Pepe also bought Ron back when *he* ran away,' Beverley leapt in, quick to defend her precious pooch.

'So you said.' There seemed to have been an awful lot of running away in Beverley's family. She had relayed some tale of Annabelle's ex-husband appearing at the holiday home they were renting, and Ron buggering off and going back on the streets because he didn't want to get in the way of them giving their marriage another go. But Pepe had followed him, forcing Ron to bring the dog back, and by then Annabelle had already told her ex to take a hike… It was all rather convoluted and quite complicated. Andrew supposed you had to have been there. 'He's definitely got a mind of his own, hasn't he?'

'Pepe or Ron?' Beverley shot back.

'Both, by the sound of it. So, Ron met Annabelle, your niece, when all of you went on holiday to Wales, and now Ron has come into some money and has set up a dog training school, and he and Annabelle are getting married in the summer. Have I missed anything?'

'No, that's about it.'

'Running away seems to be a theme in your family,' Andrew he couldn't help saying. 'First Kate, then Ron—'

'Ron had been running away for years before he met Annabelle,' Beverley pointed out. 'But you can't run away from yourself, can you?'

Andrew silently agreed. It had taken him a long time to figure that out.

Since Vivienne died, Andrew often felt like running away from his grief. But Beverley was right – it was impossible to run away from your feelings. No change of scenery could change what was in your heart.

'Everyone seems perfectly settled now though,' he observed, and Beverley nodded.

It was only much later that they would discover just how wrong they could be.

CHAPTER 3

The reality 'I still think it's too soon,' May sniffed. Beverley and May were sitting in May's flat discussing the wedding and not exactly seeing eye to eye.

'Annabelle has been divorced for ages!' Beverley exclaimed. 'How can it be too soon?'

May rolled her eyes and tutted. 'I don't mean *that*. I mean, she hasn't known Ron long. Only since August. And what do we really know about him, eh?'

Beverley could feel her feathers begin to ruffle. 'You never did like him. Just because he used to be homeless, doesn't make him a bad person.'

She thought back to the events of last summer when Ron had unexpectedly come into a nice sum of money, which should have put a stop to May's ridiculous worry that Ron was trying to con her out of her house. May had been quite anti-Ron then.

It appeared she still was.

May tutted again. 'I didn't say he is a bad person. I just think that she should wait a while.'

'For what?'

'To get to know him better.'

'And how long will that take? A year? Three? Ten? How well do we ever know another person?'

'Don't be facetious.' May pursed her lips.

Ooh, get her, Beverley thought. Just because she had got an A grade in O-level English and Beverley had only got a C, May had lorded it over her since with her big words.

'I've always been fascinating,' Beverley replied.

'Facetious doesn't mean fascinating: it means—' May stopped talking when she saw Beverley's smirk.

'Gotcha!' Beverley cried. She loved winding May up, because it was so easy to do. 'Talking about fascinating – are you going to go for one of those, or something bigger?' she asked.

'What?' May looked confused.

'A hat.'

'What about it?'

'For the wedding. I'm not sure one of those little fascinating things would suit me.'

'Fascinator.' May corrected her.

'That's what I said.'

'You didn't! You said *fascinating*,' her sister argued.

Beverley gave her that look again, the one that meant she was pulling her leg and deliberately using the wrong word. Except, this time she had made a genuine mistake. Beverley had honestly thought that those little hats were called fascinating. But she wasn't going to tell May that.

May said, 'I don't know yet. I'll have to try a few on. I'll buy the outfit first. I do hope Annabelle will do it properly this time.'

'What do you mean *properly*?'

'She had hardly any of her family there the first time. It was nearly all his. And their friends, of course. Although I think those were mostly his, too.'

Annabelle had met her first husband, Troy, when she visited Australia when she was just twenty-one. She had married him and had stayed out there, and May had forever lamented the fact that apart from herself and her husband, Terence, none of the rest of the family had been able to afford to fly out to attend the wedding. Only Annabelle's parents had been there from Annabelle's side.

At least Kate had got married in this country and had had a great big wedding with all the trimmings, so in terms of weddings, Beverley held the upper hand. May was clearly hoping to redress the balance this time around.

'Ron thinks Helen will probably be invited,' Beverley grumbled.

'I don't know what you've got against Brett's mother.' May sniffed loudly and Beverley scowled. May understood full well that such a comment would wind her up.

'You know exactly what I've got against her. I've told you enough times. That woman thinks she's better than the rest of us.'

'I might have met her only a handful of times, but she seemed perfectly nice.'

'You would say that. She's just your type.'

May bristled, as Beverley guessed she would. 'What do you mean by that?'

'Nothing,' Beverley replied innocently. 'Could Pepe have a bowl of water, please?'

'You should have left him at home. I've got brand-new cream carpets.'

'Not in the kitchen you haven't, and you shut him in there. Besides, I believe in killing two birds with one stone. It'll save me having to take him for a walk later.' Beverley paused, remembering. 'I bumped into a nice chap yesterday,' she said. 'Literally. He knocked me off my feet. Then he invited me to his house for a cup of tea and some shortbread. His name is Andrew, and he's a widower with a daughter a year or two younger than Kate. Lives just by the park. Him, not his daughter. She lives in... I forget where.' She waved her hand airily: it would come to her.

'Did you only just meet him *yesterday*? You didn't know him previously?'

'Nope. Never set eyes on him before. All those times I've walked Pepe in the park, you would have thought I'd have seen him around. You tend to see the same people all the time when you walk a dog.'

'I'll take your word for it.' May pulled a face. Like Helen, May made no secret of the fact that she didn't like Pepe.

'He keeps his house as neat as a pin,' Beverley continued. 'You would never know that he was living on his own.'

'What were you thinking of, going to a strange man's house? I don't understand you at all, Beverley. Anything might have happened.'

'Oh, lighten up. He's harmless.'

'I thought you said he knocked you over?'

'It was an accident. The dogs' leads got tangled.'

'That dog of yours is a menace.'

'That's what Andrew said,' Beverley replied cheerfully. She got to her feet, her tea long since drunk, and if there was no fresh brew on the horizon she might as well go home.

'Are you leaving already? We haven't talked about the wedding yet.'

'Got any cake?'

May's brow wrinkled. 'I've got some coffee and walnut. Would you like a slice?'

'As long as it comes with another cup of tea. And a ham sandwich wouldn't go amiss either. It's a long walk back.'

'You could have driven.'

'I told you, Pepe needed a walk. Has Annabelle mentioned a date to you?'

'No, has Ron?'

Beverley shook her head. 'Where do you think they'll hold it? In church? Or one of those places that does it all?'

She followed May into the kitchen. As far as flats went, this was lovely. May and Terence had only moved in just before Christmas and it still had that fresh-paint smell. Beverley recognised a few bits and pieces from May's old house, but much of the furniture was new. She'd say that for her sister, May had good taste.

'I've been thinking about that,' May said. 'I quite fancy Seabrook Hall. Frances Boland's son got married there last year and she said it was wonderful. Perhaps we should check it out? Or maybe the golf course? They are renowned for doing stylish weddings.'

Beverley shuddered. 'Definitely not the golf course. How about that tower thing near the beach?'

May looked appalled. 'Good grief, no! I can't think of anywhere worse. Fancy getting married five hundred feet up in the air. It's so… gimmicky.'

'Different,' Beverley countered. 'Or how about the converted church in whatshisname street? You know… near to those new council offices,' she added, when she saw May's confused expression. 'They'll have the best of both worlds – a church vibe but you don't have to drive to the reception.'

'Hmm. I'm not sure. I was thinking more country house.'

'Lewes Castle does weddings,' Beverley said. 'So does the Royal Pavilion.'

'I can't see Ron in the Royal Pavilion, somehow,' May snorted, taking the ham out of the fridge.

Pepe looked on, concentration and hope written across his face. Beverley prayed he didn't jump up and try to snatch it out of May's hand. Ron had done a wonderful job with the dog and Pepe was loads better than he had been, but the little sod still had his moments.

Beverley narrowed her eyes. 'Ron isn't going to turn up in a beanie hat and a scruffy overcoat,' she said. 'He'll be wearing a suit – a morning one, I expect. Yes… I can just see him in it, maybe with a top hat.' She brightened. 'Jake could wear a matching one! I assume he'll be a page boy.' Annabelle's son would look so cute.

May shuddered. 'You can't dress the poor boy up like little Lord Fauntleroy. He'll look ridiculous.'

Her sister had a point, Beverley conceded reluctantly. It might be too twee, and at nearly eleven years old, Jake probably wouldn't appreciate it.

Maybe Pepe could wear a top hat instead? The dog would look adorable if he had a bow tie, too. Assuming she could persuade him to keep it on…

'I've got an idea!' she declared, clapping her hands. 'Pepe could be the ring bearer.'

'You *what*?' May's mouth dropped open.

'It's brilliant, isn't it? I can see him now, trotting down the aisle with a little velvet pouch in his mouth.'

'*No*! No way. That dog is *not* coming to my daughter's wedding.'

'I think you'll find it's Ron's wedding too. Anyway, Pepe has got to be there. If it hadn't been for him, Ron and Annabelle wouldn't be together now.'

'I rest my case.'

'Pepe *is* going to the wedding.' Beverley was firm. She rarely went anywhere without her dog.

'Over my dead body!' May's expression was furious.

Beverley drew herself up to her full height and took a deep breath. 'If that's what it takes...'

***

'Grr,' Beverley growled, sounding not a little unlike her dog. May had always been able to push her buttons, right from when they were little. They should have grown out of it by now. But if May thought that by saying 'over her dead body' it was going to put her off, her sister had better think again. Challenge accepted, Beverley thought, running through all the ways she could bump her sister off.

She didn't mean it, of course, even though she was sorely tempted, and not just because she would undoubtedly get caught and have to spend the rest of her life behind bars. She did love May, but sometimes that woman could test her patience.

Beverley viciously wrenched open a box of fish fingers, and one fell on the floor.

Like a bolt of fluffy black lightning, Pepe darted between her legs, grabbed it and bolted into the living room.

'Oi! Give that back!'

Too late; the dog was crunching into it, not caring that the fish finger was still frozen solid.

Crossly, Beverley wagged her finger. 'Naughty Pepe. Bad dog.'

Pepe ignored her as he gulped down his ill-gotten gains.

With a resigned sigh, she returned to the kitchen to arrange the rest of the fish fingers on a baking tray. There had been ten in the box: six for Ron, four for her. Three, actually, because she would have fed Pepe one from her plate, despite Ron telling her that she shouldn't.

Pepe had eaten his early, that was all, she told herself. It irked her a little that the dog was perfectly behaved for Ron but could still be a little tyrant when it came to his behaviour with her.

It was her own fault: she had spoilt him. But he had been such an adorable puppy, and for years he had been her only companion. It looked like he was going to be her only companion once again when Ron moved out.

'Are you going to move in with Annabelle or will you buy somewhere new together?' were the first words out of Beverley's mouth when Ron walked through the door a short while later.

'Hello to you, too,' Ron chuckled, giving her a kiss on the cheek. 'Fish fingers? My favourite.' He hung his jacket in the little lobby between the kitchen and the back door, removed his boots, and then he greeted the dog, who was bouncing around his feet. 'Have you been a good boy?'

'No. He ate a fish finger.' Beverley glared at her pooch. 'Where can I get hold of some cyanide? I hear it's quick.'

'That's a bit drastic, don't you think? It was only a fish finger.'

'Not for Pepe, for *May*.'

Ron washed his hands in the sink, a smile playing about his lips. 'What has she done now?'

'She doesn't like my idea of Pepe being a ring bearer.' Out of the corner of her eye, she noticed Ron grimace, and she guessed that he might not be too keen either. Never mind, she was sure she'd be able to talk him around.

'And that's grounds enough to do away with her?' He wiped his hands on a towel and popped it back on the radiator.

Beverley could tell he was trying hard not to laugh. 'She said *over my dead body*,' Beverley explained. 'Maybe poisonous mushrooms would be easier to get hold of? I could sneak them into her fridge.'

'Terence might eat them. You don't want to kill him as well.'

'Collateral damage. Is that enough chips for you?' She pointed at the overflowing baking tray.

'Plenty, thanks. Too many, actually.' He pulled out a chair, sat down at the kitchen table and asked, 'Are you worried about anything? Is something on your mind?'

'What do you mean?'

'You seem to be preoccupied with murder. You accused that guy you met in the park of wanting to bump you off.'

'I was just being cautious.'

'Not cautious enough. You went to his house.'

'Don't *you* start. I had enough of that from May'.

'How is my soon-to-be mother-in-law?'

'Annoying.'

'She probably says the same about you.'

Beverley grinned. 'I expect she does. You didn't answer my question – Annabelle's house or somewhere new?'

'We haven't decided yet.'

'Date?'

'No thanks, I've got a fiancée.'

'For the *wedding*.' She tutted and flapped her hands at him.

'26th of June.'

'Venue?'

'Registry office, I expect.'

'Don't you dare! May wants a big wedding and so do I. You deserve it.'

'Ah, so you and May do agree on something,' he smirked.

'You need a wedding planner.'

'A what now?'

'Someone to plan your wedding. I can do that for you,' she offered, with what she hoped was a winning smile.

'I think Annabelle and I can manage. But thanks, anyway.'

Beverley wasn't so sure. 'I wonder if you can get married on the pier.'

Ron blinked. 'No!'

'That's a shame.'

'I meant, no we're not getting married on Brighton Pier'

'It would be fun. You could tie the knot on the roller coaster.' She caught his disbelieving expression and added hastily, 'Just kidding.'

'Good.'

Pity, she thought – it would have been fun, and Ron's life had been sorely lacking in fun for a few years. Annabelle's kids would have loved it, as well. Maybe she would check it out anyway – it was bound to be better than any of the stuffy places May would suggest.

She bent down to peer through the oven door, even though she had only just popped the chips in so there was no chance they would be done yet.

'Anyway, you've got to book places like that well in advance. You could always push it back a year,' she suggested hopefully. 'Give yourselves plenty of time to plan.'

'I don't think so. As I said, there's no point in waiting.'

Beverley thought there were lots of points, the most important one being that Ron would carry on living with her for that much longer. She knew she was being selfish, but...

'You won't get anywhere nice at this short notice,' she warned. 'I bet The Royal Pavilion is booked solid for the next twelve months. Longer, even.'

'We don't want to get married in the Royal Pavilion.'

'Where, then?'

'I told you, the registry office will be fine.'

'Over my dead body.'

'Do you know where I can get my hands on some cyanide?' he shot back, with a grin.

Beverley's filthy look made him laugh. But she would bet her last pound coin that he wouldn't be laughing when he realised that if he and Annabelle didn't decide on something soon, their only option would be to hold the reception on a bench on the promenade, with the guests eating fish and chips out of newspaper. So, yes, for once she and May *were* on the same page, even if they couldn't yet agree on which order the sentences went.

Ron and Annabelle needed someone to sort this wedding out sharpish, and Beverley was just the person to do it. With a little help from May – *if* her sister behaved herself.

CHAPTER 4

It was the dog that caught Andrew's eye first, because its owner was bundled up like an Arctic explorer and it was impossible to tell if it was a man or a woman from this distance.

Mind you, the weather did warrant a couple of layers. It was blowing a gale today, with a sharp easterly wind flowing from Russia. He didn't think any snow was forecast, but he wouldn't be surprised if they saw some of the white stuff. It was certainly cold enough for it.

'I thought it was you,' he said, when Beverley was close enough for him to see her face properly.

The dogs greeted each other in the time-honoured doggy fashion. They seemed as pleased to see one another as Andrew was to see Beverley. After she had left the other day, his house had seemed even quieter than usual. Who would have thought that such a small person could fill his kitchen so thoroughly?

She peered at him. 'I've never seen you in the park before, and now I bump into you twice in one week. Are you stalking me?' The tip of Beverley's nose was red. Except for her eyes, that was all he could see of her.

'Maybe you're the one who is doing the stalking?' he countered.

'Impossible. I bring Pepe here most days.'

'I've only got your word for that,' he argued as he fell into step beside her.

Her eyes crinkled and although he couldn't see her mouth because of the scarf wrapped around the lower part of her face, he was certain she was smiling.

'Fancy a cuppa?' she asked.

'Are you inviting yourself to my house?'

'No, I'm inviting you to *mine*.'

'Aren't you worried I might be a mad axe murderer?'

'Not in the slightest. Are you worried that *I* might be?'

'Now that you come to mention it...' he teased and received an elbow in the ribs for his trouble.

'Come on, I haven't got all day,' she instructed, turning sharply on her heel and marching off.

He hobbled to catch up. This cold weather didn't half play havoc with his knee, and the rest of his joints fared only marginally better. If it wasn't for Twinkle needing a daily constitutional, Andrew strongly believed he mightn't have ventured outside at all between November and March.

'Is it far?' he asked, echoing the question Beverley had asked him the other day, and marvelling at how briskly she could walk when she had a mind to.

'Just around the corner,' she replied, and he could hear the amusement in her voice.

'Déjà vu,' he said.

'No, Staley Avenue.'

'Very droll.'

'I'm good, aren't I?'

'I wouldn't give up the day job just yet, if I were you,' he advised.

They walked in silence for a while, their breath misting in the air above their heads. He was tempted to catch hold of her elbow when they crossed the road, but he didn't think she would appreciate the gesture. Beverley struck him as fiercely independent, and he guessed she might resent even the smallest indication that he thought she needed any help.

'I think it might snow,' he said, as a conversation starter.

'I hate the cold,' she replied. 'I hate this time of year, full stop.'

'It's not so bad. Look, there are snowdrops in that garden!' To Andrew, the small nodding white flowers were welcome harbingers of spring, as were the daffodils which wouldn't be far behind.

'It still gets dark too early. I'm fed up with winter. And if we get any more rain, I'm going to scream.'

'I think everyone is ready for a bit of sun,' he said, adding, 'Are you always this grumpy?'

Beverley came to an abrupt halt. 'I'm doing it again, aren't I? I promised myself that I wouldn't, and I haven't. Not for a long time. It must be because of Ron.'

'What are you sorry about?'

'Being a miserable cow.'

'I didn't say you are miserable.'

'You don't need to. I know I am. My grandkids used to complain about it. Not to my face, you understand. But I knew they did.' She resumed walking and Andrew fell into step with her again. 'Did I tell you I've got three?'

'I can't remember. You might have done. I've got two. Both boys. Twenty-one and eighteen. Men, technically, but they're not men though, are they? I wasn't a man at that age, no matter how much I pretended I was. How about you?'

'I've never been a man,' Beverley replied, deadpan.

Andrew guffawed and slapped his thigh. 'How can you claim to be miserable? You're the funniest person I know.'

'All the others have passed on, have they?'

'See! You're doing it again – being funny.'

'I'm not doing it on purpose,' she said.

'It doesn't matter. You make me laugh anyway.'

'I'm glad I amuse you.'

'Not in a bad way,' he hastened to assure her. 'In a good way.'

He realised he was telling the truth. This daft, dippy lady had brightened up his life. Which made him feel kind of sad and pathetic. It should have been bright enough without having to rely on an eccentric old biddy to cheer him up.

But if he was being honest, his life had lost its light when he had lost Vivienne. She had taken it with her, leaving him in self-pitying darkness. But if she were here now, he knew what she would say. She would scold him six ways to Sunday for being such a miserable, pathetic old sod. But she wasn't here, and miserable and grumpy was all he could seem to manage these days.

'I bet my grandsons think the same of me,' he admitted. 'Is miserable the default setting for old people?'

'Less of the old,' Beverley snapped.

They turned off the main road and into a side street with a sign for Staley Avenue screwed into a wall. It was a street of Victorian terraced houses with bay windows, recessed porches, and small bailey-style gardens to the front.

Genteel, respectable, quietly run-down. Unfashionable. A bit like him. Perhaps he should sell up and buy a place here? He would fit in just fine.

'I don't like being old,' she said, opening a wrought-iron gate and stomping up a short, cracked path. 'I'm not old in my head.'

'I like your tiles,' he told her, absently. They lined the open porch and he suspected they were original. 'Very pretty.'

'If that's not an old comment, I don't know what is. Come in, and mind you wipe your feet.'

Andrew duly wiped, but Twinkle ignored the bristled mat by the front door, as did Pepe.

Beverley headed into the depths of the house, unlayering herself as she went. The scarf, hat and gloves were discarded on the stairs, her coat was flung over the back of the sofa as she passed through the sitting room, and her boots were unzipped and left on the kitchen floor for the unwary or unobservant to trip over.

Andrew discretely shoved them to one side with his foot.

Beverley hadn't finished.

She removed a gilet next, and then a cardigan, so now she was half the width she had been and considerably less rotund.

Surely it hadn't been that cold?

Andrew unwrapped his scarf and shrugged awkwardly out of his heavy-duty anorak, the one with the fancy name and the fancier price tag. He had bought it in the January sales a couple of years ago, and so far it had kept its promise of being waterproof and windproof.

Twinkle had one to match, and Andrew bent down, struggling to remove the dog's coat.

'She won't feel the benefit of it when we go back outside if I don't,' he explained when he saw Beverley watching.

'Pepe refuses to wear one. Tea? Or is it coffee? Or…' her eyes lit up, '…a nip of brandy?'

'It's eleven in the morning.'

'So? It's Baltic out there. A drop of brandy will warm your cockles.'

His cockles were warm enough already, thank you, so he said, 'Just tea, please,' and thought he heard her mutter 'spoilsport', but he couldn't be sure.

As she bustled about, filling the kettle and drying some mugs which were on the draining board, Andrew took the opportunity to look around, without his nosiness being too obvious.

Beverley's house was far more lived-in than his own, with notes attached to the fridge door by pretty magnets, a stack of letters and flyers propped up by the side of the microwave, and a pile of folded laundry on the countertop next to it. A vase of dusty plastic flowers sat on the windowsill, along with a pair of yellow rubber gloves and a chipped ceramic bowl half full of coins.

She had slung her gilet and cardigan on one of the worktops, but when she saw that he was still holding his coat, and Twinkle's too, she said, 'Give those to me.'

Andrew handed them to her, and she hung both items up in a little lobby off the kitchen.

'Cherry Bakewell or French Fancy?' she asked.

'Ooh, I haven't had a French Fancy in years,' he enthused. He used to love those little cakes, the pink ones especially.

'I bet you haven't!' Her wicked cackle made him wince as she added, 'Make yourself useful – they're in there.' She jerked her chin at one of the wall cupboards on his left as she lifted the kettle and poured boiling water into a teapot. 'Plates are in that one over there.'

More chin jerking, her hands busy giving the pot a stir, then she popped a tea cosy over the top. He didn't realise people still used tea cosies, and it reminded him of the early days of his marriage when tea was always made with loose tea leaves, and in a pot. Vivienne had loved a tea cosy. He might still have one in the attic that she had crocheted about thirty years ago.

Andrew stepped closer to have a proper gander at Beverley's. 'Is this handmade?'

'It is. I knitted it with my own fair hands.'

'My wife used to love to knit and crochet. She always had something crafty on the go.'

'She sounds like a woman after my own heart. I've always got some needles in my hand. Here.' She passed him a chunky earthenware mug. 'Grab your plate and we'll go into the sitting room: it's more comfy.'

Andrew waited for her to take a seat before sitting down himself, guessing she would have a favourite. Then he lowered himself into an armchair, being careful not to spill his tea.

'Is Pepe behaving himself?' he asked, taking a bite of his cake.

'He's been as good as gold,' Beverley said. 'He even behaved himself when I took him to visit my sister. Mind you, he didn't have much choice, because May shut him in the kitchen. New cream carpets,' she explained, with feeling.

'Ah.' He could see her sister's point. Cream carpets and doggy paws weren't the best of bedfellows.

'Don't you dare take her side,' Beverley warned. 'Not after what she said.'

'What did she say?' Andrew was trying his best not to smile, but Beverley looked so indignant that he had trouble keeping a straight face.

'When I suggested that Pepe could be the ring-bearer, she said '*over my dead body*'. Hers, not mine. I'm seriously considering taking her up on the suggestion.'

'I see.' He screwed up his face, hoping his expression portrayed sympathy and not that he was struggling to hold back a laugh. 'Look at those two,' he said, keen to change the subject, and he used the last morsel of cake to gesture towards the two dogs before popping it into his mouth.

Twinkle and Pepe were curled up in Pepe's basket together.

'Aw, they're so sweet. Pepe doesn't usually take to other dogs.'

'He seems to have taken to Twinkle,' Andrew pointed out.

'We ought to make a thing of it,' Beverley said.

'Sorry?' Andrew wasn't sure what she meant.

'Meeting in the park, then having a cuppa afterwards. It'll give the dogs a chance to socialise.'

Andrew wondered whether Beverley was hoping it would also give her a chance to socialise. She might appear to be forthright and in-your-face, but he had a feeling she was a little lonely. And reading between the lines, he got the impression that once Ron was married, she might be even lonelier.

He was lonely, too. If his daughter lived nearer, it wouldn't be so bad. And he had also discovered that since he'd lost Vivienne, he hadn't wanted to bother with other people much – which didn't help his loneliness in the slightest.

'Good idea,' he said. Then for some inexplicable reason, he took it a step further. 'Fancy a spot of lunch one day?'

Beverley's eyes widened. 'Maybe,' she replied. He could hear the caution in her voice. 'Where are you thinking?'

'Somewhere on the front? Or maybe in The Lanes.'

'With the dogs?'

'Naturally.' It would seem too much like a date without them, and he didn't want her to get the wrong idea.

'Good. Wherever I go, Pepe goes. He gets lonely on his own.'

Andrew raised his eyebrows. He loved Twinkle to bits, but he didn't take his dog *everywhere*.

'When?' she asked.

'How about Sunday?' It would be a treat to have a Sunday lunch out – as long as he could find a pub that allowed dogs which was also easy to get to using public transport. He hadn't driven for several years, and he no longer owned a car.

Beverley frowned. 'I usually do a roast for me and Ron on Sundays, and I believe he mentioned that Annabelle and the kids would be coming this week.'

Andrew could feel his spirits sinking. Ah, well, he supposed it was only to be expected. She had a family and would want to spend time with them.

Almost as though she could read his mind, she said, 'Would you like to join us?'

'Oh, no, I couldn't possibly.'

'Why not?'

His mind went blank. He couldn't actually think of a reason.

'I always cook far too much, and end up having bubble and squeak the next day with the leftover potatoes and veg,' she persisted.

'What will Ron say? Will he mind?'

'Why should he?'

'He doesn't know me.'

'That doesn't matter. He's a friendly chap.'

'I don't like to intrude.'

'Suit yourself. The offer is there. It'll be roast chicken this week.'

To say he wasn't tempted would be a lie – although he might regret it if Beverley turned out to be an awful cook.

It was very kind of her, but he would feel like he was intruding. He couldn't begin to imagine how Judith would react if the shoe was on the other foot. His daughter would be both shocked and appalled. Shocked, because he didn't cook Sunday roasts, and appalled to think that he had invited a total stranger to join their family meal.

The last thing Beverley said about it before the conversation moved on was, 'You don't have to make a decision now. Just turn up. It'll be on the table at one-thirty.'

Andrew knew he wouldn't go. 'Maybe another time.'

***

'Don't be alarmed,' Beverley said to Ron as they ate their cottage pie later that evening. 'I've invited Andrew to Sunday lunch. I doubt he'll come, but I thought I'd better warn you in case he does decide to turn up.'

Ron's brow furrowed. 'Andrew?' Then it cleared as he realised who she meant. 'The guy whose house you went to for a cuppa the other day.' He frowned again. 'Why?'

'I think he's lonely. He asked me out.'

'I take it you bumped into him again today?'

'Not literally. We stayed upright this time.'

'Glad to hear it.'

'I brought him back here for a brew, as it was my turn.'

Ron was gazing at her with a concerned expression. 'Be careful.'

'Like everyone warned me to be careful with you?' She arched a brow, and Ron pressed his lips together.

'They were right. You didn't know a thing about me,' he said.

'I could tell you were a good man who just happened to be down on his luck. And they weren't right at all.' Helen had been horrified when Beverley had invited Ron to stay with her in Brighton for a couple of weeks.

Beverley remembered the look on the woman's face as though it were yesterday. Helen's disapproval had made Beverley even more determined because Helen's reaction had more to do with the fact that Ron was homeless, rather than outrage that Beverley was going to be sharing her house with a man none of them knew that well. Apart from Kate. Kate had assured her mother-in-law that Ron was harmless. But that hadn't stopped Helen from bumping her gums about him whenever she got the chance.

May hadn't been any better. She had actually informed Beverley that she thought Ron was trying to get his foot in the door so he could get his hands on Beverley's house. Which was ridiculous: for one thing Ron wasn't a conman, and for another Beverley had already signed her house over to Kate, so there wasn't anything for him to get his hands *on*.

And now look at him, she thought proudly. He had a thriving dog training business, enough money in the bank to put a substantial deposit on a house of his own, and was engaged to be married.

However, May still wasn't keen on her prospective son-in-law, although she did her best not to air her dislike in front of Annabelle. And Helen positively couldn't stand him.

Poor Ron… He had done nothing to deserve it. But some people had prejudices that they liked to hang on to.

Ron said, 'I hope Andrew does come for lunch; I'd like to meet him.' He gazed at her appraisingly. 'Do you know that your face lights up when you talk about him?'

Beverley's mouth dropped open. 'It does not!'

Ron's lips twitched.

'It does not,' she repeated.

Wisely, he didn't say another word on the subject, but with the seed planted in her head, she wondered if he might be right.

She still hadn't worked out what impulse had driven her to invite Andrew for lunch. She had guessed he was lonely (although he hid it well), but was that any reason to invite a comparative stranger to share a meal with her family?

But his poor little face when she had told him that she couldn't go out with him for lunch on Sunday had tugged at her heartstrings. For a second, he had looked so crestfallen that the invitation had just popped out of her mouth before she'd had a chance to consider what she was saying.

Anyway, he had politely refused, so it was unlikely he would turn up, and even if he did, it was too late now: she could hardly *un*invite him.

If she was truthful, she hoped he *would* come to lunch. There was something about Andrew that spoke to her. She just wasn't sure what it was saying.

CHAPTER 5

When he woke on Sunday morning Andrew didn't have any intention of going to lunch at Beverley's house.

He still didn't have any intention as he walked up her path, his finger poised over the doorbell.

He hadn't meant to come, but his feet had taken him in this direction without much conscious guidance from his brain. So here he was, about to sit down for a meal with a bunch of total strangers, apart from Beverley. And he didn't know her that well, either.

Twinkle whined at him to hurry up, but Andrew hesitated.

He wasn't certain about this at all. Although his tummy might be rumbling, his heart wasn't in it. He could just as easily satisfy his hunger by going home and making himself a sandwich.

Still dithering, he inched towards the bay window and cautiously peered through it, hoping the curtain was hiding him, and he winced when he saw two children, a boy and a girl, sitting on the sofa, staring at the TV. Thankfully they didn't notice him, so he took a chance and moved nearer, craning his neck at an uncomfortable angle as he tried to see without being seen.

A man came into view and Andrew shrank back, but not before he had caught a glimpse of his face. The bloke looked pleasant enough, late forties perhaps, neatly trimmed beard, and crinkly eyes. Andrew assumed that must be Ron.

He swallowed, edging back to the front door, but at the last second his courage deserted him, and he turned on his heel.

'Come on, Twinkle.'

His shoes made little noise on the path, as he tiptoed lopsidedly towards the gate, hoping no one was watching. He looked as guilty as sin, and as soon as he reached the pavement he put his stick to the ground and limped back the way he'd come.

Beverley would understand about him not turning up today. He could say that Judith had paid him an unexpected visit, and he would have phoned Beverley to tell her he wouldn't be coming but he didn't have her number.

Yes, Beverley would understand, he was sure of it.

Anyway, he guessed she might be relieved that he hadn't turned up. It was kind of her to ask him, but he was positive it had been a gesture born out of politeness rather than a genuine invitation.

***

'Aunty Beverley, why was a strange man looking through your window?' Izzie asked, when she and her brother were called to the table.

'What man?' Beverley was emptying a sieve full of peas into a serving dish, and she paused to look at her great-niece.

'A strange one.'

'When? How long ago?'

'Dunno.' Annabelle's daughter wrinkled her nose.

'A minute? Five?'

'Not sure.'

Beverley dropped the sieve into a saucepan and dashed to the front door. Maybe the bell wasn't working? She would be cross if that was the case because it was only just over a year old. Was nothing made to last, these days? She swore to God that manufacturers put microchips in things to make them stop working as soon as the warranty was up!

Beverley yanked the door open, expecting to see Andrew on her step, but he was nowhere in sight.

With a frown, she trotted down the path, scanning the pavement, but there was no sign of him.

She stood there for a moment, wondering if it could have been a delivery driver at her window, but she hadn't ordered anything and the postman didn't deliver on Sundays.

It had to have been Andrew.

Turning back to the house, she tested the bell and heard a ding-dong from deep inside.

It wasn't the bell then.

So why hadn't he—?

'Beverley, do you want me to carry on dishing up?' Annabelle called.

'Coming!' Crossly, she went back in and shut the door, but not without another quick scan of the street.

It probably hadn't been Andrew after all, but a random person.

'What did he look like?' she asked Izzie.

Izzie shrugged. 'Old. Really old.'

'As old as me, old?'

'Older, maybe. I'm not sure.'

'Did he have a dog with him?'

Another shrug.

'Was he limping?'

Izzie stared at her. 'Dunno.'

Still feeling disgruntled, Beverely tried to put it to the back of her mind.

'Have you thought about a venue yet?' she asked Annabelle, as she began eating her lunch. For some reason the gravy wasn't as nice as usual and neither was the honeyed parsnips, and she scowled at her plate. Everyone else was tucking in with gusto though, so that was a relief.

'For what?' Annabelle asked.

'Your *wedding*.' Duh, Beverley almost said.

'I thought Ron had told you? We are getting married in the registry office.'

'You'll still need somewhere to hold the reception,' she pointed out.

'We thought we'd go for a nice meal somewhere, just the seven of us.'

'Seven?' Beverley echoed.

'Me and Ron, obviously,' Annabelle laughed. 'The kids, you, and my mum and dad.'

'What about Kate? She'll want to come. I thought you got on well with her?'

'I do, and so does Ron. But we only want a small wedding.'

'Does your mum know this?'

'I did mention it.' Annabelle speared a roastie and popped it into her mouth.

'What did she say?' Beverley already knew that May wanted Annabelle to have a big fancy wedding, but she was curious as to how May had dealt with this news.

'I'm not sure she was listening, to be honest,' Annabelle said, chewing. 'She was too busy pointing out wedding dresses. She'd bought a whole load of magazines.'

'White?'

'I think she's leaning towards ivory.'

'More flattering,' Beverley said. May couldn't have heard, otherwise she would have definitely voiced her objections. 'You'll look lovely.'

'I'm not going to wear a wedding dress. Not the kind you're thinking of. I've been there, done that, and sold the blasted thing.'

May wasn't going to like that, Beverley guessed, as she asked. 'What *are* you going to wear?'

'I thought I'd wait until the new season's dresses are in the shops and see what I fancy.'

Ron spoke up. 'I've been there and done that too, the only difference being that I have no idea what happened to my suit. Louise probably gave it to a charity shop. Or cut it up into little pieces.'

'Why would she do that, Ron?' Izzie asked.

'Because she was cross with me. But she's not mad at me anymore,' he added, hastily. 'Sometimes, when people get mad, they do silly things. Like when you kicked the wall in the playground and hurt your toe.'

Izzie sighed theatrically. 'I'm not a baby, Ron. You don't have to mansplain everything.'

Ron's eyes widened and he shot a look at Annabelle, who was screwing her mouth up, trying not to laugh. 'Mansplain?' he mouthed. 'Do I mansplain?'

'I can hear you, you know,' Izzie said. 'And yes, you do. All men do. That's why it's called *man*splaining.'

'Where did you hear that?' he asked.

'Can we get back to the subject of the wedding?' Beverley tutted.

Unlike her sister, Beverley fully appreciated that it was up to Ron and Annabelle where they got married and what the bride wore, and she could see a storm brewing on the horizon when May realised her dreams of her daughter having a big wedding were about to be thwarted. Beverley would like them to have that too, if she was being truthful.

Ron and Annabelle exchanged a look as Beverley continued, 'This might be a second marriage for both of you, but that doesn't mean you shouldn't celebrate it properly, and I know Kate would love to celebrate it with you.' Kate and Annabelle had developed a close friendship since the holiday last summer and Beverley knew that Kate would be upset if she wasn't invited to the wedding.

Annabelle worried at her bottom lip. 'OK, Kate, then.'

'And Brett. You can't leave him out. He is Kate's husband after all.'

'And Brett,' Annabelle agreed, shooting Ron an apologetic glance.

Beverley was about to add that Kate and Brett's children should also be invited, but she held her tongue, vowing not to interfere. She had already said more than she should and felt guilty to have railroaded Ron and Annabelle into inviting more guests than they had originally planned.

But a wedding wasn't just about the two people who were getting married, it was about their families, too. And Beverley wanted Ron and Annabelle to celebrate it with everyone who loved them.

Beverley would do her utmost to ensure the happy couple had the wedding they wanted and not the one that she or May felt they should have, but she had a premonition she and May were about to butt heads.

***

Considering Andrew was supposed to be hungry and considering he had been looking forward to a roast dinner, his appetite wasn't as sharp as it could be. He was sitting in a pub in Meeting House Lane an hour or so after running away from Beverley's house, Twinkle lying expectantly at his feet, and he was eyeing his plate of roast turkey and all the trimmings with a great deal less enthusiasm than he had anticipated when he had ordered it.

It tasted nice enough – very nice – but he seemed to be feeding as much to his dog as he was eating.

Telling himself that he was merely checking the place out in case Beverley fancied a bite to eat here at some point, he forked some cabbage into his mouth and chewed.

Had Beverley served up cabbage today, he wondered. Would her gravy have been better than the gravy here? Had she hoped he would turn up, or had she forgotten she had invited him? If he had rung the bell, would she have been pleased to see him, or dismayed?

He wished he knew, because at this very moment he was feeling a bit of a heel: she had been kind enough to invite him and he had thrown her hospitality back in her face.

He was exaggerating slightly, but that's what it felt like to him, and that was most likely the reason why this perfectly good lunch was going down in lumps.

Still, it had to be better than the alternative of returning home and making a sandwich. Only marginally better, mind you, because Andrew felt almost as alone amongst all these diners as he would have done if he had been in his own living room.

He should have rung that blasted bell.

How bad could lunching at Beverley's have been?

No worse than this, surely?

Twinkle tapped him on the leg with her paw, and Andrew slipped her another morsel of turkey.

Turkey wasn't Andrew's favourite meat. He preferred chicken.

Well, you should have rung that damned bell, shouldn't you? a voice in his head remonstrated. He could have stuffed his face with chicken and been all the happier for it. But he had chickened out.

Snorting sadly to himself at his play on words, he tried to analyse why he hadn't gone through with it. It was hardly a big deal – a spot of lunch with an acquaintance, that's all, not a marriage proposal.

And if the experience had been awkward, it couldn't be any more uncomfortable than him sitting on his own in the pub like Billy No-Mates. He had caught a couple of sympathetic glances directed his way from some of the other diners, and he hoped they didn't feel sorry for him.

He should have brought a book to bury his nose in.

But then again, he hadn't expected to be dining here, had he?

He had made a right hash of today, but the one consolation was that Beverley didn't know about it. He'd go with his first idea and tell her that his daughter had paid him an unexpected visit. She would understand.

*****

Hurt? A little. Annoyed? A tad. Confused? *Definitely.*

Ron had gone home with Annabelle and the kids after having a heated discussion about the possibility of Jake and Izzie having a dog after the wedding. Jake had argued that it didn't 'send the right signal' for a dog trainer not to have a dog of his own, and Izzie had given Ron puppy dog eyes and had pleaded, 'Please, please, please,' continually.

Poor Ron had resembled a deer in headlights, stuck between the pleas of his step-children-to-be and the not-so-happy expression on the face of his fiancée, who didn't seem too thrilled at the idea of owning a dog and had argued that it was hard work and a responsibility not to be taken lightly.

Beverley knew how difficult it had been for Ron to be around dogs (the loss of his beloved dog, Dolly, when he had been in the army had contributed to the breakdown he had suffered shortly after he had left the military) and although he had happily lived with Pepe for over a year and was now training other people's pooches, it was a different matter altogether to lose his heart to a dog of his own. Annabelle was also aware of Ron's background, which was another reason she might be vetoing the idea.

They had still been bickering when they'd left, and Beverley was now feeling quite exhausted.

At least Ron and Annabelle had done the washing up between them, allowing Beverley to put her feet up, but now that they'd gone the house was overly quiet, giving her time to dwell on Andrew's non-appearance. Which was why Beverley found a Tupperware box and a plastic beaker with a lid, and proceeded to fill them with leftover food and gravy, then she bundled herself up in her coat, hat, scarf and mittens, grabbed Pepe's lead, and marched out of the house, taking the plastic containers with her.

Heading for the park, Beverley stomped along the pavement, rehearsing what she was going to say to Andrew, but nothing sounded right in her head. She would just have to wing it and see what came out of her mouth when she got to his house and hope she didn't make a tit of herself.

The shocked expression on Andrew's face when he opened the door and saw her standing on his step made the trip worthwhile.

'Hello.' She beamed at him.

'What are you doing here?'

'Lunch.' She held up a bag with the Tupperware containers. 'It was lovely. Shame you missed it, so I've brought you some.'

'I've had my lunch.'

'Bet it wasn't as nice as this.'

He was giving her a sideways look, his head tilted, and his eyes narrowed. She shook the bag gently, to encourage him to take it, and he grasped it, somewhat reluctantly.

'Any chance of a cup of tea? I'm gasping,' she announced. There was no way she was going to let him leave her standing on the doorstep like an annoying politician canvassing for votes.

He pursed his lips, clearly not happy about it, but he stood to the side so Beverley took that as a win and unclipped Pepe's lead. The poodle trotted ahead, in search of Twinkle.

Walking into the kitchen Beverley sniffed, scanning the room, but no cooking smells lingered in the air and there were no tell-tale dishes drying on the draining board. If Andrew had cooked himself a proper lunch, she would eat her woolly hat. And the matching mittens.

He pushed past her and popped the bag on the worktop, then flicked the switch on the kettle. She noticed he was avoiding looking at her and seemed uncomfortable that she was there.

Tough. She fully intended to get to the bottom of his non-appearance today. Because the more she thought about it, the more convinced she was that it *had* been Andrew outside her house earlier.

'You were seen,' she said abruptly, then broke off. So that's what she was going to lead with, was it? She had been wondering.

'Seen where?' Andrew had his back to her, but she noticed the increased stiffness in his back and shoulders and knew she'd touched a nerve.

Beverley huffed and plopped into a chair, but not before she had taken her coat off. 'Outside my house,' she replied, praying that he wouldn't say 'it wasn't me, it must have been someone else'.

'I can explain,' he began, turning to face her. 'I was just about to ring the bell when my daughter called. She was wondering where I was. You see, I had forgotten she was coming down to Brighton for the day, and she was already sitting in a pub in The Lanes, waiting. Silly me! My head is like a sieve, these days. Anyway, I had to dash off and I didn't *definitely* say I'd come to yours for lunch, so....' He ground to a halt.

'What did you have?' she asked.

'Turkey. It was either that or lamb, and there's always a risk lamb will be too pink for my liking.'

'Was it nice?'

'Very.' His face told a different story.

Beverley had a feeling he wasn't being completely honest.

Izzie said he'd been looking through the window, so had something scared him off? Not the kids, surely. Probably not Annabelle either.

Therefore, it must have been Ron, although Beverley couldn't think why. Ron was an absolute love and wouldn't harm so much as a fly.

'Did you take Twinkle?' she asked.

'I did.'

'Good, that means we can go there together sometime. How about Wednesday?'

He handed her a cup of tea.

'Ta.' She took it and put it on the table.

'Biscuit?' he asked.

'No thanks.' She patted her tummy. 'I'm still full. Apple crumble with cream,' she added.

He glanced hopefully at the bag she'd brought, reinforcing her suspicion that he was lying about something.

'Sorry, there was none left. Ron had seconds. I can make you one, if you want?' she offered.

'Thanks, there's no need. It was kind of you to bring me lunch. I'll have it tomorrow. It'll be OK in the fridge until then, won't it?'

'It will. Best to warm it up in the oven and not the microwave though; it'll be nicer that way. Wednesday?' she reminded him.'

'I… er… OK.'

'That's settled. Lunch on Wednesday, with the dogs. You'd better let me have your phone number and I'll give you mine, just in case anything comes up. But I'm warning you now, don't you dare try to find an excuse to get out of it.'

She didn't know why she was so adamant that they went out to lunch, but now that the idea was in her head, she was determined to go.

Telling herself it was because she didn't get out as much as she liked these days, especially now that Ron had a business to run and a new family to spend time with, she swapped phone numbers with Andrew, and when that was done she slurped the last of her rapidly cooling tea, then got to her feet.

'Remember to put that in the fridge.' She jerked her chin at the bag containing the Tupperware. 'You can give me the tubs back when I see you on Wednesday. Oh, and if you're wondering, I'll be walking Pepe along the front tomorrow in case you fancied joining me. I promised him some sea air. Cheerio – I'll see myself out. Come on, Pepe, it's time to go home.'

Pepe stood up, stretched, yawned, and shook himself, before padding over to her.

Beverley bent down, clipped the lead onto his collar, and as she was straightening up she noticed Andrew wincing.

'Knee playing up?' she asked.

'A bit.'

'I'd offer to give it a rub for you, but there's a programme I want to watch, and it starts in half an hour. Maybe next time, eh?'

She wasn't sure whether the noise he made was an actual word, but she had great fun seeing his shocked expression.

Good. He needed a bit of livening up – and she was just the person to do it.

***

Andrew closed the door firmly behind Beverley and staggered into the sitting room. God help him, the woman was off her trolley. Fancy offering to rub his knee! Goodness gracious. Apart from his dentist, who was female, and the nurse in the doctor's surgery who checked his blood pressure, no woman had laid a finger on him since Vivienne had passed away. A hug from Judith didn't count.

There had been a twinkle in Beverley's eye as she'd said it though, so she might have been teasing. The problem was, it was difficult to tell. He'd not met anyone quite like her before.

Going out to the kitchen and popping the used mugs in the sink (he had hardly touched his tea), Andrew mused on how strange the day had been. He'd not had one this eventful in a long time. Not even the day Beverley had knocked him over had been this strange, and at the time he would have bet his last pound coin that none could be any stranger.

He clearly would have lost his money.

The thought made him chuckle and the unexpected noise gave him pause. He didn't often chuckle when he was on his own. He didn't have much cause to.

The sound of his landline ringing made him jump and he hurried to answer it, smiling when he saw the number displayed on the little screen.

'Judith, how lovely!'

'Hi, Dad, how are you?'

'Not bad. You? How are Duncan and the boys?'

'Oh, you know… busy, busy, busy. Look, I've got to be in London on Wednesday morning for a meeting, so I thought I could pop down and see you afterwards. Shall we say about lunchtime? My meeting is at nine – don't they realise I've got to come all the way from Peterborough and I'll have to get up at the crack of dawn just for one hour in blasted Head Office. Anyway, I thought I could jump on the train to Brighton and come and say hello. It's ages since I saw you.'

And whose fault was that, Andrew wondered, uncharitably. He drove the thought away. 'That would be lovely.'

'Would a late lunch be OK? I thought I could do some shopping in Oxford Street first, then mosey on down for about two? How does that grab you? We can meet in town and go for a bite to eat somewhere,' she said. 'It would save you cooking.'

'Good idea. I'd like that.' Judith was right – it was ages since he'd seen her. Christmas was the last time. He knew that both she and Duncan led busy lives, but it was hard when he didn't have enough to keep him occupied. As a result, he spent far too long staring at the four walls and wishing his daughter lived nearer.

Once or twice it had occurred to him to suggest that he sold up and moved nearer to Judith, but this house held so many memories of Vivienne that he didn't think he could bear to leave it. Then there was also the added factor of whether Judith would appreciate him living on her doorstep, and even if he did move closer, there was no guarantee he would see any more of her than he did now.

Still, he was grateful that he would be seeing her soon. It was a pity she couldn't bring the boys with her, but it was term time and Leo was in university and Mark was in his last year at school, facing A-levels in the summer. He was so proud of them. Bright lads, and good looking too, they were a credit to Judith and Duncan. Every now and again, they would give him a call and he was always so very pleased to hear from them. He didn't understand half of what they said, mind you, when they talked about bands they had been to see and the gaming they did, but it was still lovely to speak with them.

Suddenly Andrew remembered he was supposed to be meeting Beverley, and he slapped a hand to his forehead.

Damn. He was going to have to phone and apologise… but what could he say to her to get out of it? If he hadn't fibbed about going out to lunch with Judith today, he could have told her the truth, but two lunches with his daughter in four days would sound suspiciously like he was trying to wriggle out of his lunch date with Beverley. And he also didn't want her to realise that he had been lying about today. She would think he was a right idiot to make up an imaginary meal with his daughter.

Then it came to him. He would already be in town with Beverley: what if they had an early lunch, then he could meet Judith in the same pub later?

It would mean two meals in a very short space of time, but he was sure he could wangle it somehow. Judith only ever ate sparingly anyway – too intent on keeping her figure – so she would never notice if he ordered something light.

The tricky part would be getting rid of Beverley in a timely manner. She might expect them to walk home together, considering that they lived in roughly the same direction.

However, he was sure he could come up with something plausible.

CHAPTER 6

Twelve noon was a little early for lunch, Beverley thought, but she reasoned that at least the food would be fresh. She had hoped that she and Andrew would meet in the park so they could make their way into town together; or, more preferably, that Andrew would call for her like a true gentleman. But he hadn't. Instead, he had phoned her yesterday to tell her that he would meet her there.

Beverley didn't like tardiness, either in herself or other people, so when she entered the pub at five minutes to twelve, she was pleased to find Andrew already there.

She supposed the other advantage of being here shortly after the pub opened – aside from the freshness of the food – was that they got their pick of tables, and she noticed that Andrew had bagged one in the corner. It was out-of-the-way, cosy and intimate, near to both a window and the fireplace. It was a pity the log burner wasn't real, but at least the heater was on, which meant she should be warm and toasty. These days she felt the cold more than she used to, which was why she always wore so many layers. Shucking off her coat, she hung it on the back of her chair. Her trusty gilet followed. She would keep her cardigan on for the time being, she decided.

Twinkle was lying quietly under the table, but stood up when she spied Pepe, her little tail wagging furiously. Beverley was delighted that the two dogs had become such firm friends: it made getting to know Andrew so much easier. And she really *did* want to get to know him better.

For an older gent, he was rather handsome, and he must have been a real looker in his day. He was also far kinder than his initial gruff persona let on.

Beverley felt an odd tightening in her tummy as he stood up to greet her, and she wondered whether it had been wise to have drunk such a large glass of orange juice with her breakfast. It didn't appear to be sitting right, and she hoped it wasn't about to give her indigestion: it would spoil her lunch.

'Can you drive?' she asked, as Andrew pulled out a chair for her. She appreciated the gentlemanly gesture, plopping down onto the seat with a grunt. Then stood again to take the cardi off because the pub was quite warm, and she popped it on the floor next to her bag. Pepe immediately claimed it for his own, circled around three times, then curled in a ball on top of it.

'Yes, I can,' Andrew said.

'Have you got a car?' He hadn't mentioned one, but that didn't mean he didn't have one, and there were probably loads of other things he hadn't mentioned. It was going to be fun to get to know him. Ooh, she did enjoy meeting new people and making new friends.

'No,' he replied.

'Why not?'

'Gammy knee. Why the interest?'

'Just wondered. I drive and I've got a car.'

'That's good to know.'

She couldn't tell if he was being sarcastic. 'If ever you want to go anywhere, I can give you a lift,' she offered.

'Did you drive here today?'

She shook her head. 'Walked. Exercise is good for you. If you don't use it, you lose it. Anyway, I hate driving in the city centre and there's nowhere to park if I do. And why drive when I've got a bus pass?'

'That's true. Drink?' he asked, as a man came over to take their order.

'Gin and lemonade, please.'

'I'll have a half of Speckled Hen.'

'A real-ale man, are you?' she asked, thinking she might get some in and stick a bottle or two in the fridge, just in case. You never know…

'I like a drop now and again.' He picked up his menu and fished a pair of glasses out of his shirt pocket. 'What are you having?'

Beverley reached into her handbag for her specs. 'I was hoping to try the turkey,' she said slyly, 'but I see it's only available on Sundays.' She traced a finger down the list of dishes. 'I think I'll have the Caribbean chicken with rice,' she said. 'What about you?'

'Um… the salmon with new potatoes, please,' he said to the waiter.

'Shall we share a portion of onion rings, to go with?' Beverley was partial to an onion ring, especially the beer-battered ones.

Andrew pulled a face. 'No thanks, but don't let me stop you.'

Beverley thought he might consider her greedy if she ordered a portion just for herself.

'Forget the onion rings,' she said to the waiter, somewhat regretfully. She certainly would be greedy if she guzzled a whole portion all by herself, which she could do with ease, and what would Andrew think of her then? She didn't understand why, but his good opinion was important to her.

She studied him. 'This is nice.'

'It's not bad, is it?' He was looking past her, his gaze roving around the room.

'I meant this.' Beverley gestured to herself first, then to him. 'Us. Here. Having lunch together. We must do it again.'

'Ah, I see. Yes, we must.'

He fell silent and Beverley hunted around for something else to say. It wasn't like her to be so tongue-tied, and she wondered why.

'Tell me about Judith,' she said at the same time as Andrew asked, 'Did you enjoy your walk on the beach the other day?'

'You first,' he said, gallantly.

'I did, thanks. It was bracing.' She had been hoping she might have seen him, considering she had told him where she'd be. But then, she hadn't specified a time and the beach was rather long.

'It is only February,' he pointed out.

'It'll be March before we know it,' she replied.

Silence reigned again for a moment.

'Judith?' she reminded him.

Andrew jerked. 'Where?'

'Pardon?'

'Judith.' He was staring over her shoulder, his eyes bulging a little as they darted about.

'I asked about her?' Beverley reminded him.

He subsided. 'Oh, yes, so you did.' Picking up a beer mat, he began playing with it. 'She's, let's see, just turned forty-seven and is married to a nice fella by the name of Duncan. He's a sales executive, and she's something big in crisps—'

'Crisps?' Beverley interjected.

'Yes, you know, the potato snacks that come in foil bags in a variety of flavours.'

'That's what I thought you meant, but I wanted to check. Go on.'

'They live in Peterborough, and I think I told you that they have two boys.'

Beverley looked up as the waiter placed their drinks on the table. 'Thanks.' She turned back to Andrew. 'Eighteen and twenty-one?'

'That's right. Mark and Leo. Leo is the eldest.' His face lit up as he mentioned their names. 'I wish Judith was bringing—' he began, then stopped abruptly and dropped his gaze to his hands.

That beermat wasn't half getting a bashing, she noticed, wondering what was up with him. Andrew appeared to be incredibly nervous for more than a simple bite to eat on a Wednesday lunchtime.

'Never mind,' he said. He picked up his glass and swallowed half the contents in one gulp, as though he needed some fortification.

Then again, she thought, it was only a half – barely more than two mouthfuls. But she couldn't help wondering what he had been about to say, or why he seemed so jumpy. Was she making him nervous? She hoped not. He hadn't seemed nervous the other occasions they'd met. He had seemed positively belligerent, especially that first time when he had knocked her over, and she tried to think what might have changed.

Their food arrived and the conversation focused on that for a while, to Beverley's relief.

'How is your chicken?' he asked, as they munched their way through their meals. Beverley seemed to be doing most of the munching though, and Andrew seemed to be doing more picking, and she wondered whether he had problems with his teeth. At their age, teeth issues weren't beyond the realms of possibility.

'Nice,' she replied. 'What about your salmon?'

'Good, good.'

It came with a Hollandaise sauce and a separate dish of new potatoes with their skins on, plus two packets of foil-wrapped butter. Beverley noticed that he had only taken one of the potatoes, and she itched to help herself but thought she'd better not. Just because he had only put one on his plate, didn't mean he wouldn't eat the rest. And again, she didn't want to appear greedy, but she couldn't help it if she had a healthy appetite: unlike Helen, who pecked at her food like a chicken scratching for seed. May could be a bit like that, too. Which probably explained why Beverley was plump and why May and Helen could audition as skeletons at Halloween.

Andrew didn't add any more potatoes to his plate and he also refused dessert, although he was quick to say that she should have something if she wanted.

As if! There was no way she was going to stuff her face with the Belgian waffles she fancied, while he watched.

Beverley settled for a cup of tea instead, and Andrew had a coffee.

'Not hungry?' she asked after their drinks arrived. 'I noticed you didn't eat much of your lunch. Or were you fibbing about the food here?' She thought her meal had been well tasty and the portions had been generous, too. But maybe his salmon hadn't been as nice as her chicken.

'I thought I was, but...' He drifted off.

Beverley pursed her lips as he glanced at the clock hanging on the wall behind the bar. That was about the fifth time he'd looked at it in as many minutes.

'Got somewhere else to be?' she asked sharply. 'You keep checking the time.'

'Ah, yes.' An expression of relief flitted across his face. 'I've got an appointment, here in town. Two o'clock.'

'Is that why you wanted to eat so early?'

'Yes.'

'We could have gone out for lunch another day,' she said.

'You told me not to make an excuse!' he protested.

'It wouldn't have been an excuse,' she pointed out. 'You should have said.'

'I didn't know until after we'd made our arrangements.'

Guiltily, Beverley guessed she must have come over a bit forceful. She had a habit of doing that. No wonder the poor bloke hadn't wanted to rearrange. When would she ever learn…?

'I want a glass of sherry,' she announced.

'What, *now*?' Andrew looked shocked.

'It's only one-fifteen,' she said. He would have plenty of time to get to his appointment.

'Sherry is supposed to be drunk *before* a meal.' Andrew looked so affronted that Beverley chuckled.

'Who says?' she asked.

'Er....'

'Go on, have another half and stop being such a misery-guts.' It made a change for her not to be the miserable one, and she felt quite superior. Andrew, she realised, brought out the best in her. Or should she say, the *better*... She didn't think she had been her best for a very long time.

'Just one,' he conceded.

She called the waiter over and ordered a round of drinks, and when they arrived she took an appreciative slurp of hers and said, 'We'll drink these, then I'll walk with you to your appointment.'

'What? Er, that's OK, you don't have to. It's in the opposite direction. Out of your way,' he added.

Hmm... There was a hint of awkwardness in his eyes that made her think he was hiding something. He had stuttered and stammered a bit as well, another sign. But was he telling porkies about having an appointment because he didn't want to spend any more time in her company, or did he have an appointment and he didn't want her to know what it was about or who it was with?

A horrid thought suddenly struck her. What if it was a *medical* appointment? What if he was ill?

The more she thought about it, the more she was convinced she might be right. It would explain why he seemed unable to settle today and also why his appetite was lacking.

Beverley didn't want to poke her nose in where it wasn't wanted and she understood that his health was none of her business... but, darn it, she was worried about him.

And if she could do something to help, she would.

But first of all, she had to find out whether her suspicion was right, or whether she was barking up the wrong tree entirely, before she jumped in with both feet.

The thought of Andrew being unwell made her heart flutter uncomfortably and her mouth became dry. She hoped she was wrong. He was such a nice bloke – it would be a real shame if he had something seriously wrong with him.

***

Phew, that was close, Andrew thought as he said goodbye to Beverley soon after he had swallowed his last drop of ale. Congratulating himself on dodging a bullet, he stood outside the pub and watched her walk off down the lane, Pepe trotting at her side.

Once the pair of them were out of sight, he turned on his heel and hurried away in the opposite direction, Twinkle happily scuttling along next to him.

'We'll take a little walk for a few minutes, shall we?' he said to the dog, who looked up at him with her tongue lolling out.

His relief was profound, which was silly.

Andrew had been concerned that Beverley wouldn't believe him, and he had been quite surprised that she hadn't – in her blunt and forthright manner – asked him straight out who he had an appointment with and why. Maybe she had thought, quite rightly, that it was none of her business, and he was thankful that it had saved him from having to tell her an outright lie – because so far he hadn't told her an untruth. He *did* have an appointment: he just didn't want Beverley to know that the appointment was a

77

lunch date with his own daughter in the very pub he and Beverley had just vacated.

If she ever found out, she would think him a right prat.

That would teach him not to fib. If he had come clean about why he hadn't rung her doorbell on Sunday, he wouldn't be in this position now.

Checking the time, he saw that he had about twenty minutes before he was due to meet Judith, so he headed down to the front and onto the pebble beach to give Twinkle a chance to stretch her legs, have a sniff around, and do a wee. It couldn't be much fun for the dog to have to lie under a table for a couple of hours, but Andrew consoled himself with the knowledge that it was better than being left at home in her basket in the kitchen.

With a few minutes to spare, he headed back the way he'd come and returned to the pub he hadn't long left. The place had filled up, and ironically the only spare table was the one where he and Beverley had sat earlier.

He should have suggested to Judith that they dine at a different establishment, but he knew this one allowed dogs. He also knew that Judith loved mooching around in The Lanes with its maze of twisting alleyways and wonderful mix of shops, from antique and jewellery shops to clothes and shoe shops. The pub's location would be perfect for her, and at least he knew that the food was good. He wasn't sure he could face another meal though, even if he hadn't managed to eat much of the salmon.

He grabbed the vacant table and sat down.

No sooner had he done so, than he spotted his daughter as she walked in. Impeccably dressed in a navy business suit and a white blouse, her glossy brown hair bouncing on her shoulders, she scanned the room with a quick darting glance.

The sight of her made his heart clench. She looked so much like her mother, and with every year that passed the similarity grew more pronounced.

Judith saw him and he waved, beckoning her over, and when she arrived at the table he got up and gave her a hug.

He must have clung onto her too tightly because when she pulled back she scoured his face, her expression filled with concern. 'How are you, Dad?'

'Good, I'm good.' He sat down and she followed suit.

She was carrying a black woollen coat over her arm, and she folded it neatly and rested it on top of a large bag which she placed on the floor by her feet. 'You've brought Twinkle,' she said, sounding surprised. 'Hello, girl.'

Twinkle stood on her hind legs, her front paws on Judith's lap, and she briefly patted the dog on the head, before pushing her down and brushing at her skirt with her hands and turning her attention back to Andrew.

'You're looking well,' she observed, cocking her head to the side.

'I feel well. How was your meeting?'

And for the next couple of minutes she regaled him with how her morning had gone. Not well, apparently.

'At least I got to see you today, so that's one good thing to come out of it,' he said.

Judith's aggrieved expression immediately softened. 'That's true. So what's been happening with you? Any news?'

They spoke a couple of times a week on the phone, but the calls were usually hurried affairs, so it was nice to be able to sit down and have a proper chat with his daughter.

He said, 'Nothing much. Same old, same old. Twinkle has made a new friend: a poodle.'

Judith shot him a look. 'What about *you*?'

'Oh, she's not really a friend. More of an acquaintance.'

'Who is?'

'His owner.'

'I see.' But from the expression on Judith's face, she didn't see at all. 'Shall we order?' She plucked a menu from the holder and scanned it. 'I think I'll have the salmon.'

Andrew shuddered, debated whether to try the Caribbean chicken, but settled for the steak and mushroom pie, despite not fancying it much.

Order given, he leant back in his seat, feeling distinctly odd about this whole situation. It didn't help that the very same waiter who had served him and Beverley no more than an hour ago, was now serving him and Judith. The man's brow wrinkled and he was about to say something, but Andrew widened his eyes and shook his head. Luckily the waiter took the hint and thankfully, Judith didn't notice. She had been too busy scrolling on her phone and simultaneously telling him about the new contract that Duncan was knee-deep in.

He listened with half an ear, part of his mind on Beverley and part on why his daughter needed to recount every single smidge of information about people he'd never met and didn't think he'd even heard her mention before, when Twinkle let out a whine and tugged on her lead. Andrew had wrapped it around the leg of the chair he was sitting on, and he glanced down to see what was wrong with his dog, only to find her peering up at the window, her tail wagging furiously.

Andrew looked up, wondering what had caught the terrier's attention, and nearly fell off his chair.

Beverley was outside, peering through the window, her hands cupped around her eyes and resting on the glass as she tried to see inside. Her mouth was open and his heart sank when he took in her shocked expression as he caught her gaze.

'Who is that?' asked Judith.

'Beverley,' Andrew said. Unsure what to do and at a loss for anything to say, he stared at his friend.

Beverley stared back for a second before giving him a cross look, then turning on her heel and stomping off.

'Beverley who?' Judith wanted to know.

'Pepe's mum.' His reply was faint.

'Who is Pepe? Have I met him?'

'He's a dog. A poodle. I told you, he and Twinkle are friends.'

'And you're friends with this Beverley person?' Judith was studying him.

'Not really. I hardly know her. We've met a couple of times, that's all. When walking the dogs. In the park.'

'Why did she look so cross?'

'Did she? I didn't notice,' Andrew fibbed. Crumbs, he had always considered himself a truthful person, but in the last few days he had told enough lies for his nose to have doubled in size.

'Here you go, salmon for you, sir and Caribbean chicken for you, madam.' The waiter placed the meals on the table.

'Sorry, we didn't order a Caribbean chicken: we ordered a steak and mushroom pie,' Judith said. 'And the salmon was for me.'

The waiter blinked. 'Are you sure? I could have sworn—' He shook his head. 'My mistake. I'll change it for you immediately.' He retrieved the chicken dish. 'By the way, I'm glad you came back, sir – the lady you were with earlier has forgotten her cardigan. I'll bring it over.' He glanced at the plate he was holding. 'Steak and mushroom pie coming right up.'

Andrew closed his eyes and drew in a slow breath.

When he opened them, it was to find Judith staring at him, a confused expression on her face.

'What did he mean – *earlier*?' she asked. 'When were you here? And who were you with?'

'Er... I... Oh, dear...'

'Dad?'

Andrew gathered his thoughts. It was time to come clean. What did it matter if he had met with a friend before he met Judith? 'I popped in here for a bite to eat a couple of hours ago.'

'*You've already had lunch?*'

He nodded.

'Why?'

'It was arranged before I spoke to you on Sunday.'

'Why didn't you say something? We could have just had a coffee.'

Hmm, why *hadn't* he said anything...? Oh, yes, he knew the reason: because if he had confessed to having another lunchtime date, Judith might have changed her mind about coming to Brighton today and he wouldn't have got to see her at all.

'It was with *her*, wasn't it? That woman who was giving you daggers through the window.' Judith's brows lowered. 'Was she cross about you meeting me? I thought you said you didn't know her that well? What's going on, Dad?'

Andrew sighed. 'I suppose I'd better explain.'

'I think you should,' Judith said, sounding as though she was talking to one of her boys, and not to her father. Since when had that become a thing?

Andrew realised it was happening more and more frequently. It had begun before Vivienne died but was slowly escalating. Almost a role reversal – like he was the child and she was the parent – and he didn't like it.

'I don't know her well, but that's how things start, isn't it? By not knowing someone, then, getting to know them.'

'But you had lunch with her and lied about it. Is there something going on, Dad? Something you're not telling me?' She looked worried, and he immediately felt guilty.

'There's nothing going on. I'm trying to get out a bit more, that's all.'

'With this Beverley woman?'

'At least 'this Beverley woman' isn't too busy to fit me into her schedule,' he snapped, and instantly regretted it. 'Look, I don't want us to fall out over this. It's something of nothing. I didn't say anything to you because it wasn't a big deal. Anyway,' he took a deep breath, 'I wanted to have lunch with my daughter. Is that such a bad thing?'

'One steak and mushroom pie,' the waiter said. 'And one cardigan. Enjoy. The meal, not the cardigan.'

Andrew and Judith stared at him. The waiter gave them a smile that was more of a grimace, and they watched him slink away.

'Let's eat,' Andrew said, even though his appetite was non-existent, and by mutual silent agreement he and his daughter picked up their cutlery.

But even as the conversation moved on to other things, Andrew had a feeling he hadn't heard the last of this from Judith, and he knew without a shadow of a doubt that he wouldn't have heard the last of this from Beverley.

He would just have to do his best to explain and hope she would understand.

CHAPTER 7

May scowled as she shut her car door. From the back seat Pepe scowled back. For a dog, he had a very expressive face, and it was as clear as day that he didn't appreciate having to sit in the car whilst his mistress and May traipsed all over Brighton and surrounding areas, looking at wedding venues.

For her part, May didn't appreciate Beverley's insistence that the dog came along.

'He likes going out in the car,' Beverley said when May arrived to pick her up. Her sister hadn't been at all happy to see Pepe ready and waiting, with his collar and lead on.

'He might be sick,' May argued.

'He won't.'

'What if he decides to cock his leg over my back seat?'

'He won't.'

'They won't allow him in,' had been May's final shot, before giving in and bowing to the inevitable.

We'll see about that, Beverley thought. If the venue didn't allow dogs on the premises, then it wasn't the venue for them. Or rather, for Ron and

Annabelle, because how could Pepe be the ring bearer if he wasn't allowed inside?

'Where are we going first?' she asked. She had a scribbled list of possibles in her bag, but she wanted to see what May had come up with before she shared them with her sister. She had a feeling none of May's suggestions would include the Sea Life Centre, or the police cells at the Town Hall. She didn't seriously believe that Ron and Annabelle would hold their wedding in any of these places, but it would be such fun to see the look of horror on May's face when she suggested them.

'Have you told Annabelle what we are doing today?' Beverley asked, after May had explained where they were going and confirmed what she already suspected – boring, expensive, and not what Ron and Annabelle would want at all. Did the woman never listen? May seemed determined to steam on ahead with plans for the wedding, without any consideration for what the couple in question wanted.

Guilt flashed across May's features. 'I thought I'd tell her when we've narrowed it down. After all, they're cutting it fine, so they'll be hard pressed to find somewhere nice at this late stage.'

The reception might have to take place on Brighton Pier after all, Beverley mused.

And after visiting three very posh venues and being told in no uncertain terms that bookings were now being taken for at least a year ahead (two years in the case of the country manor house on the other side of Hove) May was fast becoming dispirited.

'We should have phoned instead,' she lamented, when they had stopped along the route for coffee and cake. 'But I so wanted to see the place for myself first.'

'You've gone about this all wrong,' Beverley agreed, slipping Pepe a generous morsel of Victoria sponge.

May eyed the action with disapproval. 'You spoil that dog.'

'So?' Beverley's reply was belligerent.

May tutted but didn't say anything further. May was good at tutting. And eye-rolling. She was also good at lip-pursing.

'I've got a couple of suggestions,' Beverley began, scrabbling around in her bag for the list of venues she had come up with, and handing it over.

May took it eagerly, but the hope in her eyes swiftly dimmed. 'No,' she muttered, scanning down the page. 'I don't think so... Definitely not...' and ending with, 'What were you *thinking*?' She thrust the sheet of paper across the table as though it was coated in something unmentionable. 'They might be your idea of perfect wedding venues, but they certainly aren't mine.' May wrinkled her nose. 'A *games* room? With *laser lights*? Ugh.'

'It might be fun,' Beverley protested, thinking that it really might be. The kids would have a whale of a time, and so would the adults – apart from May and Helen, although Beverley was still holding out hope that Ron and Annabelle wouldn't want Brett's mother there.

'Fun? Weddings aren't about having *fun*.' May shot her an incredulous look.

That was where Beverley begged to differ. In her day, weddings had been damn stuffy affairs, but things were different now. A wedding didn't have to be about canapes and inviting long lost Cousin Gertrude who no one had spoken to for a decade. It could be a lighthearted celebration of a new future together, filled with love and laughter.

She slurped her coffee, deliberately making a noise that she knew would wind her sister up, then smirked as May rolled her eyes.

But however much the two of them disagreed on most things, Beverley couldn't deny that she and May wanted Ron and Annabelle to have a wonderful day, a day to remember for the rest of their lives.

The problem was, May had very firm ideas on what that wonderful day should entail, and Beverley's thoughts kept coming back to where the reception would be held. May was right in that time was ticking along. One consolation was that the 'best' places (the ones May favoured) would all be booked up, so maybe Beverley's more unusual venues were in with a chance.

They had better hurry up, though, or Ron and Annabelle would be holding the reception in a pub down the road. Or in The Lanes, she thought sourly, as an image of the one she and Andrew had dined in popped into her head. The one that she and Andrew, and then *Andrew and his daughter* had eaten in, she amended, scowling.

'Don't sulk,' May commanded.

'I'm not.'

'You are; just because I poo-pooed your suggestions.'

'That's not the reason I'm sulking.'

'Ha! So you admit that you *are* sulking. Your face will stay like that,' May cautioned when Beverley's scowl deepened.

'Yours already has,' Beverley shot back.

'Don't be so rude.'

Beverley would normally have hunted around for a suitable retort, but today she couldn't be bothered. Her mind was on Andrew. To think that she had got herself all worked up and worried because she'd thought he was ill, when there hadn't been a thing wrong with him apart from his gammy knee. If she saw him again anytime soon, she might be tempted to kick his good knee, to even things up.

Fancy him brushing her off so he could have lunch number two with his daughter!

When Beverley had followed him to the beach, making sure to keep well enough back so he didn't spot her, she had been curious and confused. When she had seen him retrace his steps and return to the pub, she had assumed he had forgotten something, so she had waited in a shop doorway, poised to dash inside if he headed in her direction when he emerged. She had scooped Pepe up, so he wouldn't make a fuss – and the shop staff would be more inclined to let her in if her dog was in her arms rather than on the floor, and as she'd waited she had considered buying a voluminous handbag to pop Pepe in so she could smuggle him into those places he wasn't allowed to go.

It was only when she had got as far as imagining whether the bag should be made out of fabric or leather, that she realised Andrew was still in the pub, and she wondered what he could be doing in there considering his appointment was imminent.

She had put Pepe down and slowly walked towards it, debating whether to go inside. But if he had been in there, she hadn't wanted him to see her, so she had sidled up to one of the windows, cupped her hands around her eyes and had peered inside, her nose almost pressing against the glass.

Her surprise when she had seen Andrew sitting at the exact same table where she had sat with him a short while earlier, and that he was with another woman, knew no bounds. Gobsmacked was an understatement.

Andrew's expression had mirrored her own, but his had harboured undertones of dismay and maybe even guilt. He had reminded her of Kate when her daughter was tiny and had been caught doing something that she knew she would be scolded for.

It had taken every bit of willpower Beverley possessed not to march into the pub and give him a piece of her mind. Instead, she had backed away from the window, almost treading on Pepe in the process, and walked off.

She hadn't seen Andrew since.

She wasn't sure she wanted to if she was honest, and so had been avoiding the park. Which was a nuisance because the park was so convenient.

But even though she was still cross with him, she recognised that most of her ire was aimed at herself.

Andrew didn't owe her anything, and certainly not an explanation. If she had jumped to the wrong conclusion regarding his appointment, that was down to her, not him.

Maybe if she had asked, he would have told her who he was meeting; although somehow she didn't think so. He had clearly been caught on the back foot, and she had got the feeling that he hadn't wanted her to know.

The question was, why? She had recognised Judith instantly, having seen her photo on Andrew's kitchen windowsill, and surely there was nothing wrong with a father meeting his daughter for lunch?

Beverley wasn't sure what had been going on, but she was determined to find out, so it was time to put her hurt feelings to one side and ask him.

CHAPTER 8

Andrew hadn't been this down in the dumps for a long time, and it was all Beverley's fault. If she hadn't railroaded him into going out to lunch, he wouldn't have had to play silly buggers. But if he was honest, he had no one to blame except himself. He should have told Beverley he couldn't make it as soon as Judith phoned him. He might have guessed that it would backfire.

He had been hoping to bump into Beverley on his daily dog walk, but he'd gone from seeing her at every turn, to Beverley seeming to have disappeared off the face of the earth. It had been a week since their lunch debacle, and he'd not seen hide or hair of her since.

Once or twice he had been tempted to phone to explain, and at one point he had got as far as dialling her number, only to hang up before the call connected.

He had even considered popping around to her house to explain in person, but he hadn't been able to pluck up the courage.

Instead, he had lingered on his walks in the park, doing more laps than usual, his knee aching abysmally. The walks had taken so long that even Twinkle had been glad to get home, but Beverley hadn't shown her face, and he was surprised to discover that he missed seeing her.

As he limped around the park yet again Andrew scowled, thinking that if he missed a grouchy, opinionated woman like Beverley, he really should get out more. He should meet people, socialise more, and make new friends. Or, at least, see more of the ones he had. He couldn't remember the last time he had met up with the boys for a pint and a natter.

The *boys* indeed! Even for the youngest of the men, boyhood had been over six decades ago. They were all retired now, although Kevin did have a part-time job in a DIY store to supplement his pension.

Maybe that was something Andrew could look into? He didn't need the money, but it would get him out of the house and he'd have some company. Whilst Vivienne was alive, the thought of going back to work hadn't crossed his mind because he had been content with his life as it was, and after she had passed his grief had been so deep that he'd had trouble getting out of bed in the morning. If it hadn't been for Twinkle, Andrew didn't think he would have ventured outside for days on end.

He had a sudden unsettling thought – did this idea of finding a job mean he was starting to get over her?

He stopped in his tracks, remorse and guilt sweeping over him. He didn't want to 'get over' her, as though she had been a nasty incident that he should put behind him. He wanted to wallow in his misery, because that was what kept Vivienne's memory alive.

However, there had been several occasions lately when he had gone a good few hours without his wife constantly on his mind, and those occasions were when he had been in Beverley's company.

The realisation floored him.

Was that a good thing, or a bad thing? He couldn't make up his mind whether he welcomed this change, or whether he hated it. A bit of both, maybe.

He couldn't shake off the expression on Beverley's face – confusion, hurt, perhaps a hint of disbelief – and he couldn't work out why it was affecting him like this. It wasn't as though he had been untruthful (not that time, at least). He *had* had an appointment. The fact that it had been with his daughter was neither here nor there.

He had to admit though, it must have seemed odd.

Another thought struck him, and he groaned at not realising before now how it must have looked to Beverley. She had probably thought he was seeing someone else. She wouldn't have known that Judith was his *daughter*, despite the obvious age difference. You did hear of these things, and although he never would have described himself as a sugar daddy, Andrew supposed it wouldn't be outside the realms of possibility that a woman of forty-seven might be interested in someone his age. He still had a good head of hair and all his own teeth, and if he ignored his gammy knee, he was relatively fit and healthy. He had a house, a decent pension and a fair amount of savings in the bank. He might be considered a catch to some women, despite his advanced years.

Looking back, there hadn't been a lack of female visitors in the months after Vivienne had died, and he had thought it very considerate of the ladies to go out of their way to chat with him and ask after his health. Until, that is, one of 'the boys' had told him, almost resentfully, that Andrew would now be considered fair game in the love-interest department. Richard had pointed out that the older one became, the fewer men there were, as the women outlived their male counterparts by ten to one.

Andrew hadn't been sure of the accuracy of the statistic, but he was aware that there were more widows than widowers, and for his generation unattached men seemed to be a scarce commodity. Men his age were dropping like flies, leaving their wives or female partners alone and lonely. Which was another reason why he had tended to avoid social situations after Vivienne died. The requests for him to come take a look at a drippy tap, or listen to a strange rattle in a car, or even change a bulb in a ceiling light, had all been thinly veiled attempts to worm their way into his affections. As had the invitations to accompany them on day trips, or to the cinema, or, most memorably, to a funeral. Whoever heard of a plus-one at a funeral!

Needless to say, he had politely declined each and every one, until the invitations had eventually dried up. The fact that he had retreated further and further into his shell had also been a contributing factor, and now he was so far into it that he thought it would take a pulley and winch to drag him out of it.

Then he had met Beverley. Independent, outspoken, full-of-life Beverley, who was unlike any woman he had ever met.

Vivienne would have described her as a breath of fresh air.

'What do you think, my love?' he asked his wife's photo. Her face gazed happily back at him, her expression unchanging.

He touched a finger to her cheek. Three years, nearly four… It seemed like both yesterday and an eternity since she'd left him.

He lowered himself awkwardly into his favourite armchair and Twinkle immediately jumped onto his lap. Absently stroking the dog's head, Andrew asked himself the question that had been preying on his mind recently: did he want to carry on living like this for the remainder of whatever time he had left on this earth? There was no mistaking that he was miserable, his crushing loneliness only partly alleviated by the love of a good dog.

Would it be so wrong to cultivate Beverley's friendship, or hope that it might turn into something more? He suspected it would be unlikely though, because he was as certain as he could be that she didn't have designs on him, and friendship was the only thing on offer.

Aw, sod it. He would have to go round to her house. He was the one in the wrong, not Beverley, so it was up to him to put it right.

Whistling to Twinkle, Andrew put on his coat, clipped the lead onto her collar, grabbed his walking stick and made for the door.

But just as he opened it a fist nearly caught him on the nose and he staggered back, lost his balance, and tripped over Twinkle.

'For crying out loud!' he yelled, glaring up at Beverley whilst trying to fend off an excited poodle. 'I could have broken a hip.'

'Have you?' Beverley asked, peering down at him.

He checked himself over. 'No thanks to you.'

'Hmph. You're in a fine mood. I wish I hadn't bothered coming to see you.'

'Why have you?' he demanded.

Beverley stuck her nose in the air and sniffed. 'I don't know, I'm sure.'

Andrew remembered where he had been going and why, and he softened. 'I'm sorry,' he said, struggling to get his feet underneath him.

Beverley held out a hand and Andrew took it. This hauling each other up off the floor was getting to be a bit of a habit, but he was grateful for the help. The sooner he had his knee replacement operation the better, but he hadn't been given a date yet and the waiting list was horrendous.

'Did you want to come in?' he asked.

'I'm not sure I'm welcome,' Beverley tutted.

'You are. I was just on my way over to yours, in fact.'

'Run out of women to have lunch with, have you?' Beverley's reply was acerbic.

Andrew supposed he deserved that. 'I owe you an explanation.'

'It's none of my business who you have lunch with,' Beverley said, in direct contrast to her previous comment.

'It's not,' he agreed, 'but I do think I should explain. Judith, the woman I was with, is my daughter.'

Beverley scoffed, 'I know.'

'You do?'

'Photos,' she said.

Ah, of course. Now she came to mention it, he remembered her looking at the photos on his kitchen windowsill. She'd thought he hadn't noticed her nosiness, but he had.

'Are you sure you don't want to come in?' he offered again.

'I suppose I might as well, seeing as I'm here,' Beverley replied grudgingly.

He went to go back inside but Twinkle whined pathetically. Andrew glanced down at the dog and pulled a face.

'I tell you what, why don't we take a walk so Twinkle can stretch her legs, and we'll find a coffee shop on the way?'

'Good idea.'

'My treat,' he added.

She waited for him to gather himself together and lock the front door, but as soon as they started walking she went in for the kill.

'What was all that about?' she asked. 'I thought you had a medical appointment or something.'

Andrew pursed his lips. He was aware that Beverley might have jumped to that conclusion?

'Or if not medical, something formal, like a visit to a solicitor,' she carried on. 'When one says appointment, one doesn't normally mean meeting up with one's daughter for lunch.' Beverley stuck her nose in the air.

He took a deep breath. It was time to come clean. 'That Sunday when you invited me for lunch, I got as far as almost ringing the doorbell, but… I don't know… something held me back.'

'Was it Ron?'

'Of course not, why do you say that?'

'It had to be something, or someone, and I didn't think you'd be scared to meet the kids, or Annabelle, so I assumed the reason must be Ron.'

'I don't know what it was,' he admitted. He was trying to be truthful, but Beverley sent him a sceptical look.

'He doesn't bite, you know,' she said.

'I think it's because we hardly know each other,' Andrew began. 'It just seemed a bit...' He ground to a halt.

'Too soon? You do realise I haven't got designs on your body,' Beverley chuckled.

Andrew blushed. 'I didn't think you did,' he protested, then the memory of her offering to give his gammy knee a rub popped into his head and made him blush even more.

'Or is it that you've got designs on mine?' she laughed, and Andrew spluttered.

'Certainly not,' he retorted. Then he realised how that sounded, and he spluttered even more. 'I mean… it's not that you're...' He sighed. 'Oh, dear.' She was laughing, and after a pause Andrew joined in. 'We are a pair of idiots, aren't we?' he said.

'Speak for yourself,' she shot back. 'I'm not the one who had two lunches in one day.'

Andrew snorted. 'I've done that twice,' he admitted. 'I didn't meet Judith that Sunday, but I did go to that pub in The Lanes, and I did have lunch there. The meal was good, but I didn't enjoy being on my own.'

'I thought there was something up!' Beverley was triumphant. 'Don't tell me – you ate the food I brought round for tea that evening?'

He nodded.

Beverley began to wheeze. She was laughing so hard, Andrew wondered if she was in danger of having an asthma attack, but she gradually got a hold of herself and her laughter finally tapered off into an occasional snort.

'You are an eejit,' she said.

'I know.' He carried on with his explanation. 'After you and I made plans to go out to lunch, Judith phoned. She had a meeting, a real one—' he shot Beverley a look out of the corner of his eye '—in London, and she suggested popping down to Brighton and meeting up for a bite to eat.'

'You should have said.'

'You told me I wasn't to make any excuses!'

She gave him another one of her looks. 'You think I wouldn't have believed you?'

'Would you have?'

Beverley shrugged. 'Possibly not. Oh what a tangled web we weave,' she misquoted. 'How did you get on with lunch number two?'

'I didn't. After seeing you peering through the window, then the waiter mixing up the order, and you forgetting your cardi – remind me to give it to you – I lost my appetite.'

'I wondered where that had got to. Did your daughter see the funny side?'

'Not so much,' Andrew said, although he thought that might have more to do with the fact that he had lied about knowing Beverley, and then had been forced to admit that he knew her well enough to have lunch with her.

He had seen the worry lurking behind Judith's eyes, and he hoped she didn't think he was in the early stages of dementia. He knew it was a fear of hers, because Duncan's father had suffered from it for years before he passed away.

'Shall we go in here?' Andrew asked as they neared a café.

He was very familiar with the establishment, having on occasion called in for a morning cuppa and a chat with the boys. This was where they usually hung out, but he knew they would have left by now. He hadn't joined them for ages, and he felt a little guilty about it. But it just seemed too much of an effort these days, somehow.

Looking back over the past few years, he realised how insular he had become. Before Vivienne died, he had made her a promise that he would look after himself, and that he wouldn't mourn her too badly. He had let her down. He wasn't looking after himself nearly as well as he should, and he was mourning her far more than she would have wanted.

In the beginning he had made an effort to go out and meet with friends, or play cards in the pub now and again, but his heart hadn't been in it, and gradually everything had tailed off, until the only times he went out these days was when he took Twinkle for a walk, or to go to the shops. Plus the occasional visit to the doctor or the dentist, of course.

Was that why he had been so reluctant to have lunch at Beverley's house?

Then, ironically, he had found himself eating out three times in the space of a couple of days. Go figure.

He ordered their drinks and a cake because a drink was too wet without one, then settled back in his chair, feeling happier than he had done for a while. It was good to be out, and it was even better to have some company.

'What have you been getting up to?' he asked.

Beverley glowered. 'Checking out wedding venues,' she said with venom.

'Oh, dear. Not going well, I take it?'

'You could say that. May dragged me all over Brighton and Hove, looking at suitable places. The problem is that they are all booked up, some of them years in advance. And she ignored all of my suggestions.' Her expression lifted. 'She might have to reconsider them now she has realised that her first choice ones aren't available.'

'I remember when Judith got married. She and her mother were running around like headless chickens for months beforehand. Bridezillas I think they call them these days: you know, when brides sort of behave like monsters.'

'Annabelle isn't in the least bit like that,' Beverley said. 'She's the opposite. Far too laidback for her own good. It's her mother who is the bridezilla. They want to have the ceremony in the registry office, but May's having none of it.'

'Why not?' he asked, then he flinched when he saw Beverley's expression.

'May reckons they deserve a proper wedding with all the bells and whistles. Remember me telling you that she felt a bit cheated because Annabelle got married in Australia the first time? Anyway, she wants the whole shebang to be held somewhere posh, but instead they're talking about a registry office ceremony and going for a quick meal afterwards, instead of having a proper reception.'

'What do you think they should do?'

'I must admit, I would like them to have a proper reception, somewhere more memorable than nipping to the nearest boozer, because I think they might regret it if they don't. And I suspect May will railroad them into it anyway. I just hope she doesn't go too overboard.'

'I'm sure it will all turn out well in the end.' Andrew did his best to reassure her, but weddings weren't really his thing and he hoped they could chat about something else instead.

He noticed Beverley eyeing him speculatively, and he shifted uneasily in his seat, wondering what she was thinking. He soon found out.

'I've got an idea,' she said. 'How about you coming to look at wedding venues with me?'

'Me?'

'It would be better than taking May. I don't think she'd come anyway. She doesn't like the pier.'

'Excuse me?'

'Brighton pier – they do weddings. May won't entertain the idea, so I know she'll refuse to come with me. But she might find that she's running out of options, so I want to be able to jump in when she realises that Ron and Annabelle won't be able to get married in a fancy castle or one of the big hotels on the seafront, like she's hoping for.'

'I don't know the first thing about weddings,' Andrew protested. He wasn't sure how much use he would be.

'That's OK, you don't have to say anything. I'll just feel better if I have someone with me.'

'All right,' Andrew agreed reluctantly. What harm could it do? And it would certainly get him out of the house. He couldn't remember the last time he'd been on the pier. It must have been when his grandsons were small, and he guessed it had probably changed a fair bit.

'What about Pepe?' he asked. Twinkle was happy enough to be left on her own for a couple of hours, but he knew that Beverley usually took Pepe everywhere with her.

'I suppose I'll have to leave him at home. He's not going to like it.'

'Why don't you bring him here, and he and Twinkle can keep each other company.'

'That's a brilliant idea. You're not just a pretty face, are you?' She reached across the table to pat his cheek, and Andrew tried not to flinch at the unaccustomed contact.

'When do you want to go?' he asked.

'How are you fixed for tomorrow?'

Andrew didn't have anything planned. He rarely did. 'Tomorrow is good for me.'

Beverley beamed at him, and Andrew found himself beaming back.

Yes, she definitely was a breath of fresh air.

CHAPTER 9

Beverley stuffed a hot vinegary chip into her mouth and savoured the taste. Nothing could beat a cone of proper chip-shop chips eaten in the fresh air. And she did mean fresh! It was blimmin' bitter on the end of the pier. But then again, what did she expect? It was only March, a month famed for its blustery winds and grey skies. Add a grey roiling sea beneath their feet and a stiff north-easterly breeze blowing in from the continent, and it was enough to make her wish she'd doubled up on her thermal undies.

Although it was bracing, it wasn't unpleasant. The smell of the sea, the sound of the waves as they pushed and pulled at the pebbles, and the wheeling seagulls overhead with their raucous cries, was so quintessentially British seaside. As was the aroma of frying onions and the sweet smell of sticky pink candyfloss, and the clink and clank of coins being fed into the slot machines.

Beverley loved it, but she knew how much May hated it. Her sister had never been a fan, not even when they were kids. Too stuck up and snooty for penny arcades and Punch and Judy shows, May had no sense of fun.

Andrew, on the other hand was having a whale of a time. He had headed straight for a push-shove machine, feeding it two penny pieces with the same enthusiasm as Beverley was shovelling chips into her gob.

He hadn't won anything, of course. And neither had he managed to hook a cuddly toy from the grabby thing.

She had steered him away from the slot machines but had failed to divert his attention from the air hockey table, and he had insisted on having a game. He had looked so hopeful that she didn't have the heart to refuse him, so they had played best of three and she had let him win, although he claimed he'd won fair and square.

Once he had satisfied his arcade games itch, he had been more than happy to carry on, heading out to the other side of the arcade to explore the rest of the pier, although she did have to keep chivvying him along because he continually wanted to stop to look over the side.

'Anyone would think you haven't been on a pier before,' she grumbled.

'It was so long ago, I'd forgotten what it's like,' he said. 'The boys were quite young the last time I brought them here. Their mother preferred more educational places, like museums.'

Beverley took her own grandchildren to the pier whenever they came to Brighton, and she had brought Annabelle's two here last summer. They'd had a great time, as had Beverley, and she had enjoyed spoiling them rotten. She just wished Kate lived nearer, so she could bring Ellis, Portia and Sam here more often.

Saying that though, Ellis was eighteen now and in university, and Portia was sixteen and too cool to accompany her nanna anywhere, so that only left Sam, and he was growing up fast.

Thankfully, Andrew hadn't suggested going on any of the rides, so Beverley was finally able to concentrate on what she had come here to do – check the place out as a wedding venue.

She had never been in any of the bars or restaurants here before, so she had a really good look around, but eventually she was forced to admit that May was right.

'I don't think this is the place for Ron and Annabelle,' she concluded, even though the venues themselves were lovely. She just couldn't see shy Ron being comfortable here, and neither could she envision Annabelle walking down the pier in her wedding dress.

'Where next?' Andrew asked. Oblivious to her disappointment, he was clearly having fun.

She drew in a breath, said, 'I was thinking about that place at the marina – they have laser light rooms that have their own themes…' and ground to a halt when she saw his expression. 'They're not going to like that either, are they?'

'I don't think so,' he replied gently.

'There's that cabaret place?' She stared at him hopefully, then added, 'Maybe not. I suppose we'll have to go with somewhere more traditional, after all.' Suddenly the day lost its lustre and she began to flag. 'Let's go home,' she said.

'OK.' He looked almost as disappointed as she felt, but she suspected it was for a different reason – he was enjoying himself, despite all the walking.

'Shall we have a stroll along the front before we head back?' she suggested. The sun was poking through the clouds and the weather was trying its best to brighten up. 'We can have a coffee in one of the cafés on the way.'

He perked up again at that, and she felt quite mean for having promised him a day out looking at wedding venues, only to call it off after visiting only one place. But she hated being wrong, and she hated May being right even more. Not that she would tell her, of course. May didn't need to know that Beverley had come to the pier today with the intention of checking it out as a possible wedding venue.

Beverley slipped her arm through Andrew's as they set off along the wide promenade, aware that he hadn't complained in the slightest at having to walk from the bus stop to the seafront and wanting to give him something to lean on as well as his walking stick. She hadn't wanted to drive into town, not with traffic being so bad and the parking even worse. Anyway, they both had bus passes, so they might as well use them, which was what they had done.

He wasn't complaining now, but she noticed his limp was becoming more pronounced, and he was leaning on his stick more heavily. She hoped she could offer him some support, without him realising what she was doing.

Despite the weather being typical for early March, there was a surprising number of people taking the air along the promenade, from dog walkers to people pushing prams, workers on their lunch breaks, and older people like herself and Andrew, who were out for a stroll. She noticed that the majority of older people were bundled up just as much as she was, which made her feel slightly better, even if she did resemble an Easter egg in shape.

Beverley had always loved the seafront, with its golden pebbly beach, paved walkway, and pretty iron balustrade. She also liked the double-headed streetlamps. It was all very genteel and Victorian, especially with the impressive buildings lining the other side of the road. Many of them were private residences, mostly flats, and May lived in one of the side streets in a building very much like the ones Beverley was currently staring at.

Not long after Annabelle had returned from Australia with her two children to make a new life for herself in the UK, May and Terence had decided to sign their house over to their daughter and use their not-inconsiderable savings to buy a flat near the seafront. Excuse me, Beverley thought, *apartment* not *flat*.

Beverley had done roughly the same thing herself when it came to her own house and daughter. Having heard loads of horror stories about the elderly having to sell their homes to pay for the fees if they had to live in assisted accommodation, Beverley had decided several years ago that there was no way she was going to allow her house to fall into the hands of the council, when she had worked hard all her life. Therefore, she had transferred ownership of her three-bedroom Victorian terrace to Kate, on the understanding that Beverley would live in it until the end of her days, or until she was no longer able to cope with living on her own – whichever came sooner. Touch wood (she tapped herself on the head) she was able to care for herself just fine, and long may it continue.

She and Andrew had been strolling for about half an hour and had covered some considerable distance, when she said, 'The bandstand has got a café. How about we go in there? It will be just like being on the beach but in the warm.'

'That's a terrific idea,' Andrew said, and she heard the relief in his voice.

They made their way slowly down the steps, Andrew grunting slightly, and she knew that there was no way they were catching the bus back. She wasn't even sure whether he'd make it as far as the bus stop. They would grab a taxi, she decided, feeling quite decadent. She hadn't treated herself to a taxi for quite some time, and she was rather looking forward to it.

She was also looking forward to having a sit down with a nice hot drink, in a nice warm café, with a view of the sea.

The bandstand was an octagonal structure, painted white with green accents, and decorated with gorgeously ornate wrought iron. It seemed to balance on the edge of the promenade, the view out to sea uninterrupted. Underneath, holding it up, was another octagonal structure which was where the café was located.

This was where Beverley and Andrew headed, going inside because it was too chilly to eat on the terrace.

A blast of delightfully warm, coffee-scented air hit her as she opened the door, and she sniffed appreciatively. Despite the chips she had eaten, her tummy rumbled.

'I fancy a cheese toastie,' she announced when they sat down. 'Would you like one?' She took the opportunity to shuck a layer or two, wanting to feel the benefit when she went back outside.

'Go on, you've twisted my arm,' Andrew said, and they ordered a toastie each and a hot drink.

Whilst they waited for their food, Beverley's attention was caught by a young couple strolling hand-in-hand across the pebbles. The girl was gazing up at her fella with total adoration on her face, and Beverley's heart clenched. She remembered gazing up at Kate's dad like that once. It had been so long ago, in a different life, when she had been someone else entirely.

She caught Andrew looking at her and she smiled brightly. She didn't want to get maudlin – it didn't suit her. Grumpy was more her thing. But these days grumpy didn't sit well with her, either; not since Ron had come into her life. He might be nearing fifty, but he had needed lots of TLC and she had been happy to provide it.

She scanned Andrew's face, and wondered whether she was seeing the same need in him as she had seen in Ron. Was that why she was so determined to befriend him? Because he filled her own need to be needed?

Bloody hell, those were deep thoughts to be having just before a toastie, she chided silently.

'I hope Pepe is behaving,' she mused, trying to distract herself. 'I don't leave him on his own very often.'

'He'll be fine. He's got Twinkle to keep him company.'

'I can't believe how well the two of them get on. Pepe can be a miserable little sod.' She chuckled. 'Just like me.'

Andrew shook his head. 'You're not miserable, at all. Argumentative, maybe, but not miserable.'

'I'm not argumentative,' Beverley argued. 'I just have firm opinions.'

'See, you are arguing now,' he laughed.

'No, I'm not.' Her own laugh was heartfelt. Andrew was right – she could be argumentative, and downright ornery too, when the mood took her.

She swivelled in her seat to glance around the café, liking what she saw, and when she spotted a canine figure on the floor next to its owner, she tapped Andrew on the arm.

'We can come here again, and bring the dogs,' She jerked her chin, and Andrew followed her gaze.

'That would be nice. It'll be lovely in the summer, and we can sit outside.' He beamed at her and she grinned back, pleased that he was assuming their trips out would carry on.

Her attention was caught by a lovely photo of a bride and groom hanging on the wall, and she squinted at it. Getting her glasses out of her bag, she popped them on and leaned forward for a closer look.

It had been taken on the bandstand, which had been decked out with flowers and billowing white fabric, and looked absolutely gorgeous.

Beverley had heard the expression 'a light bulb moment' but she had never experienced it herself until now.

She gasped and slapped a hand to her chest, her mouth dropping open.

'Beverley? Are you all right? Beverley!'

'What?' She brought her thoughts back into focus. 'Yes, yes, I'm fine,' she said impatiently. 'I've got it!'

'Got what?' Andrew looked so worried, she burst out laughing.

'The wedding. I know where it should be held.'

He blinked owlishly. 'Where?'

'Here.'

'The café?' He did a little circular motion with his finger.

'No. The bandstand.'

Andrew's brow wrinkled, but when she pointed to the photograph on the wall, it cleared.

'Perfect, isn't it?' she cried.

'What if it rains? Are you sure an outdoor wedding is a good idea?'

Beverley's face fell and just as she opened her mouth to agree with him, a young woman placed two large mugs of coffee on their table and said, 'We've already thought of that. If rain is forecast, we move the ceremony to inside the café.'

Beverley's gaze roamed doubtfully around the café before coming to rest on the waitress.

'Wait a sec, I'll show you.' The woman darted away.

Beverley plopped three cubes of brown sugar into her drink and stirred, her thoughts whirling.

The woman returned with two cheese and tomato toasties plus a salad garnish, and a brochure.

'Scan in the QR code on the back,' she instructed, turning the brochure over, 'and it'll take you to our website. Click on 'Gallery' and you'll see loads of photos of the weddings we've held.'

'QR code?' Beverley had heard of them, but she had no idea how they worked.

The waitress showed her what to do, then left her to it, adding that she would be happy to answer any questions she might have.

Although Beverley was keen to have a look at the photos, she didn't want her toastie to get cold, so she ate that, finished her coffee, and ordered more drinks first.

Then she shuffled closer to Andrew, holding her phone between them so he could see the screen, and she began scrolling.

'This is perfect!' she cried delightedly. 'I know Ron and Annabelle wanted a registry office ceremony but look how lovely this is. I'm sure they would love to get married on the bandstand; although it still doesn't solve the problem of where to hold the reception.' She began counting on her fingers, muttering, 'Ron, Annabelle, the kids, me, May, Terence—'

'What are you doing?'

'Trying to work out how many guests there will be. The bandstand only caters for forty in total, but I reckon that'll be OK. Neither Ron nor Annabelle has a big circle of friends. I wonder if they allow dogs? Excuse me, miss?' Beverley called the waitress over. 'Do you know if dogs will be allowed?'

The young woman laughed. 'I don't see why not. As long as it is well-behaved.'

'He is,' Beverley assured her. 'My son, Ron, is a professional dog handler.'

'I'm sure that'll be fine.'

'What do you think, Andrew?'

'It looks lovely,' he said.

'Right. That's decided. How do I book?'

The woman was smiling. 'I'll just grab the diary. Have you got a date in mind?'

'26th of June.'

The waitress hurried off to fetch the diary and came back to their table holding a tablet. 'I take it we're looking at next year,' she said. 'Or is it for the year after?'

'It's for *this* year.'

The woman's eyes widened. 'Hmm, let's see.'

Beverley held her breath, expecting the worst but hoping for the best.

'It's free,' the waitress announced, sounding surprised and Beverley exhaled slowly. 'I wouldn't hang about though,' she advised. 'The bandstand is usually booked up a year in advance.'

Beverley nodded. It was a familiar refrain. But would Ron and Annabelle go for it? She respected their decision to marry in the registry office, but this place was so them. And there was always the risk that May would railroad them into going for something much grander and much more expensive. Her sister would undoubtedly insist on paying for it, too.

Beverley made a decision.

'How much deposit do you need, and can I pay it now?'

CHAPTER 10

'**Y**ou've done *what?*' May was aghast and her horrified expression lifted Beverley's spirits. They didn't actually need lifting – they were already perky enough – but May's disbelief and shock was an added bonus.

'It's perfect,' Beverley insisted. 'Andrew thought so, too.'

'Andrew?'

'You remember me telling you about him? We bumped into each other in the park? We were having a bite to eat in the café under the bandstand, when we realised they did weddings.'

'We? I didn't know you were a *we*.'

'It's not like that,' Beverley began, but May didn't let her finish.

'Oh, well, if *Andrew* likes it, then it must be nice.'

Beverley huffed. 'All I'm saying, is that it's not just me who likes it.' She wished she hadn't mentioned Andrew now, but the damage was done.

'I'm not having my daughter getting married in a café,' May stated firmly.

'She won't be getting married in a café.' Unless it rains, Beverley thought but didn't say. She had to sell her sister the bandstand idea first before she tackled the possible problem of inclement weather. 'The ceremony would take place on the bandstand,' she clarified. 'Here, look at these.' She hurriedly brought up the images on her phone and studied her sister's face carefully.

May's expression, initially closed, gradually opened up as she scrolled through the photos of happy couples saying their vows under the canopy of the bandstand, toasting each other, and sharing a first married kiss with the sea glittering in the sun behind them.

Looking beyond the bride, the groom and their guests, Beverley hoped that May could appreciate how nicely the bandstand had been decorated, how stylish it looked, and how it seemed almost exotic with the blue sky and the darker blue sea in the background.

'What about the reception?' May asked. 'I hope you're not suggesting they hold it in the café?' The horrified tone had returned.

'Not at all. The café will provide the drinks both before and after the ceremony, and canapes if needed, but we can hold the reception somewhere else.'

'Where?'

'Um, any number of places.'

'I wanted them to have the whole thing in one place, not to have to traipse all over Brighton.'

'Is that any different to getting married in church? Because if they did that, they would still have to hold the reception elsewhere,' Beverley pointed out.

'But they're not getting married in a church,' May argued.

'No, they're getting married on the bandstand. May, you saw for yourself how hard it was to find anywhere nice. This is the perfect alternative.'

'You keep saying that word – perfect,' her sister grumbled.

'That's because it is. With the bandstand booked, we can widen our search for a reception venue. We aren't limited to only those places that are licenced to hold wedding ceremonies.' Beverley knew she'd won when May's expression became thoughtful.

'I've always liked The Willow Tree,' May said. 'They do fabulous afternoon teas. Celia Hughes and her husband went there the other week for her birthday. I think they have private rooms. Of course, it means hiring wedding cars and whatnot, because parking will be a nightmare.'

Beverley had already thought of that. 'Charabanc,' she blurted.

'Did you just sneeze?'

'Bus,' Beverley translated. 'One of those vintage ones.'

'I was thinking of a Bentley or a Rolls Royce.'

'You won't fit everyone in a Bentley.'

May's tone was scathing. 'For the *bride and groom*. You really are hard work, Beverley. We'll need two, of course – one for Annabelle and Terence, and one for the bridesmaids and myself.'

'What about me and Ron?'

'You'll have to make your own way there. As for Ron, I'm sure it's the best man's job to get him to the church on time.'

Beverley let that go for now and asked, 'Who is the best man, do you know?'

'No idea. That's for Ron to sort out. I've got enough on my hands with the bridesmaids.'

Bridesmaids? *Plural?* This was news to Beverley. 'Who else, besides Izzie?'

'I'm not sure, but Annabelle can't just have the one: that would look silly.'

'It'll have to be Ellis and Portia,' Beverley said, feeling smug to think that her granddaughters would get in on the act.

'Does Portia still wear black lipstick?' May shuddered. 'It did nothing for her.'

'That was her Goth stage. She's moved on.'

Last summer Portia had still borne some Goth traits, but the black-dyed hair had mostly grown out and the girl no longer looked like death warmed up. She had still worn a lot of black though. At least it must make getting dressed in the morning easier if you didn't have to worry about what went with what, Beverley mused, as she glanced down at her purple skirt and red jumper, and thought how much more colourful she looked compared to May's boring beige and cream outfit.

May began to look happier. 'Glad to hear it. A pretty girl like her shouldn't be dressing as though she's going to a funeral. There'll be time enough for that when she gets to our age. I've lost count of the number of funerals I've been to lately. Dropping like flies, they are. Talking about funerals, we had better have a word with the bride and groom. Annabelle will kill me if we spring this on her at the last minute. Anyway, she was talking about making an appointment with the registrar soon, and I might be wrong, but I believe they have to state the place where the ceremony will take place.'

Ah, now... that was the bit Beverley wasn't looking forward to. She had a feeling it wasn't going to be as easy to convince Ron and Annabelle that getting married on the bandstand was a good idea, as it had been to convince May.

***

'Something smells nice,' Ron said when he walked into the kitchen that evening. Pepe danced around his legs, uttering little yips of joy, until Ron bent down to fuss him.

'I'm doing you a nice mixed grill,' Beverley told him. 'Have you had a good day?'

'Pretty good.' Ron rinsed his hands in the sink and then wiped them on a towel hanging on a hook next to the radiator. 'I spent a couple of hours with a Doberman and his owner, who wouldn't stop pulling on the lead – the dog, not the owner,' he joked. 'Then, a yappy Jack Russel who needed to learn to tone it down a bit, and after that I had a puppy training class.' He seemed tired but happy, and she loved that he had found his niche in life.

They chatted about this and that until it was time to eat, but when Beverley placed a piled-high plate in front of him and said, 'I want to talk to you about something,' Ron looked worried.

'Please don't tell me you're ill,' he begged.

'It's nothing like that. It's about the wedding.'

'What about it?'

Beverley was aware that she had to choose her words carefully. She picked up her fork. 'I know this is a second wedding for both of you and neither of you wants a fuss, but have you considered everyone's feelings?'

'What do you mean?'

'A wedding is a special day, even if you have done it before.' Beverley smiled winningly.

Ron eyed the morsel of steak he had just been about to pop in his mouth, and put it down. 'I don't understand.'

Beverley thought swiftly. 'May wants you and Annabelle to have a big fancy wedding.'

'She can want all she likes,' Ron said with a sigh. 'She's not going to get it.'

'How about a compromise?' she suggested.

'Like what?' he asked suspiciously.

She said, 'Even if you do get married in a registry office, everyone is going to want to come, right?'

'By everyone, you mean...?'

'Annabelle's parents, me, Kate, Brett and their kids.'

'Okaay.'

'And you've already said you're happy to go for a meal afterwards.'

'Ye-e-es.'

'So that's not too different to what May wants. She just wants your wedding to take place somewhere nice.' Beverley held up a hand as Ron opened his mouth to speak. 'Hear me out,' she pleaded.

He sat back, his meal forgotten.

'Me and May have been looking at wedding venues,' Beverley said, hurrying on before he could object. 'Don't worry, we didn't find anything. Well, we did, but they were all booked up months and months in advance.'

'Good.' His voice was flat.

'We also thought about the pier or that laser room place, or even the tower, but I didn't think it was your kind of thing.' She thought it was best to start off with the worst-case scenario in the hope that Ron would be more amenable when she confessed to what she had done.

'No, it isn't.' He was still looking at her warily.

'I've booked the bandstand for the ceremony,' she ended.

A heavy silence hung in the air. Beverley was too afraid to break it.

Eventually, Ron did. 'What on earth possessed you?'

'Because it's romantic and it's practically on the beach, like when you and Annabelle first met and—'

'We met in a *house*.'

'True, but you were on holiday, and it was at the seaside. And the bandstand is really pretty. Annabelle will love it. Take a look? Please?'

She fetched her phone and showed him the photos.

Ron studied the images for such a long time that the meal she had so lovingly prepared went cold.

'It does look nice,' he grudgingly conceded.

'It's still small and intimate, like the registry office,' Beverley insisted.

Ron snorted. 'That's not intimate. Every Tom, Dick and Harry can see.' But he didn't sound as dismissive as she thought he might.

'There are some lovely restaurants nearby where you can hold the reception,' she continued.

Ron let out a long sigh. 'We'll see. I'll have to have a chat with Annabelle. You've already booked it, you say?'

'I had to, otherwise the date might have gone. In fact, it definitely would have: it's very popular. Let me warm your food up,' she suggested, guessing it might be wise to back off and let him think about it.

She had done as much as she could – the rest was up to Ron.

***

Beverley didn't mean to eavesdrop. She had just folded a pile of ironing and was about to put it in the airing cupboard on the landing when she heard Ron's voice. He was in his bedroom, but the door was partly open and, thinking he was speaking to her, Beverley paused outside.

A soft laugh quickly made her realise that he wasn't, and she was about to walk away when she heard her name mentioned.

'I think Beverley really wants this,' he was saying. 'She has been so good to me… Your mother?... Yeah, I know. It might be *our* wedding, but I suppose we owe it to everyone else... I agree, it does look lovely, but this has to be right for us... No, I don't honestly care where we do it. I'm marrying *you*, not your family.' He sighed and continued, 'Beverley does though, I can tell... You're sure you don't mind?... OK, the bandstand it is.' Another laugh, low and intimate. 'I love you, too.'

Hastily, Beverley moved out of earshot, her cheeks flaming. She ought not to have been listening, but she was glad she had heard that Ron and Annabelle were going to go with the bandstand option. May mightn't have got exactly what she wanted, but hopefully, in her sister's eyes, the bandstand was preferable to the registry office.

123

Now all they had to do was find a place to hold the reception.

Oh, and she needed to buy a dress – a *nice* one.

***

Beverley lifted her face to the sun and closed her eyes. Orange and red flickered behind her eyelids and the warmth on her skin was welcome. The park was alive with birdsong and she let nature's music ebb and flow around her.

'Boiled sweet?' Andrew nudged her arm, and she heard the crinkle of a packet.

'Better not. I don't want to risk it with my teeth.'

'I suck 'em to death,' he told her.

'I haven't got that kind of self-control.'

'But you eat bon bons,' he pointed out, the words muffled by the sweet.

'That's different.'

'How?'

'It just is.'

'You're strange.'

'I know.' She smiled, her eyes still closed. She had a feeling Andrew quite liked her being strange.

Over the past couple of weeks they had taken to meeting every morning in the park. If the weather was nice, they would sit on a bench for a while and natter. If it wasn't, they would head to the café and treat themselves to a cake and a pot of tea.

'Do you ever go out in the evening?' he asked.

'Never. Nowhere to go and no one to go with.'

'Me, neither. What do you do?'

'Watch telly and knit.'

'I watch telly, but I don't knit.'

'You should. It's very therapeutic.'

'I told you that Vivienne used to knit, didn't I?'

'You did.'

Beverley opened her eyes and uttered a contented sigh. Their chats were hardly riveting, and most people would say they were boring, but she looked forward to them. Seeing Andrew broke up the monotony of her day now that Ron was out of the house more often than not. He still slept there (mostly) and he usually joined her for tea, but he was at work all day and he also wanted to spend time with Annabelle, which meant that Beverley was often at a loose end.

'Could you dog-sit for me?' she asked, as an idea for something to do on Saturday occurred to her.

Ron was spending the day with Annabelle, and for some reason the thought of being on her own was more unpleasant than usual. Beverley supposed she could always drop around to her sister's house for a while, but May had Terence and Beverley didn't want to feel like a spare wheel.

Andrew stared at her. He did that a lot. Mind you, she seemed to have that effect on most people, and she guessed it was due to her being a bit scatter-brained. She was aware that she had a tendency to leap from one topic to the next, and people often had trouble keeping up, but she couldn't help it if they were slower-witted than her.

'Of course,' he said. 'When?'

'Saturday. I'm thinking about going shopping for an outfit.'

'This is for the wedding, I take it?'

She nodded. 'I thought I'd get a head start, seeing as the spring fashions have hit the shops.' Squinting at him, Beverley asked, 'Your Vivienne – was she a smart woman?'

Andrew blinked. 'I'd say so, yes. She had a good brain in her head.'

'That's as may be, but I meant did she dress well?'

He screwed up his eyes. 'Yes. Why?'

'That's OK, you don't need to dog sit after all. I'll drop Pepe round to yours, and he and Twinkle can keep each other company while we're out.'

Andrew was giving her that look again – the bemused and slightly wary one, as though she was an insect he had never seen before, and one which might sting him if he got too close.

'We can go dress hunting together,' she explained. 'You can help me choose.'

'Er… I don't think that's such a good—'

Beverley leapt in before he could say anything further. 'I know my dress sense isn't the best, so I was hoping you will reel me in.'

'Rein you in.'

'Whatever.'

'Wouldn't you prefer to go with your sister?'

'Not on your nelly! She'll have me in beige. I hate beige. Or navy. I don't like navy much, either. I like bright colours.'

Andrew's reply was faint. 'You don't say…'

CHAPTER 11

Andrew hadn't been dress shopping since long before Vivienne died, and he wasn't sure he wanted to go now. It had never been his favourite activity – hanging around outside ladies' fitting rooms with the other poor husbands and boyfriends wasn't his idea of fun. He would have much preferred to slouch on the sofa watching the footie. Even a spot of gardening beat dress shopping with the wife.

But that was then and this is now, and what was the alternative? Sitting at home alone, staring at drivel on the telly? He had lost interest in sport around the time Vivienne had become ill, and he'd lost interest in everything else after she had passed away, so he didn't have anywhere to go and nothing to do on Saturday. Therefore, he may as well accompany Beverley in her quest for the ultimate mother-of-the-groom outfit, and try to steer her away from anything too garish.

The day that she had told him he was going with her (she hadn't asked – she had *informed*) Beverley had been wearing a gold lame anorak that had probably been in fashion in the 1970s, a pair of lime green slacks, and pink trainers. He had done his best not to smile when he'd seen her, thinking that at least she brightened up the park, which had yet to fully embrace spring.

However, for their shopping trip today she was more conservatively dressed, much to his surprise, and seemed to be wearing a few less layers.

'Where first?' he asked when they got off the bus in Western Road. At ten thirty on a Saturday morning, the city centre was already buzzing with shoppers.

'I'm not sure. I usually shop in Primark, but I doubt if they'll have anything suitable for a wedding.'

'Shall we try Marks and Spencer?' Vivienne used to shop there a lot. She especially liked their food hall.

'I was thinking of somewhere a bit more weddingy.'

'A proper wedding shop, you mean? One that sells wedding dresses?'

'They sometimes sell mother-of-the-bride dresses, too.'

'OK, lead on Macduff.'

Beverley barked out a laugh. 'It does feel like I'm about to go into battle,' she said. 'Let's hope we both survive.'

'Eh?'

'Macbeth. Shakespeare. We did it in school. I don't remember much of my English lessons apart from that and a silly poem about a flea.'

'John Donne?'

'That's the fella. Why would anyone want to write a poem about a flea? Shall we try The Lanes? There are bound to be some wedding shops there.'

Andrew bit back a smile. Beverley was always doing that – flitting from one subject to another. It made for interesting, if sometimes odd, conversations.

A short walk down North Road and then into Duke Street provided them with their first target.

Eagerly Beverley darted inside, only to drag him swiftly back out again, her face grey when she saw the prices. 'Erm, maybe something not so expensive,' she said faintly.

'I'm sure there are plenty more shops we can try,' Andrew said, offering her his arm: she looked as though she was about to keel over. 'Were they really that pricey?'

He had hung back to allow her to peruse the rails by herself, whilst a sales assistant had hovered around, trying to impress upon him that they should have made an appointment and that they didn't do 'walk-ins'.

'Seven thousand,' Beverley hissed out of the corner of her mouth.

'For a *dress*?'

'A wedding dress. I didn't get as far as the mother-of-the-brides ones. I didn't see the point.'

'No…' Andrew felt like sitting down himself. He was pretty sure Judith hadn't paid half as much as that for her wedding dress. Mind you, it had been over twenty-five years ago and prices had gone up a lot since then. But seven thousand pounds was an awful lot of money.

Several shops later and he could tell that Beverley was starting to flag. Heck, he had been flagging more or less since they had got off the bus.

'Lunch?' he suggested. 'My treat.'

'Oh, no, you don't. We're not starting that malarkey. We go halves. I pay for me, you pay for you. Agreed?'

'Agreed,' Andrew said, amused.

Beverley was certainly an independent lady, and he admired her for that. A lifetime ago, when he'd been courting Vivienne, it had been the done thing for the man to pay, no matter whether he could afford it or not. He supposed the idea was that if you couldn't afford to pay for your girl's meal, then you weren't much of a marriage prospect. Nowadays, things were so very different. He quite liked it, though. Despite Beverley being his age, give or take a year or two, she seemed quite modern in her outlook. Or was it that he was old fashioned and hadn't been able to keep up with the times?

He guided her into a little bistro, a place that didn't look too expensive but was one up from the cafés he usually frequented. Although 'usually frequented' was a bit of a misnomer. He didn't *usually frequent* anything, only the park or his sofa.

'Didn't you see any dresses you liked?' he asked.

'I saw loads, but I refuse to pay a silly amount of money for something I'm only going to wear once.'

'You never know, you might end up going to another wedding,' he said.

She snorted. 'I don't know whose; Ellis is the only one in the family who is anywhere near old enough to get married and she's only eighteen, so I should imagine it would be a good few years before she settles down.'

'Well, then, in that case, everyone will have forgotten what you wore to Annabelle and Ron's wedding, so you could give it another outing at Ellis's.'

Beverley arched an eyebrow. 'You're being silly.'

'I'm not,' he protested. 'I'm being practical.'

'You do realise that women like my sister and Helen will remember exactly what I was wearing the last time, even down to the earrings.'

'Really?' Andrew was incredulous.

'How long were you married?'

'Fifty-one years.' Gosh where had all that time gone, and how quickly it had flown.

'In that case, I would have thought you would know better. Didn't Vivienne teach you anything? Women don't usually dress for men, they dress to impress other women.'

Yes, he had heard that, but he hadn't been sure how true it was. Andrew had always laboured under the impression that Vivienne had dressed to impress *him*. He had certainly liked to look smart for *her*, favouring shirts and ties whenever they went out. He wasn't wearing a tie now though: he'd only worn one a handful of times since Vivienne died.

There was that phrase again – *since Vivienne died.* He hadn't realised how often he thought it. His life had been neatly dissected into before Vivienne and after Vivienne. Everything before his wife's death had seemed so much lighter and brighter. Then again, he supposed grief could do that to a person.

During those first few days after the funeral, when he had to face a new normal without her, he had looked it up on the internet, hoping for some reassurance that his deep sadness and feelings of hopelessness would lift. He hadn't been particularly encouraged. He had expected some miracle timeline when, at a certain point, he would suddenly begin to feel that life was worth living again. But that hadn't happened. Despite outward appearances – for Judith's sake mainly, because he didn't want to worry her – he was not much further forward.

Until recently.

Ever since he bumped into Beverley, in fact.

It felt like she was slowly bringing him out of the shadows and into the light when he was with her. And when he wasn't, the world didn't feel quite as bleak as it once did.

Lunch was a lighthearted affair, and Andrew found himself laughing along with her as she recounted some of Pepe's antics – and her own. Beverley was as mischievous as her dog when she had a mind to be, and Kate's mother-in-law certainly brought out the imp in her.

'I'd like to meet this Helen,' he said, wiping tears from his eyes as she got to the end of a funny story about the pair of them squabbling over bedrooms. Beverley acted both parts, making the other woman out to be hoity-toity and rather up herself. He could easily imagine Beverley going out of her way to wind Helen up, just for the sake of it.

She had already told him the story of how Ron had come to move in with her, and she had touched on the holiday to South Wales last summer when Ron and Annabelle had met and fallen in love, but over lunch she had gone into more detail until he almost felt as though he knew the people she described.

'I want to see if she's as bad as you make out,' he added.

Beverley looked at him in mock horror. 'Don't you believe me? I think you'll find that *you're* the one who tells porkies.'

'Fair cop,' he said. 'But I promise I won't tell any more fibs. I'll be honest with you from now on.'

'Even when it comes to my fashion sense?' She was smiling to show she was teasing.

'It is rather… eccentric,' he said.

'I know and I don't care. I think it's a rebellion against May's beige, navy and black. May always did dress conservatively, and our mum used to try to get me to be more like her. The more Mum tried, the more I resisted. I can dress nicely when I have to, you know.'

'I think you dress nicely anyway,' he replied, and when she raised her eyebrows he added, 'I'm not lying, honest. You're like a breath of fresh air.'

'Thank you, kind sir. Now, how about we settle the bill and carry on with my quest for a wedding outfit? We'll give a couple more shops a go, and if I can't find anything we'll call it quits for today.'

Andrew was happy enough to agree, as long as they took it slow and she didn't go charging off at a rate of knots. For a woman her age, she could certainly motor when the mood took her. It was a pity he couldn't keep up.

Thankfully she walked at his pace, and when they arrived at the next likely looking shop, she asked the sales assistant for a chair for him to plonk his backside on (Beverley's words, not his).

He lowered himself onto it gratefully, content to watch Beverley trawl through the racks. This shop seemed more to her liking, and he guessed that the prices were more reasonable. Not only that, she also hadn't had to make an appointment.

'Will you be OK there, while I try these on?' she asked, holding an armful of dresses in plastic wrappers. The sales assistant who had been helping her also had her arms full of brightly coloured outfits, and the two of them looked like a pair of butterflies waiting to unfurl their wings.

Another lady brought him a cuppa and he settled back to wait.

'Have you sorted yourself out with a suit yet?' the young lady asked. He called her young, but she was probably around the same age as Judith.

'For what?' he asked blankly.

'For the wedding.'

'Oh, I *see*. I'm not going.'

'Aren't weddings your thing?'

'I've not been invited, and I don't expect to be,' he added, seeing her face.

'Sorry, I didn't mean to put my foot in it. I automatically assumed that as the lady was looking for a mother-of-the-groom dress, that you were the father-of-the-groom. My mistake.' A blush had bloomed on her cheeks, and she looked mortified.

'Beverley and I are just friends,' he explained. 'I'm here for moral support and to make sure she doesn't pick anything too outlandish. She likes bright colours.'

'I'm sure she'll look stunning whatever she chooses,' the sales lady said diplomatically. 'Ah, here she comes now.'

She stepped aside to give him an uninterrupted view, and Andrew's breath caught in his throat.

Beverley looked amazing. Classy, elegant… *beautiful*.

The dress was fitted, but didn't cling, emphasising her waist and flaring a little at the hips. The soft slate-grey hue suited her colouring perfectly, and the beading and lacework provided plenty of glamour but not too much. The sales assistant was holding a matching jacket and she held it up for Beverley to slip on.

'What do you think?' Beverley sounded nervous as she did a twirl, unsure of herself. It was most unlike her, and he found it endearing.

'It's lovely,' he said, then realised lovely wasn't good enough. 'You look beautiful.'

A hint of pink spread across her cheeks and her gaze dropped to the plush carpet. 'You're just saying that.'

'I am not,' he replied firmly. 'That dress is wonderful on you. You look amazing.'

She lifted her head, and her eyes met his. 'I do?'

'You do.' He nodded to emphasise the point.

A big beaming smile spread across her face and her pleasure made his heart sing.

'I'll take it,' she said. 'Do you do hats? And I'll need a pair of shoes to go with it, and a bag.' She clapped her hands. 'Ooh, this is so exciting!'

Andrew watched indulgently as she tried on several hats, until eventually she decided on a cream side-of-the-head affair, with a flurry of ribbons and feathers on the top. A bag and shoes in a deeper shade of grey completed the outfit, and Beverley nearly cried when she was told that the shop could add lengths of ribbon to the hat in the same shade as the bag and the dress, to tie all the colours together.

'Are we done?' he asked as she emerged from the fitting room in her normal clothes. The assistant was carrying her purchases and Beverley nodded as she followed the woman to the cash desk.

He waited patiently while everything was neatly packaged in tissue paper and boxes, and then he held out his hand for the bags. Beverley handed one of them over with a smile. She hung onto the others.

'I can't believe I found something,' she said. 'Are you sure I looked OK?'

'You looked more than OK. You looked flipping gorgeous.'

'I want to do Ron proud,' she said. 'If his mum was still alive it would be different, but she's not. I don't want him looking at the photos in a few years' time and feeling disappointed in me.'

'Ron could never be disappointed in you.' Andrew hadn't met the man, but from what Beverley had told him Ron sounded a lovely bloke.

Beverley gasped, clapping a hand to her mouth. 'Photographs!' she exclaimed. 'We need to hire a photographer. And the cars. And the charabanc!'

'Charabanc?'

'Didn't I say? It's probably the easiest way for the guests to go from the bandstand to the reception.'

'Have you decided where the reception will be held?'

Beverley wrinkled her nose. 'Not yet. But we will.' She sounded confident.

'At least you've got your outfit, so that's one less thing to worry about,' he said.

'I think we'd better have a family get-together,' Beverley mused. 'Make a list of what still needs doing and divvy it up. I can't believe the wedding is only four months away, and there's such a lot to do.'

Andrew had an idea. 'I might be able to help with the photographer,' he said. 'Did I ever mention what Leo is studying in university?'

Beverley shook her head. 'No, I don't think you did.'

'Photography!' Andrew announced triumphantly. 'His course should be finished by the date of the wedding and as far as I know he hasn't got a job lined up. I could always ask him?'

'That would be fantastic. Do you think he'll say yes? We'll pay him of course.'

'I'll phone him now.' Andrew took his phone out of his pocket and stabbed at the screen with a finger. 'It's ringing,' he announced. 'Leo? It's Grandad. Yes, yes, everything is fine...' His eyes found Beverley's and he smiled. 'When does your course finish?... That's good... Have you got anything lined up?... Right, right... How do you feel about earning a few bob?... No, I don't want you to dig my garden. This would be proper paid photography work. A wedding... Ha ha, don't be daft. A friend of mine's son is getting married on the 26th of June and they haven't got a photographer. What do you say?... Brilliant! I'll let them know. Bye, Leo.'

Andrew poked at the screen a few times to make sure the call had ended, then he looked up and said, 'He'll do it. Weddings aren't his usual thing, but I can assure you he'll do a damn good job.'

'Phew, that's one less thing to worry about. Thank you, Andrew. Right, let's get off home and take those poor dogs out for a walk.'

As they made their way back to his house, Andrew realised that he had enjoyed today. Not only had he felt useful, but Beverley was also great fun to be with. Really good company.

But what stuck in his mind later, as he made himself a sandwich for supper, was how lovely she had looked. Beverley was a handsome woman and seeing her in all her finery had brought it home to him.

Something he hadn't felt for a very long time stirred in his tummy…

He fancied her!

The feeling was so unexpected that he had to pour himself a little nip of whiskey to get over the shock.

CHAPTER 12

Beverley felt strange sitting in Annabelle's kitchen. Ever since May and Terence had tied the knot, they had lived in this house. But not any longer.

She gazed around curiously, noting the subtle changes. The units were still the same and so were the white goods, but the bread bin had gone and the microwave was no longer the plain white one she was used to – Annabelle's was a lovely shade of pink. There was a new blind at the window, and where the clock had once hung there was now a rail with hooks with assorted kitchen implements dangling from it. A mean-looking coffee machine sat on the furthest worktop, and it was currently burbling to itself. The kitchen had also received a lick of paint and was now bright yellow. It was certainly preferable to May's signature magnolia.

Beverley wondered whether it would be rude to ask if she could see the rest of the house.

Deciding it would, she held her tongue and accepted a cup of tea instead.

May sat next to her at the table, along with Terence, and Ron was leaning against a worktop with his arms folded whilst Annabelle made the drinks.

Beverley could hear the children thundering around upstairs, and she hoped she would get to see them before she left. She had taken quite a shine to them, Izzie especially. The little girl had been very shy and rather withdrawn when she had first met her, in contrast to Jake's anger. Jake hadn't been happy to leave Australia to come to live in the UK, and it had taken him quite a while to settle, although both of them seemed happy and well-adjusted now.

May took charge. 'Right,' she said in a firm voice. 'Thanks to Beverley we now have a venue for the ceremony.' She shot Beverley a venomous look.

Beverley smirked behind her mug. She clearly hadn't been forgiven for booking the bandstand without consulting her.

'It does look lovely,' Annabelle said. She smiled at her mother, who scowled back, and Beverley guessed they'd already had words about it.

'Yes, well,' May huffed. 'We still need to find somewhere to hold the reception.'

Ron piped up, 'I'd be quite happy to pile into the nearest pub.'

May gasped and slapped a hand to her chest. 'I do hope you're joking,' she said frostily.

Ron caught Beverley's eye and looked away. He clearly hadn't.

'Of course he's joking,' Annabelle said. 'But in a way he's right: we don't want any fuss. Holding the ceremony on the bandstand is fuss enough.'

'Having a reception is hardly a *fuss*,' May protested. 'Tell her, Terence.'

Terence looked flustered. 'Um...'

'See, your father agrees.'

Beverley didn't believe Terence had agreed at all, and she took another sip of her tea, enjoying the show.

'I do wish you'd have waited a year,' May said with a sigh. 'You've made this very difficult for everyone.'

'Difficult for who?' Annabelle asked. 'Certainly not for me and Ron.'

Beverley could see that Annabelle was holding her tongue and she guessed the reason. Annabelle's parents had been so good to her since her enforced return from Australia, not only opening their house up to her and the children, but signing it over to her so that she had a place of her own. Beverley knew how grateful Annabelle was and how generous May and Terence had been, but that didn't mean Annabelle's mother had the right to enforce her expectations and wishes on the wedding.

'How about if you and Ron pop out next weekend and have a little look at a few places?' Beverley suggested to Annabelle.

'But—' May began.

Terence shushed her. May's mouth dropped open and she raised her eyebrows, but when Terence gave a small shake of his head, she said instead, 'We've been thinking that a charabanc would be a good idea, to get you from the bandstand to the reception. Well, not you and Ron, because you will be in the wedding car and so will the bridesmaids, but the rest of the guests.'

'The rest of what guests?' Ron asked.

'Kate and Brett obviously, and the children. And you have to invite Helen if you're inviting Brett.'

Ron's lips twisted. 'Why – do they come as a pair?'

'Don't be silly. It just wouldn't be fair to leave her out.'

The look Ron gave Beverley told her that he thought it would be very fair, but he didn't say anything.

'Then there's your cousin Wendy,' May said. 'You'll have to invite her and her husband. And what about Aunt Madge?'

'I didn't know she was still alive,' Annabelle said.

'Neither did I,' said Terence.

His wife dug him in the ribs with her elbow and continued, 'Madge will probably have to bring someone from the care home with her, and I doubt she will stay all day. That reminds me, you'll have to find somewhere that's wheelchair friendly.'

'Who is Madge?' Ron asked.

May provided the answer. 'She's Terence's father's sister. Terence's father died years ago of course, but there was a bit of an age gap between him and his sister. Fifteen years, wasn't it, Terence? Anyway, she's still going strong at ninety-five.'

Annabelle protested, 'Why should she be invited? You haven't mentioned her once since I've been back in the UK.'

Her mother pulled a face. 'There was a bit of a falling out and some bad blood, but that was years ago, and just because I don't talk about her doesn't mean Aunt Madge isn't part of the family.' She tapped the table. 'Right, let's see… That's me and your father, Beverley, Kate, Brett, the three children. How many is that so far?'

'Eight, Ron said. 'I'm assuming you want to include me and Annabelle, Jake and Izzie? That makes twelve. Unless you intend to have the reception without us?'

'Ron,' Annabelle said in a warning voice, and Ron huffed.

May ignored him. 'Helen, Aunt Madge, plus the carer… Who else?'

'That's it,' Beverley said. 'There is no one else, unless Ron and Annabelle want to invite their friends.'

'Of course!' May clapped her hands. 'Have you kept in touch with any of your old school friends?'

Annabelle's brow wrinkled. 'Not really. I haven't seen any of them since I was about twenty, although I've kept in contact with one or two via social media.'

'You can invite them, then. I'm sure they will be delighted to see how well you are doing for yourself. Ron, is there anyone you would like to invite? Louise, maybe?'

Beverley inhaled sharply. What a crass thing to say, she thought. Ron might be on speaking terms with his ex-wife, but that didn't mean Annabelle would appreciate having the woman at the wedding.

'No,' Ron said, through gritted teeth.

'If you want to invite her, I don't mind,' Annabelle told him.

'I know you don't, my love, but I don't think it's appropriate, do you?' He sent a stern look in May's direction.

'Maybe not Louise,' May conceded. 'Anyone else?'

'No.' Ron turned his back and reached into the cupboard for a glass and proceeded to run the tap. Beverley had a sneaking suspicion Ron was wishing it was hard liquor that he was drinking, not water.

'You'll have to invite Heather Gouden,' May said. 'I went to their daughter's wedding. And Cheryl Strickland; her son got married a few years back.'

Annabelle straightened up. 'Are you suggesting that I invite a load of *your* friends to *my* wedding?'

Her mother said, 'I'm simply returning a favour. And it's not as though we've got many other guests. It'll swell the numbers.'

Annabelle tilted her head back and stared at the ceiling. 'I don't want the numbers swelled,' she said slowly. 'I want this to be a celebration of our marriage with people we love, with our family. Not with strangers.'

'Cheryl isn't a stranger! She used to look after you when you were in junior school. Remember? You used to go to her house for tea sometimes. Surely you remember her son, Edward? The pair of you used to make mud pies in his garden.'

'I was a child: I wouldn't recognise him now if he jumped up and bit me.'

'Talking about being bitten,' May said, 'Can you please tell Pepe to stop chewing Jake's trainer? I see that dog still hasn't learnt any manners, Ron.'

'Bloody hell, you sound like Helen,' Beverley muttered.

'Well, he hasn't. Considering Ron calls himself a dog trainer, I would have thought that dog would be better behaved.'

'Don't start, Mum,' Annabelle said.

'I'm not starting anything,' May protested.

'Photographer!' Beverley announced, keen to avoid an all-out slanging match. 'I've sorted one.'

'Do we *need* a photographer?' Ron asked.

'Is he any good?' This was from May.

'Yes, you do need a photographer,' Beverley said to Ron. 'It's all well and good if people take snaps, but you want some decent photos to remember the day.'

'I'm hardly likely to forget it,' Ron retorted. 'I won't need photos to remind me.'

'But they're nice to have,' Beverley insisted. 'Anyway, I've sorted the photographer, and I'll pay for him.'

'As I said,' May interjected, 'is he any good?'

'Beggars can't be choosers,' Beverley shot back. 'With only three months to go to the wedding and June being peak wedding season, I doubt if there are many available.'

'So why is this one free?' May asked, reasonably.

'He's in his last year doing a photography course at university,' Beverley explained.

May sneered. 'A *student*? How did you find him? Graffiti on a wall?'

'Andrew recommended him.'

'Is that the chap who didn't turn up for lunch the other Sunday?' Annabelle asked.

'Yes, there was a perfectly good reason for that. For one thing, we didn't make it a firm invitation – I told him to drop in if he felt like it – and for another, his daughter was down from Peterborough for a visit.'

'How does he know if this boy is any good?' May was certainly persistent, Beverley thought.

'He is his grandson.'

'Ah, I see.' May gave her a smug look.

'You don't see anything. We can at least give Leo a go. Why don't I ask Andrew if his grandson can send us a sample of his work?'

'That's a good idea,' Annabelle said soothingly. 'Shall we hold off booking him until we've seen it? He might be far better suited to photographing buildings than weddings.'

'Fine.' Beverley folded her arms. She was getting rather fed up with this whole wedding business. If it wasn't for May being so interfering and insisting that Ron and Annabelle had the wedding she wanted them to have, Beverley would be quite happy to let them pop to the registry office, sign on the dotted line and pile into a pub afterwards.

Then she remembered her outfit and Andrew's expression when he had seen her in it, and she was thankful for an excuse to wear it. It was just a pity he wouldn't be there on the day to see her with some lippy on and her hair done.

Never mind, she thought, at least he had got to see her in something dressy for a change.

The little gathering wound up fairly quickly after that, May having issued tasks to everyone. Hers was to find a venue for the reception, Beverley's was to sort out the photographer and the charabanc, considering it was her idea, and Ron and Annabelle were to sort out the wedding dress, the groom's suit, Izzie's bridesmaid's dress, the wedding cars, the cake and the flowers. Oh, and May had also assigned herself the task of drawing up a list of guests to be invited – with Ron and Annabelle having the final say, of course.

Beverley simply knew that Helen's name was going to be on it. But at least Beverley had a gorgeous outfit, so hopefully that would be a poke in the eye for Kate's mother-in-law. She couldn't wait to see the woman's face!

***

'Do you know how difficult it is to find a charabanc?' Beverley asked Andrew, a few days later.

Andrew didn't. It wasn't something he had ever thought about. In fact, he had forgotten such a thing existed until Beverley mentioned it that day in the café under the bandstand.

'No, but I think you're going to tell me,' he said, with a smile.

They were in the park as usual, enjoying a stroll in the spring sunshine. They hadn't seen each other for a couple of days because the weather had been abysmal, high winds and driving rain keeping Andrew indoors and only venturing out for quick little walks so Twinkle could stretch her legs.

'Bloody impossible,' Beverley said. Then she beamed at him. 'But I managed it!'

'Good for you. How are the wedding preparations coming along?'

'Don't ask.' Beverley rolled her eyes.

'That good, eh?'

'We had a family meeting the other day,' she said, 'and May insisted on taking charge. Anyone would think this was *her* wedding, not her daughter's. She has put herself in charge of finding somewhere to hold the reception, and compiling the guest list.'

'That sounds ominous.' Andrew made a sympathetic face.

'It is. God only knows who she is going to invite. She was rabbiting on about asking some of her friends to come, just because she had been invited to their offspring's weddings. I think Annabelle will put her foot down, though.'

Andrew was glad all this wedding nonsense was behind him. He'd not had much to do with Judith's nuptials, thankfully, having left all that to Vivienne. He had simply turned up for suit fittings when he was told to, and walked his daughter down the aisle on the day. That had been his contribution – oh, and an eyewatering injection of cash.

'Did Leo send through those photos he promised?' Andrew had told his grandson to email some of his work to Annabelle. He hoped they were suitable. He knew Leo specialised in arty shots of run-down city centres and derelict buildings, and he wasn't sure how Annabelle would react to those kind of images – they were hardly weddingy or romantic.

'He did. I haven't seen them, but Annabelle said they were very atmospheric. She liked them.'

Andrew breathed a sigh of relief. It was always a risk when you recommended someone, especially when that someone was family.

'It'll be Easter in a couple of weeks,' Beverley said, her mind flitting onto another topic, as was her wont. 'I'm going to visit my daughter.' She looked as pleased as Punch, and Andrew was delighted for her, despite the little twinge of envy he felt. He'd not seen his grandsons since Christmas, and Judith's last visit had been fleeting. It was doubtful whether he'd get to see her over Easter.

'I'm so looking forward to seeing Kate,' Beverley was saying. 'I haven't seen her since Christmas. It's a bummer when they live so far away, isn't it?'

'It certainly is.' Andrew's reply was heartfelt.

'I don't know how May coped when Annabelle lived in Australia. Kate living in Pershore is bad enough. We should make a greater effort to see our families more often. It's not like Pershore and Peterborough are at the ends of the earth.'

Beverley's words gave Andrew food for thought, and he mulled over them during the rest of his walk and continued to mull for the remainder of the day.

Bugger it, he said to himself that evening after he had eaten his tea whilst sitting in front of the telly, a tray balanced on his knees and Twinkle's pleading gaze following the arc of every forkful from his plate to his mouth, and back again.

He washed up the dirty dishes first, dried them and put them away, then grabbed his courage and reached for the phone.

'Judith? It's me, Dad.'

'Hi, Dad. Is anything wrong?'

'Not at all. I can phone for a chat, can't I?'

'Of course you can. Duncan, can you turn the oven down, please?'

Andrew heard Duncan's muffled response.

'Shall I ring back? Is this a bad time?' But whatever time he called, it always seemed to be a bad time. Judith and Duncan were just so busy.

'No, it's fine. Are you sure everything is OK?'

'I'm sure. How are the boys?'

'Mark is out somewhere.' She sounded disapproving. 'I keep telling him he needs to concentrate on his studies, but he's so blasé about it. He should be revising – his exams start in a few weeks.'

'I'm sure he's on top of things,' Andrew soothed. 'He's a bright lad, he knows what he's doing.'

'And as for Leo,' she grumbled, 'I haven't spoken to him in ages: I'm lucky if I get to hear from him from one week to the next!'

Welcome to my world, Andrew was tempted to say. The same thing could be said for him and Judith. Now she knew how it felt.

She continued, 'When he does bother to message me, it's usually a photo. Nothing meaningful, like what he's been getting up to.'

'His photos are meaningful to him,' Andrew pointed out. After complaining that she hadn't heard from her son, he didn't like to tell her that he had spoken to Leo just a few days ago.

'Yes, but is he eating properly? And is he getting enough sleep? And—'

'He's young and he's a student, so I doubt it.'

'I worry about him. Both of them!' she exclaimed.

'Of course you do. I still worry about you.'

'There's no need to worry about *me*,' Judith laughed.

'No matter how old they get, you don't stop worrying about your children,' he said. 'Anyway, I expect he'll be home for Easter.'

'Absolutely. He'll want a term's worth of washing done.'

'Not going anywhere?' he asked, about as subtly as a train at full speed. Judith, Duncan and the boys had been known to jet off for a week at Easter.

'Not this year. Mark needs to revise, and with the best will in the world, he's not going to get much done sprawled on a sun lounger.'

Andrew thought it was now or never and steeled himself to say, 'In that case, I thought I might come to yours for a few days, to see you and the boys.'

'Oh.' Judith's surprise was evident. 'Are you sure? We won't be doing a great deal. I don't know how much fun it will be for you.'

Andrew didn't want to have fun: he wanted to see his daughter and grandsons. He wanted to spend some time with his family.

'I'm sure,' he replied firmly. 'Just for a few days,' he added, in case she thought he was going to descend on her for the full two weeks of the school holiday.

'OK, then, if you want, we'd love to have you.'

Relief caught in his throat as he said, 'I'll check the train times and let you know when to expect me.'

'Great. I've got to go, Dad, Duncan needs me in the kitchen. I hope he's turned the oven down like I asked him to.' She sounded harried, so he let her get on, his mission accomplished.

He was going to spend Easter with his daughter, and he couldn't wait!

CHAPTER 13

Beverley lifted Pepe onto her lap, gathered up her little wheeled case, her coat and her handbag, and struggled down the train's far-too-narrow aisle towards the doors.

She was looking forward to spending a few days in Pershore with Kate and the grandchildren, even though she guessed she wouldn't see much of the girls. Ellis and Portia would no doubt be out with their friends, but Sam, at twelve, wasn't quite old enough to do his own thing for hours on end, so she would get to spend some time with him. He was growing up so fast and the years were speeding by as swiftly as the train she was about to disembark, that she wanted to enjoy every precious moment with him.

This year was flying by, too, and she couldn't believe it was April already, and spring was well and truly here. She had loved seeing the lambs skipping in the fields as she peered through the train's window, and the fresh green of the new leaves on the trees. Blossom was on the hawthorn, and more than once she had spotted a magnolia tree or an ornamental cherry in full bloom as she had sped past urban gardens.

The train trundled into the station with a jaw-clenching squeal of breaks, and as soon as it came to a standstill she repeatedly stabbed at the button to open the doors. Pepe, bless him, was huddled into her legs, not liking this part of the journey one little bit, and she wished her hands were free so she could pick him up.

A nice young man helped lift her case off the train, and after thanking him Beverley made her way out of the station and onto Worcester's Foregate Street, hoping Kate would be there to meet her as promised. Pepe didn't like taxis – the last time he'd travelled in one he had been sick.

Beverley had considered driving, but it was such a long way and over the years she had lost her confidence when it came to distances and fast roads. The train was much less hassle and Pepe, bless him, had been as good as gold. He was happy to stretch his paws though, and he trotted at her side with his tail held high and a jaunty spring in his step.

'Kate!' Beverley yelled, spying her daughter. 'Coo-ee!'

Kate saw her and hurried over. 'Hello, Mum. Did you have a good journey?'

'It was OK. I could murder a cup of tea,' she grumbled, then gave herself a mental shake.

She was doing it again – being grumpy. There was no need for it, and she vowed not to be so miserable. But complaining had become her default setting and it was a hard habit to break. She didn't do it as much these days though, not since Ron had come to live with her, and she certainly wasn't miserable when she was with Andrew.

As his image floated into her mind, she wondered how he was getting on: he was also visiting his family this Easter and she hoped he was having a good time.

'Here, let me take your case,' Kate said, and Beverley happily relinquished it. 'You're looking well,' her daughter told her.

'Are you saying I looked ill before?' Beverley asked, and when she saw Kate roll her eyes, she hastened to add, 'Thank you. I feel it.'

A surprised expression flitted across her daughter's face, quickly suppressed.

Kate said, 'I thought we could have a lazy day tomorrow, seeing as it's Good Friday, and a girly shopping day on Saturday. We could look for a wedding outfit for you.'

'I've already got one,' Beverley announced, as they crossed the street, Kate's car flashing its lights when she pointed the key at it.

'You have?' More surprise. Beverley's dislike of clothes shopping wasn't a secret. 'What's it like?'

As Beverley described her dress, she recalled Andrew's look of admiration when he had seen her emerge from the fitting room. It made her feel all warm and tingly inside. It was a long time since anyone had looked at her like that, and she had basked in it for days.

She got into the car and settled Pepe on her lap.

'Did Annabelle or May go with you?' Kate asked, lifting the case onto the backseat, then getting in herself.

'No, Andrew did.'

Yet more surprise. Beverley found she was enjoying it.

'You must tell me more about him,' Kate said.

The car pulled out into the traffic as Beverley wondered where to begin. Beverley had phoned Kate the day she and Andrew had met, to tell her about the strange man who had knocked her off her feet and then invited her to his house for a cup of tea. And she had mentioned him several times since, but she hadn't gone into a great deal of detail.

'Have you got a photo of him?' her daughter asked.

Beverley snorted. 'We're not like you young ones, taking selfies every five minutes and posting them on the internet for the whole world to see.'

'That doesn't stop you from taking the odd picture,' Kate pointed out.

'He's not odd,' Beverley replied, deadpan.

Kate began to protest that wasn't what she'd meant, when she realised Beverley was teasing her. 'You like him, don't you?'

'Of course I do! I wouldn't bother with him if I didn't. What a daft thing to say.'

Kate didn't speak for a few minutes as she negotiated the city centre traffic, and Beverley gazed out of the window at the impressive tower of the cathedral looming above a row of small shops and businesses, and thought what a pretty city Worcester was. She would enjoy poking around the shops with her daughter and having a bite to eat in one of the little bistros. That one down by the river was nice, or maybe they could find a little place on Friar Street. She loved Friar Street with its Tudor buildings and cobbles. It felt like stepping back in time.

'Tell me if I've got the wrong end of the stick,' Kate said, as they headed out of the city to pick up the road to Pershore. 'I get the feeling that you and Andrew might be more than friends.'

'Stuff and nonsense. Don't be ridiculous.' Beverley's response was automatic. Since she and Kate's father had gone their separate ways all those years ago (good riddance, Beverley thought) she hadn't had much to do with men. They were more trouble than they were worth, and she had been perfectly happy on her own. She'd had a daughter to raise, and even if she did say so herself, she'd done a damned fine job. Of course, it had been hard when Kate married Brett and she saw less of her, and harder still when they'd moved to Pershore. But Kate had her own life to lead, and Beverley understood that. Although, like Andrew, she lamented the fact that Kate didn't live nearer, and Beverley didn't see as much of her daughter as she wanted.

Just like Andrew, Beverley had suffered from loneliness despite May living just up the road. May could be spiky and argumentative, and her living so close was sometimes a two-edged sword.

Spikey? Argumentative? The sisters were more alike than Beverley cared to admit, because those adjectives could as easily be used to describe her. Then Ron came along, and Beverley hadn't felt nearly as lonely.

But he was about to move out soon, and Beverley would be back to rolling around the house on her own, like a forgotten marble.

Sensing that Kate was looking at her out of the corner of her eye, she asked, 'What?'

'Would it be so bad if you liked him in a non-friend way?' Kate's attention was on the road, but Beverley wasn't fooled. Her daughter was on tenterhooks, waiting for an answer.

'I'm too old for all that nonsense,' she protested, flapping a hand in the air and making Pepe flinch. 'Sorry, poppet,' she crooned. 'Aunty Kate is being silly.'

'Aunty Kate, indeed,' Kate sniggered. 'You treat him like a baby.'

'Are you jealous?'

'Of a dog? No way. But you *are* far more lenient with him than you ever were with me.'

'That's different. He doesn't answer back like you did when you were a teenager.'

Kate rolled her eyes, then went on to tell her all about Portia's latest antics, which involved swigging half a bottle of Jack Daniels, stolen from a cupboard in the kitchen, an illicit party at a friend's house which the friend's parents weren't aware of, and being caught snogging a spotty youth on the pavement outside the house.

'All over each other they were,' Kate added in disgust.

Beverley supposed she should feel aggrieved on Kate's behalf, but the only thing Beverley could think was that at least Portia's spotty-youth snogging incident had deflected Kate's attention away from suspecting that her mother had feelings for Andrew.

***

Andrew was sitting in Judith and Duncan's lounge and feeling like a fish out of water. His daughter's household was so bewildering and busy. Take the telly, for instance. It was one of those smart TVs, similar to the one he himself owned but hadn't quite got to grips with yet and probably never would. He had no intention of subscribing to anything other than Sky, and he had no clue what the apps on his TV were for. He never pressed any buttons he didn't recognise, yet this afternoon he had been trying to watch a bit of footie when a YouTube video had appeared on the screen, and he had no idea why or how, or what he could do to get rid of it.

Apparently, Mark's phone was connected to the TV somehow, and whatever the boy had been watching had popped onto the screen. After Mark had explained what had happened, all Andrew could think of was thank goodness the lad hadn't been watching porn.

After that, Andrew had given up trying to watch football and had read the news on his phone instead, until it was time for dinner.

Dinner consisted of a takeaway, which was fine by him because he didn't get to have one of those very often – mainly because it was always too much for one person and he hated wasting food. Besides, it wasn't the same eating it on your own.

He wondered whether Beverley ever indulged in takeaways and if so, did she prefer pizza, Indian, or Chinese. Maybe when he got back to Brighton, he could suggest she popped over to his for a meal one evening. Or he could go to hers.

Both his grandsons were going out later, but with a bewildering (to Andrew) array of curries and side dishes on offer, they were eating at home first. Judith bustled around, opening cartons and decanting their contents into pre-warmed dishes and laying the table. Duncan had been tasked with pouring some drinks, and the boys were sprawled in the lounge area, doing exactly that – lounging. And playing on their phones.

Andrew had to admire the speed and dexterity of their thumbs, even as he thought they were being rude by ignoring the rest of the family. Mind you, Andrew didn't have a leg to stand on himself, considering he had been staring at his own phone's screen for the past hour.

The boys put their phones away when Judith called them to the table though, so that was something, and as he slipped his into his trouser pocket, Andrew wondered whether he should have dropped Beverley a text to see how she was doing.

Maybe he would send her one later. Or maybe not. She was probably having a lovely time with her daughter, and he didn't want to disturb her. She had better things to think about than him.

His mouth watering and his tummy rumbling, Andrew pulled out a chair and sat down. He was looking forward to this – Indian food was one of his favourites – and he began ladling rice onto his plate with enthusiasm.

He was sniffing a spoonful of channa daal and wondering whether he would like it as he hadn't tried it before, when Leo spoke.

'Thanks again, Grandad. I know that the gig you sent my way isn't my sort of thing, but the money will come in handy. I can stay with you, yeah?'

'I'll be offended if you don't.' Andrew decided he would give the daal a go and he put a dollop on his plate.

'What's this about a gig?' Judith looked from her son, to Andrew, and back again.

'Haven't you told your mother?' Andrew asked.

Leo lifted a shoulder. 'I don't tell Mum everything.'

'He doesn't tell me *anything*. What gig?' she repeated.

'Some wedding in Brighton,' Leo mumbled, around a mouthful of food.

'What wedding?' Judith gave an exasperated sigh. 'Is it a friend of Grandad's?'

'It's her son's wedding, actually,' Andrew said, and in the interests of being exact, he added, 'Her surrogate son.'

'Surrogate?' Judith placed her fork on the side of her plate, and there was a crease between her brows.

'I suppose you could say he's adopted,' Andrew explained.

'Who is this person? Do I know her? Was she a friend of mum's? What's her name?'

'Beverley.'

Judith's eyebrows shot up. 'The woman outside the pub?'

'That's the one.' Andrew helped himself to another poppadom and snapped it in two. Should he go for mint dip or chutney? He settled on the chutney and spread a generous slather over one half.

'I thought you said you didn't know her that well.' Judith had a pinched look about her mouth, and he wondered if she was cross with him for asking Leo directly without running it by her first.

'I don't. Beverley is just an acquaintance.'

'A good enough acquaintance to allow an unknown photographer to photograph her son's wedding.' Judith's tone was sharp.

'Hey, I've got to start somewhere,' Leo protested.

Judith scowled at her son. 'I thought you weren't going to do wedding photography?'

'If it pays, I will.' Leo shrugged again. 'I don't want to do it on a regular basis, but the cash will come in handy.'

'How much are you being paid?' his mother wanted to know.

'I don't know yet. It depends on what they want.'

'Not enough, probably,' Judith muttered, adding, 'I'm not sure I'm happy about this.'

'Which bit?' Andrew asked.

'All of it,' she replied. 'Surely there is a local photographer they can use?'

'Too short notice for most of them,' Andrew said.

'When is this wedding taking place?'

'26th of June.'

'Where?'

'Brighton.' Andrew eyed the bowls of food on the table, debating whether he could fit any more into his tummy. He was full, but that curry was so tasty.

'I gathered that,' Judith huffed. 'I was referring to the venue.'

'Brighton bandstand.' He decided to go for the extra portion. Goodness knows when he'd have another curry like this. Even if he suggested that Beverley join him for a takeaway, she might not like Indian food.

'Where does this Beverley woman live?' Judith asked.

Andrew had been about to pop another spoonful on his plate, but his daughter's question made him pause. He wasn't keen on her tone or the way she had referred to Beverley.

'Brighton.' His reply was short and sharp.

'Now you're just being difficult,' Judith said, ignoring Duncan's warning look.

'And you're being rude about a friend of mine,' Andrew retorted. He dropped the spoon with a clatter and pushed his plate away, appetite gone. Which was probably just as well, considering the amount he had eaten. If he wasn't careful, he would give himself indigestion.

'Sorry, Dad, I didn't mean to be. It's just... you seem quite friendly with her, yet I don't know anything about the woman. I'm trying to look out for you, that's all.'

Andrew softened. He knew she was. 'What do you want to know?'

'Where does she live?'

'The other side of the park, on Staley Avenue.'

'I assume she hasn't got a husband?' his daughter asked.

'Or a wife?' Mark said.

'No husband or wife. She has a dog – Pepe. He's a poodle. Twinkle gets on famously with him.' Twinkle had accompanied him to Judith's house and was currently snoozing on her blanket.

'Do you like, take the dogs on play dates?' Mark asked, grinning. 'Do they have sleepovers and stuff?'

Leo rolled his eyes. 'Grow up, Mark.'

'Just because you've finished your uni course.' Mark gave his brother the finger.

'Mark, don't be silly.' Judith's response was automatic, then her eyes widened, *'Sleepovers?'*

Andrew knew what was going through her mind, and it shocked him. 'We take the dogs for walks in the park together,' he said. 'So I suppose you could call it a play date. But no sleepovers.'

Without warning, an image of waking up in Beverley's bed leapt into his head. Which took him completely unawares, because he'd never been upstairs in Beverley's house and probably never would. The thought brought him out in goosebumps.

Judith hadn't noticed, thankfully. 'She's retired, I take it? She looked like she's in her late sixties, early seventies.'

Andrew cleared his throat, pushing all thoughts of sleepovers out of his head. Beverley was a handsome woman, but he couldn't allow himself to think of her in that way. It wouldn't be right. 'Yes, she's retired.'

'What did she used to do?'

'I've no idea.' He would have to rectify that. 'I told you; I don't know her terribly well.'

'Hmm.'

To Andrew's relief, Judith didn't pursue it, and the conversation moved on.

Later though, after the boys had gone out, Judith cornered him in the kitchen. 'I don't mean to pry, Dad, but I do worry about you.'

'I know.' Andrew also knew something else – that Judith was still mourning the loss of her mother and the thought of him growing close to another woman didn't sit well with her.

'You don't have to be concerned,' he assured her. 'Beverley is just a friend.'

But even as he uttered the words, he wondered whether it was strictly true on his part – because Andrew was starting to develop decidedly non-friendly feelings towards Beverley Collins.

CHAPTER 14

'Does she have to come?' Beverley grumbled, on Easter Sunday morning. Kate was preparing lunch and Beverley was dismayed to discover that Helen had been invited.

'She is Brett's mother,' Kate pointed out.

'So?' Beverley knew she sounded belligerent, but honestly! Couldn't she enjoy one visit to her daughter without Helen butting in? It might only be lunch, but in Beverley's eyes Helen's presence would sour the meal. No doubt all she would talk about would be golf, people who Beverley had never heard of, and how marvellous Brett was. Don't get me wrong, Beverley thought, Brett was a lovely chap and he and Kate made a great team, despite there having been a couple of blips along the way, but if you listened to Helen you would think the sun shone out of his backside.

Kate tutted. 'She would be on her own today if we didn't invite her, and it is Easter Sunday. Promise me you'll be on your best behaviour.'

Beverley had no intention of promising any such thing. If Helen was going to be sitting opposite her at the dining table, the woman would be fair game. If the shoe was on the other foot, Helen wouldn't make any promises to behave, either.

Sulking, Beverley plonked herself down on a squishy chair in the lounge and took out her knitting. Keeping her hands busy had always helped calm her. Anyway, she had recently begun a jumper for Andrew, and she wanted to get on with it. She'd had to guess his measurements but after studying him as unobtrusively as possible, she concluded that he was slightly shorter than Brett and about the same size around the chest. She had chosen a soft green that would complement his colouring.

Pepe was slumbering happily by her feet, but he scrambled to his paws when he heard Helen's voice in the hall, and uttered a low growl. The poodle didn't have a nasty bone in his grumpy, irascible body, and he would never bite Helen: he simply wanted to express his displeasure at her being there. The feeling was mutual. Helen didn't like Pepe, either.

Immaculately dressed as always, in a tweet skirt, fine-knit round-necked jumper and a matching cardigan, Helen swanned into Kate and Brett's living room as though she owned the place. Her nose wrinkled when she saw Beverley, followed by a tightening of her lips when she spotted Pepe.

'I hope we're not having lamb,' Helen sniped.

Beverley smiled sweetly, remembering a year last Christmas when Pepe had stolen a roast leg of lamb off the table that had been meant for dinner. The family had been forced to order pizza instead. Pepe hadn't been in anyone's good books that day, but Helen had taken it personally.

'Pork,' Beverley replied. She had made both the stuffing and the apple sauce from scratch earlier that morning.

'I hope that dog hasn't been anywhere near it.' Helen sailed into the kitchen and Beverley heard her say, 'Kate, my dear, can I do anything to help?'

Kate's reply drifted into the living room. 'Thanks, Helen, but it's all under control. Why don't you keep Mum company?'

Beverley grimaced. Her daughter was trying to make her and Helen play nice, but Beverley didn't want to.

And neither, it appeared, did Helen.

'Ron is getting married, I see…' Helen began, as she returned to the living room and perched gracefully on the edge of the nearest armchair. 'He's done well for himself.' The tone was sneering.

There was no love lost between Ron and Helen, either. Helen had mellowed somewhat when Ron had received a hefty sum of money from the sale of his former marital home, but she hadn't been able to move past Ron having been homeless for a number of years. May had also struggled with Ron's homeless status in the beginning, but she accepted him now. Which was a good thing considering he was marrying her daughter.

'He *has* done well for himself,' Beverley agreed proudly. 'Business is booming.' She knew Helen had been referring to Ron having bagged a lovely woman like Annabelle, and not the success of his business. Punching above his weight, Beverley thought the expression was, but as far as she was concerned Annabelle was the lucky one.

Helen sniffed. 'Kate seems to think they're getting married in a registry office, but I see they're having the ceremony on Brighton's bandstand, and the reception in The Gillespie Rooms. I must say, it all sounds very posh. I had to look up the bandstand on the internet as I thought it was a pub.'

'Hi, Mum, I didn't hear you come in.' Brett poked his head into the living room.

Helen's face lit up like a Christmas tree with too many fairy lights, at the sight of her precious son, but Beverley wasn't paying attention. She was trying to process what Helen had just said – something about a reception in The Gillespie Rooms...?

'Brett, darling, give your mum a kiss.' Helen raised her chin and Brett obediently pecked her on the cheek. 'Where are the children?' she asked.

'Upstairs. I'll give them a shout.' He walked to the door and yelled up the stairs. 'Kids! Your nan is here. Come and say hello. Lunch is almost ready.'

Muffled replies drifted down the stairs, but Beverley wasn't listening. 'What do you mean *The Gillespie Rooms*?' she asked. Where had Helen got that idea from?

The Gillespie Rooms were rather exclusive and very expensive. The old Georgian building had once been a large private residence, but was now an upmarket hotel with a number of different function rooms, an impressive restaurant, and a reputation for being one of the most desirable places to hold a wedding in the South East.

Helen was staring at her strangely, but her expression slowly turned to one of glee. 'Didn't you know?' Her smile threatened to split her face in half.

'You didn't, did you?' She clapped her hands in delight. 'Oh, my, this is priceless.'

'I *did* know,' Beverley lied. 'I just didn't think it was public knowledge yet.'

The triumphant expression seeped away, leaving Helen looking rather put out, but she rallied gamely. 'Annabelle and Ron could hardly keep it a secret if they're sending the invitations out, could they? You are being silly, Beverley.'

Beverley wasn't being silly. What she was being was incredulous, disbelieving and extremely cross. Ron should have told her that they had booked the reception, and he also should have told her that the invitations had gone out. It would have stopped her from almost making a fool of herself.

Then the full implication hit.

Helen had received an invite. Blast!

'You can take our RSVPs back with you, can't she, Kate?' Helen called.

Kate appeared in the doorway. She was holding a tea towel and wiping her hands on it. 'Lunch in five minutes,' she announced. 'What was that about an RSVP?'

'For Annabelle's wedding. Beverley may as well hand-deliver them. It'll save on postage.'

'Hiya, Nan!' Sam burst into the room, all gangly legs and skinny arms.

He deftly avoided Helen's kiss, slipping out of her grasp with the skill of an international rugby player aiming for a winning try.

'Don't say hiya,' Helen sniffed. 'Say hello.'

Sam made a face, which his paternal grandmother thankfully didn't notice.

'What RSVPs?' Kate asked. 'Sam, wash your hands and give the girls a shout, please.'

'Dad has already called them,' Sam said.

'It won't hurt to call them again,' his mother told him. She turned to Brett. 'We haven't had an invitation yet, have we? I'm assuming if Helen is invited, Brett and I are, too?'

'And the children,' Beverley added. She tried her best to sound normal, but inside she was fuming. Ron really should have said something.

Then Beverley suppressed a gasp as a thought struck her.

Did Ron actually *know?*

It wouldn't surprise her to find that May had gone ahead and booked the place, then sent out the invitations without discussing it with Annabelle and Ron first. That Beverley herself had done a remarkably similar thing when it came to the bandstand, was neither here nor there. She'd had good reason, and the deposit hadn't been too horrendous that if Ron and Annabelle had refused to get married there and she had lost her money, it wouldn't have bankrupted her. But for May to have sent the invitations out…

Beverley blew out her cheeks at the nerve of the woman.

'I assumed your invitation would have arrived the same time as mine,' Helen said. 'Mine came on Thursday, but I suppose with the bank holiday the post might be delayed.'

Brett slapped a hand to his forehead and said, 'Thursday's post is in the drawer in the hall table.'

Kate blinked. 'What's it doing in there?'

'You told me to tidy up,' he protested.

Ellis and Portia sidled into the room as Kate explained, 'Brett's had a few days off. I was at work on Thursday, so I asked him to dust and run the vacuum cleaner around before my Mum arrived.'

Helen muttered, 'I wouldn't have bothered,' but no one took any notice.

'You shouldn't have put the post in there,' Kate told him. 'It could be something important – like a wedding invitation.' Her laugh followed Brett out into the hall.

'Hi, Nan,' Ellis said to Helen, and Portia waved at her grandmother.

Even as Beverley seethed, she noticed how lovely her eldest granddaughter looked. She still favoured floaty clothes and continued to wear her hair loose, which fell in a mass of waves to her waist. But over these past few months her face had become more adult, her cheekbones more sculpted and her lips fuller.

Portia, too, had altered; gone was the goth look she had once favoured, and in its place was a pixie haircut in her natural light auburn shade, and her formerly pale make-up had been replaced by creamy skin with a healthy glow.

'Here you go,' Brett said, handing three envelopes and a flyer to his wife.

Kate flicked through them. 'Got it,' she said, tearing the envelope open and withdrawing an embellished card. She skimmed the contents, then handed it to Brett. 'There won't be enough room for us to stay with you,' she said to Beverley. We'll book a hotel. Remind me to do it after lunch. Helen, would you like me to book a room for you, too? I'm sure we can find a hotel with a single room. Or you could share with Sam?'

A smug expression crept across Helen's face. 'Book me a double, please. The invitation says plus-one. I will be bringing Carlton.'

The name was out of her mouth before Beverley could rein it in. 'Carlton?'

'Nan has got a *gentleman friend*,' Portia leapt in. 'Yuck.'

Helen scowled. 'Don't be rude, Portia. You won't think it's yuck when *you* have a boyfriend.'

'Purleeze, that's so different. You're *old*.'

'Not that old,' Helen said quickly. 'And you'll be my age one day.'

Portia's expression showed how she felt about the prospect.

Beverley had a feeling her own expression was broadcasting how she felt about Helen having a gentleman friend. One who she knew well enough to share a room with.

Beverley didn't think Helen went in for that kind of thing. And she was looking so incredibly smug about it too. It really got Beverley's back up.

Helen turned to her. 'Carlton is a banker. Or he used to be. He's retired now, of course. We've been seeing each other for about six months. I must say, he has given me a new lease of life. You should get yourself a gentleman friend, Beverley. It will do wonders for your temperament.' Helen simpered and Beverley itched to wipe the smirk off her face.

A whole range of emotions coursed through her — astonishment, outrage, envy... But what came out of her mouth was a total lie.

'I already have one. His name is Andrew, and I'll be bringing him to the wedding.'

The look on Helen's face was priceless. 'You *have?* Since when?'

'A few months.' Beverley played her trump card. 'He helped me choose the bandstand for the ceremony.'

'*You* chose the bandstand?'

'Ron and Annabelle are just so busy,' Beverley said, dodging the truth.

'Did you organise the reception, too?'

Beverley inclined her head modestly. She didn't exactly lie, but if Helen believed she had had a hand in it, that was fine by her.

With the wind taken out of her sails, Helen subsided into a sulky silence and the conversation over lunch was a far more pleasant affair because of it Beverley thought, and neither gentleman friend (she hated that phrase) was mentioned again.

But after Helen left, Kate cornered her.

'I knew there was more to Andrew than you were letting on,' her daughter said. 'You've got a real glow when you talk about him.'

She had? That was news to Beverley.

Kate carried on, 'I'm so pleased for you, Mum. It's about time you started to live a little and enjoy yourself. And I can see he makes you happy.'

Kate could? That was news to Beverley, too. It was amazing what people could imagine. Beverley had never glowed in her life, and she certainly didn't think of herself as happy. Content maybe, but not *happy*.

'I can't wait to meet him,' Kate was saying. 'He sounds lovely. Aw, Mum, I think I'm going to cry.'

Beverley was appalled. 'Don't you dare. There's nothing to cry about,' she began, and was about to tell Kate the truth when her daughter pulled her into a hug.

'I'm so thrilled. All I want is for you to have someone to love you and care for you... I can stop worrying now.'

Beverley drew back. 'You've been *worrying* about me?'

'I've seen how much happier you are since Ron came to live with you. I know how lonely you were before, and I was scared you'd be lonely again when he and Annabelle move in together. It looks like I don't have to worry so much, eh? Not now you've got a *gentleman friend.*'

'Ugh, don't. Portia is right – it sounds icky. Why can't Helen call him her boyfriend?'

'Maybe she feels boyfriend is too juvenile. What do you call Andrew?'

'A friend.'

Kate nudged her. 'Fibber.'

Beverley felt heat rising up her neck and into her face. She wanted to tell her daughter the truth – that Andrew *was* only a friend and she had lied because Helen had been so bloody smug and condescending – but she couldn't bring herself to. Kate seemed so happy for her, and Beverley didn't want to burst her bubble. They were having such a lovely weekend, it would be a shame to spoil it. She would tell her in a week or so. Or maybe she would leave it until after the wedding. If she told Kate beforehand, Kate might slip up and Beverley would feel like a right idiot if Helen found out she'd been lying about her relationship with Andrew.

Beverley nodded to herself. After the wedding would be best.

She could say that she and Andrew had decided they were better off being friends. At least by then she would have made it clear to self-satisfied Helen that Beverley could also have a man if she wanted one.

There was one little problem…

Whilst she was fairly confident that Andrew would agree to accompany her to the wedding, what he might be less keen on was pretending to be her boyfriend!

CHAPTER 15

Beverley had insisted they take a taxi from Andrew's house to The Gillespie Rooms, even though the price she had been quoted by the taxi firm had made her eyes water. She wanted to arrive in style – not hot and flustered by having to walk from the bus stop. She supposed she could have driven, but she hadn't been too sure about the hotel's parking situation.

She and Andrew were currently in the back of the cab, and Beverley was telling him about what May had done.

'And Ron knew nothing about it?' he clarified.

'Not a sausage. She booked it without telling either of them – which wouldn't have been so bad,' she added hastily, her own guilt at having done the very same thing clear for all to see. 'But she sent out the invitations without checking with Ron and Annabelle that they are happy with the place.'

'And are they?'

'I get the impression that they can't be bothered arguing with her. Ron sort of clams up every time the wedding is mentioned. He doesn't know we're checking The Gillespie Rooms out today. I tried to tell him, but he wasn't interested. I think it's all getting a bit much.'

'I can see where he's coming from,' Andrew said. 'They only wanted a quiet wedding, didn't they?'

'It's still not going to be a big one,' Beverley said. 'They put their foot down about May's friends being invited.' She sniggered. 'The problem was that May had already sent out the invites, so she had to tell these people that they were uninvited. I would have loved to have been a fly on the wall for that conversation.'

'Poor May.' Andrew was sympathetic.

'Poor May, my backside,' Beverley retorted. 'She should never have sent the invitations out in the first place. That was for Annabelle and Ron to do. It's *their* wedding, not hers.'

Andrew gave her a keen look and she guessed what he was thinking.

'*I'm* only trying to help,' she said loftily. 'May is trying to *take charge*.'

The taxi pulled into the kerb and Beverley took a second to examine the hotel before she alighted.

'It looks very posh,' she hissed, glad that she had made an effort with her appearance this morning. She hadn't thrown on the first thing she had laid her hands on – which was her usual method of choosing what to wear – but had picked out her plainest skirt (plain blue) and had teamed it with a lipstick-pink jumper. The colour worked well with her hair, she thought, which was still a light purple colour. Her lime green coat let the side down, but she was carrying it over her arm, so it was less in-your-face.

Anyway, so what if she liked bright clothes? If Andrew didn't mind them, what business was it to anyone else? She hadn't quite worked out why it was important that Andrew liked what he saw when he looked at her (or at least, didn't recoil in horror) but she had her suspicions, and they were quite worrying. Which was why she didn't want to examine them too closely.

The inside of the hotel was even grander than the outside, with a huge wood panelled reception desk, more wood panelling on the walls, and a carpet so deep it was like walking in quicksand. Muted voices came from the far end of a hall to their right, along with the clink and tinkle of cutlery and glassware, and a large vase of flowers filled the air with a sweet fragrance.

The whole place shouted elegance and money.

'Um... we haven't made a reservation, but we wondered if you have a table free?' Beverly asked the man behind the desk.

'For two?'

'Yes, please.'

He gave them a friendly, professional smile. 'You're in luck. If you'd like to follow me, I'll show you to your table. May I take your coat?'

Beverley handed hers to him. Andrew didn't have a coat as such, but he was wearing a smart sports jacket, with a shirt and tie, brown trousers and polished brogues. He looked very nice.

Beverley tried not to show how impressed she was with the place, as they were led to a table. The maitre'd pulled out a chair for her, then picked up one of the snowy-white linen napkins and with an expert flick of his wrist, draped it over her lap. He called a waiter over, who placed a jug of iced water with lemon slices floating on the top, in the centre of the table.

'Would you like a drink while you decide what to order?' the maitre'd asked.

'A gin and lemonade, for me, please,' Beverley said, feeling somewhat intimidated and overwhelmed.

'Make that two, but I'll have tonic instead of lemonade.' Andrew smiled up at the man, who opened the leather-bound menus and gave them one each. Andrew seemed very much at ease, to her envy.

'Flipping heck,' Beverley muttered, as soon as they were alone. 'This must be costing May an arm and a leg. I can't see Ron and Annabelle forking out for this.'

'It's certainly very impressive,' Andrew agreed.

'What did you do for a living?' she asked.

He blinked at the sudden change of direction. 'I was the MD of a manufacturing company. Why?'

'No reason.' Beverley wondered whether managing director topped banker in the employment charts.

'What about you?' he asked.

'I was a nurse.'

'Ah.' He nodded. 'That explains why you offered to massage my knee.'

'I can't remember doing that?'

'You did. When you came to my house the Sunday that I didn't turn up for lunch.'

'It sounds like something I would say,' she conceded. She tended to say a great deal she shouldn't.

Andrew asked, 'Do you miss it?'

'Sometimes. I don't miss the shifts or being on my feet all day, but I do miss the companionship and helping people.'

'Like Ron?'

She inclined her head in acknowledgement.

'You think the world of him, don't you?' Andrew said.

'He's had a hard time of it. And he's a good man.' As are you, she thought.

A waiter brought their drinks, carrying them on a small silver platter, and before he put the glasses down on the table, he placed a small paper doily underneath each one first.

Beverley giggled. This was so very May. And Helen would love it, too. Beverley was very glad she had a dress that would do this place justice. She knew that there were a number of function rooms here, from ones large enough to hold up to two-hundred people, to smaller intimate rooms suitable for twenty or so guests to dine in private, and she was dying to take a look at the one in which Ron and Annabelle's reception would be held, but she didn't think it appropriate to ask. There was one thing she did want to ask, however.

After they had finished their meal – Dover sole for her, wild boar for Andrew – she called the maitre'd over.

'Is everything all right, madam?'

'Fine, thanks. The meal was lovely. I wonder, do you allow dogs here?'

The maitre'd didn't so much as twitch an eyebrow. 'Yes, we do, but only in certain bedrooms, and never in the dining room or any of the other public rooms, although the bar isn't off limits.'

'What about a private room for a wedding reception?'

'It might be possible. Will it be madam and sir's own wedding?'

Beverley blushed. 'No, my son's. They've already booked it. It's only a small wedding – on the 26th of June.' She looked up at him hopefully.

'You will have to obtain the bride and groom's permission, but if they agree I'm sure we can come to some arrangement.'

Beverley clapped her hands. 'Goodie!' she exclaimed. 'I hate leaving Pepe on his own for too long. He's very well behaved,' she added, resisting the urge to cross her fingers.

The maitre'd gave the smallest of bows. 'I'm glad to hear it.'

'That's settled,' Beverley said to Andrew, as soon as the man was out of earshot. 'You can come with me.'

'Come with you where?'

'To the wedding. You needn't worry about Twinkle, because you can bring her with you.'

'To the wedding?' Andrew looked so confused that Beverley thought if anyone looked up the dictionary meaning of the word 'confused', it would say 'see Andrew.'

'Keep up,' she sighed. 'I want you to come with me to Ron and Annabelle's wedding as my plus-one.'

'Are you sure?' An expression of pleasure crept across his face.

'Definitely. It'll be fun. Oh, there is one thing,' she said, her hands clammy and her heart racing. 'You have to pretend to be my boyfriend.'

***

Oh, no. No, no, no. There was no way Andrew was going to pretend to be anyone's boyfriend, least of all Beverley's. He was already having inappropriate feelings for her, so for him to pretend to be all lovey-dovey when he wanted to do more than pretend, wouldn't be a good idea.

'Why do I need to do that?' he asked mildly, pleased that his inner turmoil wasn't apparent in his voice.

'Because Helen is bringing a gentleman friend.'

'I didn't think she had a partner.' Beverley hadn't mentioned Helen having a man in her life, and he'd got the impression that she was unattached.

'Neither did I,' Beverley said sourly. 'She sprung it on me with a sarcastic comment about me needing to get myself a fella. So I told her I already had one.'

'Was that wise?'

'I doubt it,' she replied cheerfully.

'Fancy a pot of tea?' he suggested, trying to gain a few extra seconds to process Beverley's request.

Neither of them had wanted any pudding – to be fair, the portion sizes of their main courses had been rather generous, which boded well for the wedding breakfast – but a nice cup of tea would be a suitable end to the meal, he thought, calling a waiter over.

Beverley continued, 'She was so smug, I could have slapped her.'

'I didn't think you were the violent type.' She had mentioned being done away with the first time he'd met her though, so he might have read her wrong.

'I'm not, but I'd make an exception for Helen,' she grumbled.

'You two really don't get on, do you?'

Beverley sent him what Andrew could only describe as a '*Duh!*' look. 'No, we don't.'

'But just because she is bringing a partner, doesn't mean you have to,' Andrew pointed out reasonably.

'I know, but it just popped out.'

'Can't you take it back?'

'And look like a total idiot? I'd prefer not, if it's all the same to you. Look at it this way, it's a free day out. I take it you've got a suit?'

'One or two.' He had several, but he hadn't worn one for ages. The last time had been at a funeral for one of his neighbours. He wouldn't wear that one though, despite a black suit being acceptable wedding attire for a man. He had a nice dark navy one that would complement Beverley's dress perfectly.

What was he thinking? He had no intention of going to this wedding. He might have considered accompanying her if she had couched it as less of a boyfriend role and more of a friend role.

Then again, what were friends for if not to help each other out? He mightn't approve of Beverley telling her arch-enemy that she had a boyfriend, but the damage was done now and he could appreciate that she would lose face if she turned up at the wedding on her own.

What harm could it do if he agreed? It wasn't as though he'd be snogging her socks off behind the wedding cake. A solicitous peck on the cheek, a hand on her elbow to guide her, or on the small of her back, a chair pulled out for her... he could manage that. And, after the wedding, Helen would most likely forget all about Beverley's supposed boyfriend, and that would be that.

Beverley was still gazing at him hopefully, but before he said yes there was someone else he needed to consider – Judith. How would she feel about him going to this wedding with Beverley on his arm? She already thought there was something going on between them and this might confirm her suspicion.

He had been rather cross with Judith for her attitude concerning Beverley. His daughter had reacted more like a teenager faced with the prospect of a wicked stepmother stealing her father's heart, than a woman in her late forties who had a home and a family of her own.

But did he really want to let Judith dictate who he can and can't see? His friends were *his* business, not hers. Anyway, he could always claim that he had been invited to keep Leo company.

'Yes,' he said, making his mind up. 'If you want me to accompany you to Ron's wedding I will, and I'll even pretend to Helen that I'm your boyfriend.'

'Um... could you pretend that you're my boyfriend from now on? For one thing, if everyone knows the truth except Helen, someone is bound to slip up.'

'And for another?' Andrew had a feeling he wasn't going to like her answer.

'Kate already thinks we're a couple and she's so thrilled that I've met someone, I haven't got the heart to tell her we're not together. So can you pretend to be my boyfriend from now until the wedding. *Please?*

When Beverley looked at him with such a pleading expression, how could he refuse?

'Ok, I'll do it,' he said, wondering what he had let himself in for and hoping he hadn't bitten off more than he could chew.

Oh, heck, what was the worst that could happen?

CHAPTER 16

Beverley had sensed that Andrew hadn't been particularly pleased about the wedding-boyfriend situation, but despite his reluctance, he had agreed to help her out.

She could have kissed him, but she didn't think he would appreciate it, so she had done the next best thing and paid for the meal. She'd had to do it on the sly, pretending to go to the loo, because she knew he would have objected. And he had, quite strenuously, trying to shove some cash into her hands. But she had refused to take it, so he had been left with no option other than to accept.

He had grumbled and grizzled about it all the way home, this time on the bus because one lot of cab fare had been enough today, and she had left him standing on his doorstep after she'd collected Pepe, still chuntering about it.

'Give it a rest,' she'd said, then had acted purely on impulse and had kissed his cheek before hurrying off.

It had stopped his moaning dead in his tracks, and Beverley was still grinning at the look on his face when she arrived home.

'Why are you so happy?' Ron asked. 'Have you won the lottery?'

'I've won something else,' she replied, getting into character as she prepared to tell Ron that Andrew would be accompanying her to the wedding. 'Andrew's heart.' Then she wondered whether she had lathered it on too strong, when Ron froze.

He was silent for a good few seconds and she was beginning to think he was upset, when a broad smile spread slowly across his face and he held out his arms.

Feeling a fraud, Beverley stepped into his embrace. 'You don't mind?' she asked.

'Mind? I'm delighted. From what you've told me, he sounds like a great guy. I'm so pleased. It's about time you had some romance in your life.' He pulled back and stared Beverley straight in the eye, his gaze intense and unnerving.

For a moment Beverley feared she had been rumbled, but when he said, 'If he doesn't treat you right, he'll have me to answer to,' she breathed a sigh of relief.

Until a wave of remorse struck her. Ron seemed thrilled for her, and she felt like a cow for misleading him and wished she had kept her big mouth shut and not squared up to Helen.

'I'm so pleased for you,' Ron continued. 'You deserve some happiness.'

'I was happy anyway,' she protested. Maybe not deliriously happy, but happy enough with her life just the way it was. She didn't need a man to make her happy.

'You are *now.*' Ron gave her a squeeze. 'You're glowing.'

Oh, dear; Kate had said something similar.

Beverley must be a better actress than she'd thought. She should have gone on the stage, and she wondered whether seventy-two was too old to be a film star.

OK, maybe not films, but she could walk the boards? She quite fancied being on the stage.

'When can I meet him?' Ron asked.

'Eh?' Bugger, she should have anticipated that, and her face fell. 'I… er… it's like this…'

Ron's brow creased. 'Don't you feel the same way about him?'

'Of course I do.'

'You looked a bit uncertain, that's all. Just because he's in love with you, it's not compulsory that you have to love him back.'

'I do love him,' Beverley insisted, mentally crossing her fingers and hoping she wouldn't be caught out in the lie.

'Good. I'd hate to think of any man railroading you into doing something you don't want to do.'

'Andrew's not like that,' she said. 'He's kind and thoughtful, a true gentleman. And he's fit.'

Ron barked out a laugh. 'Did you just call him fit?'

'He *is*,' Beverley insisted, beaming. 'He's got all his own teeth, too.'

Ron was chuckling. 'That's a bonus. '

'It is when you get to my age. He does have a gammy knee though.'

'Is that a medical term?' Ron's shoulders were heaving, his eyes creased with mirth.

Beverley joined in, thinking that she hadn't felt this lighthearted in years.

'So, when do I get to meet him?' Ron asked again a short while later when they'd both calmed down.

'Soon,' Beverley promised, and her mood turned sombre. Andrew wasn't going to be happy about this.

What was that saying about no good deed goes unpunished, Andrew asked himself a few days later as he limped along Staley Avenue. He was on his way to Beverley's house, Twinkle at his side.

Andrew's good deed had been to agree, against his better judgement, to accompany Beverley to Ron's wedding and pretend to be her significant other. Or *boyfriend*, as she had put it.

His punishment was… where should he start? Pretending to be something he wasn't, when he was beginning to wish that he was? Having to meet Ron who, Beverley had informed him, wanted to see for himself that Andrew was treating her right? Lying to total strangers? Lying to his family? Lying to *himself*?

Maybe he was being overly dramatic, but he sensed this wasn't going to end well.

He had agreed now though, and he could hardly back out without hurting Beverley or making Ron think he was a cad. He just hoped he could carry it off convincingly, without letting on to Beverley that his feelings for her had gone beyond the purely platonic.

He couldn't pinpoint when it had happened, but slowly, like an invading virus, she had crept under his skin, and he hadn't noticed until it was too late and he had become infected.

Comparing Beverley to a virus wasn't the nicest, but he hadn't been a willing participant. Like getting a cold or a bout of the flu, he hadn't wanted to come down with a dose of romantic inclinations – it had happened regardless. He wasn't yet at a point where he couldn't live without her, or even at the declaration-of-undying-love stage (such dramatic gestures weren't him) but he felt far more for her than he was comfortable feeling.

As far as he was concerned, he was still grieving for Vivienne, and he was quite affronted that Beverley had hijacked even a little part of his heart: a heart that until recently had been reserved exclusively for his dead wife. Romantic notions for another woman shouldn't have entered his head, and he was quite resentful that they had.

But that was his cross to bear, not Beverley's. She would most likely be appalled if she knew, so it was up to him to make sure she never found out. Her friendship was important to him, and he didn't want to lose it.

He was so entrenched in his widowerhood that he couldn't see himself in any other role. He was Vivienne's husband, and the fact that she had passed away didn't change anything. Which made his growing treacherous feelings for Beverley all the more incomprehensible. What did he think he was playing at?

Boyfriend – that was what he was playing at today, and he would be playing that part from now until the wedding. After which, he could hopefully fade into the background as a friend.

With benefits? his dirty mind asked, and he scowled the idea away. Just because he had pictured himself in her bed, didn't mean it would ever happen. When he was younger, he had imagined making love to Cindy Crawford on more than one occasion, but that hadn't happened either.

The voice in his head argued, *you wouldn't have stood a cat in hell's chance with the lovely Cindy, even if you had managed to actually meet her. A famous model like her wouldn't have looked at you once, let alone twice. But Beverley might.*

'Give it a rest.' he muttered, reaching Beverley's house and opening her gate, a sudden attack of nerves making him falter. This was worse than that Sunday in February not long after they'd first met, when she had invited him to lunch and he had chickened out.

He wished he could chicken out now, but he couldn't think of an excuse. Claiming that an alien invasion was about to take place wasn't a believable option, and he had already used the unexpected arrival of his daughter as an excuse, and look how that had turned out.

As he rang the bell, he wished he had suggested that he and Ron meet in a more neutral location, rather than on the man's home turf, so to speak, but it was too late now...

The door opened and he was relieved to see Beverley on the other side of it. Her mouth was smiling but worry lurked in her eyes.

Andrew guessed the reason, and he stepped forward and took her in his arms. In for a penny, in for a pound, he thought, intending to give her a quick hug and a peck on the cheek, but then he felt her warmth and softness, smelt the light perfume she wore and the scent of her hair, and his lips connected with hers and he was lost.

He had no idea how long they stood on her step, kissing like a couple of teenagers on their way home from the pub, and they might have stayed there all day if it hadn't been for a polite cough.

Andrew released Beverley immediately and they sprang apart. His horrified gaze shot over her shoulder to see a man hovering behind her in the hallway, and he was mortified. He could feel the colour draining from his face, but by some weird osmosis, pink was flooding into Beverley's cheeks, and she blushed furiously.

Before she turned around to face Ron, she looked at Andrew's, bewildered and embarrassed.

'I take it you must be Andrew,' Ron said, stepping towards him and holding his hand out. He was grinning broadly and there was laughter in his eyes.

'Gosh, yes, sorry. Um… I didn't mean for that to happen.'

'I bet you didn't,' Ron chuckled, gripping his hand firmly. 'I wouldn't want to be caught necking on the doorstep, either. Beverley, are you going to stand there all day or are you going to ask Andrew in? I think the neighbours have seen enough.'

Ron was openly laughing now, and Andrew's cheeks grew so warm that he would soon be rivalling Beverley in the blushing department. But when he'd said that he hadn't meant for that to happen, he hadn't been referring to being caught. It was kissing her in the first place that he hadn't meant to do. It had been as much of a shock to him as it had been to her. Looking back, he was surprised she hadn't pushed him away – but then again, that might have appeared odd.

Beverley shouldered past him, and he numbly followed her and Ron into the house, closing the door behind him. He could still taste her on his lips, still feel her in his arms, and his breath caught in his throat. His pulse was racing, and he felt jittery and out-of-sorts, as though he'd had three cups of coffee too many.

He made a mental note to not be so enthusiastic next time – if there *was* a next time. After what he had just done, he wouldn't blame her if she told him she never wanted to see him again. Talk about taking his role literally!

But – and this was what flummoxed him – she had appeared to enjoy it as much as he. She had melted into his embrace, her lips had parted, and—

'It's nice to finally meet you,' Ron said, breaking into Andrew's thoughts when they reached the kitchen and turning to face him. 'I've heard a lot about you.'

Beverley hurried over to the stove, picked up a wooden spoon and began stirring something in a saucepan. Andrew wished he could see her face; it might have given him some inkling what she was thinking.

'All good, I hope,' he replied weakly. He needed a sit down and a cup of tea. Or brandy. 'Twinkle!' he cried, suddenly remembering his dog and hoping he hadn't left her outside.

'She's cuddled up with Pepe in his basket. She trotted in all by herself, which was why I came to find you.' Ron grinned again, clearly remembering the state they were in when he had.

Andrew must have dropped Twinkle's lead. Thank goodness she hadn't run out into the road.

Ron said. 'Would you like a beer? I've got a couple chilling in the fridge. Beverley, what about you?'

'Not for me, thanks.' Her voice sounded strangled.

'Aw, are you embarrassed?' Ron teased, oblivious to the tension in the room. 'Don't be. I think it's sweet.' He took two stubby brown bottles out of the fridge, prised the tops off and handed one to Andrew.

'Would you like a glass?' he began, but stopped when he realised Andrew had downed half of his in one go.

Andrew wiped his mouth with his fingers. That was better. Not much, but a bit.

'You were thirsty,' Ron observed, and then sniggered. 'It must be all that kissing you were doing.'

'Ron! Make yourself useful and lay the table!' Beverley snapped.

'Yes, ma'am.'

'We'll eat in the dining room,' she instructed.

He nodded, still grinning, but opened a drawer and selected some cutlery.

As soon as he was out of the room, Beverley turned her stricken face to Andrew. 'I'm so sorry,' she hissed. 'I didn't mean to kiss you like that. I promise it won't happen again.'

'It wasn't you; it was me,' Andrew protested. 'I'm a bit out of practice. I was aiming for your cheek, but…'

'Oh, God,' she groaned. 'I was aiming for *yours.*'

'No harm done.'

'Are you sure?'

Andrew was about to say something, but Ron walked back into the kitchen, and he quickly closed his mouth.

'Stop whispering sweet nothings in his ear,' Ron said to Beverley. 'Not even me and Annabelle are that bad.'

'I wasn't,' she protested, but Ron gave her a knowing look.

'Would you like me to make myself scarce?' he asked.

'No!' Andrew and Beverley cried at the same time.

Beverley recovered first. 'I thought you wanted to meet Andrew?' she said.

'I do, and I have. I can see he's a top bloke, so if you want to have a meal with just the two of you, I can—'

'Ron, shut up.' Beverley flicked a tea towel at him.

Ron did as he was told, but the amusement lingered in his expression.

Andrew was mightily relieved when they sat down to eat. Although he didn't have much of an appetite, it gave him something to do with his hands. It also seemed to take Ron's mind off teasing him and Beverley.

Hunting around for something to say, Andrew decided that talking about dogs was a safe enough topic. 'Beverley tells me you run a dog training business?'

Ron replied, 'I do. If you've got a mutt that won't stop yapping, or a pooch that is possessive over food, then I'm your man. I must say, Twinkle is very well behaved. She's a credit to you.'

'Thank you. She's a very easy-going dog.'

'Not like Pepe,' Beverley said. 'He's a total menace. Stubborn, too.' She gazed fondly down at the poodle, who was lying under the table with Twinkle in the hope that someone would slip him some scraps.

'He's better than he was,' Ron said.

'Thanks to you.' Beverley smiled at him. 'I'm glad he's still a little bit naughty, otherwise you and Annabelle would never have got together. Did I tell you that story, Andrew?'

'Yes, you did.' Andrew turned to Ron. 'He came looking for you when you left, I believe?'

'That's right.' Ron reached down to fondle the poodle's ears.

Pepe shook him off. The dog was more interested in what was on the humans' plates than being petted.

Hoping he was being discreet, Andrew slipped both dogs a morsel of food, but when he glanced up he found Beverley watching him. He wished he could read her expression, but she was keeping her face blank.

'OK?' he mouthed at her and was relieved when she nodded.

The rest of the meal passed without incident and gradually Andrew began to relax. Ron seemed a nice chap and he clearly adored Beverley, and she, him. They were like mother and son, and it warmed his heart to see it. He knew how much she missed Kate, so having Ron around was a real bonus, and Andrew feared she was going to miss him even more than she let on after he was married, even though Ron wouldn't be living too far away.

With the meal eaten and Ron offering to do the washing up, Beverley suggested they take the dogs for an evening stroll around the park. Andrew guessed she wanted to get him on his own without the risk of Ron overhearing.

As soon as they were outside, Andrew apologised once more. 'I'm sorry. The last thing I wanted to do was to embarrass you.'

'You didn't. I was the one who embarrassed you.'

They looked at each other and chuckled. 'We are a pair of numpties, aren't we?' Andrew laughed.

'At least I can safely say that Ron is fully convinced we are an item,' Beverley said, and Andrew detected a degree of satisfaction in her voice.

'Mission accomplished,' he agreed. 'I don't think we're going to have any trouble persuading Helen either, although I don't think we should enjoy a passionate clinch at the wedding.' He bit his lip when he realised what he'd said.

'Did you enjoy it?' Beverley was back to her forthright self.

Andrew concentrated on where he was putting his feet, even though they were walking along a flat pavement. 'I did,' he muttered, reluctantly.

'So did I.'

He glanced at her in surprise. 'You did?'

'Yes, but I don't think we should repeat it.'

'No, of course not.' Andrew was quick to agree. He was already in deep enough without making it worse for himself. If he thought he had liked her before today, that kiss had cemented it.

It was an odd situation to be in. He was trying to regard her as just a friend he was doing a favour for, but in reality, he was starting to fall for her. He found it quite unnerving and somewhat distressing for two reasons. The first was because of his wife. He never thought he could feel a fraction of what he felt for Vivienne for any other woman, and he wasn't sure he could cope with all these new emotions. The second reason was Beverley herself. She might have enjoyed the kiss, but it didn't mean she wanted that kind of relationship with him. And even if she did, he didn't know whether he was able to commit to her anyway.

They were better off as friends. It was far less complicated. They would just have to get through the next couple of months until the wedding was done and dusted, then they could go back to being the way they were before.

Now all he had to do was to convince himself of that – but it was easier said than done when all he could think about was that kiss.

***

'Well, what do you think?' Beverley asked Ron, when she returned from her rather awkward walk with Andrew. Andrew had clearly been discomfited and embarrassed that she had snogged his face off, and that he had been caught in such a compromising position.

But as she had said to him, at least Ron was convinced they were an item. They probably wouldn't need any more demonstrations of physical affection apart from a quick peck on the cheek now and again, or him helping her to put her coat on… things like that. So maybe it hadn't been too bad after all, considering it had served its purpose.

She had liked it, though. More than liked it, if she was honest. He had taken her breath away, leaving her trembly and with a racing heart. God, what she wouldn't give to do it again – but she knew that wasn't going to happen. Andrew had been so incredibly dismayed, it made her feel awful.

As far as she could tell, Andrew was a confirmed widower. He didn't want a romantic liaison. He was still grieving for his wife. He might never stop grieving for her, and the last thing he needed was Beverley making him feel uncomfortable.

She hoped she had done enough to convince him she wasn't interested in him in that way. But she was lying: she was very interested indeed, and she felt like banging her head against the nearest wall. Trust her to go all these years without feeling the slightest bit of attraction to a man – apart from Brad Pitt, but any heterosexual woman with a pulse fancied Brad Pitt – only to fall for one who had zero interest in any kind of relationship.

She almost wished she'd never met him, but she couldn't bring herself to go that far. The thought of not having Andrew in her life was unbearable.

'I like him,' Ron said. 'You seem different when you're with him.'

'How so?'

'Lighter, more carefree.'

Ron was right: she did feel lighter and more carefree. Or, at least, she *had* felt lighter, until she realised she was falling in love with him. Now all she felt was depressed. But as long as Ron carried on thinking she was happy and that she and Andrew were a couple, he wouldn't worry about her so much. She realised part of the reason she had blurted out to Helen that she had a boyfriend, was so Ron would start married life without worrying about Beverley being lonely living on her own.

With that realisation came a renewed resolve not to let Ron suspect that her relationship with Andrew was anything other than committed and romantic.

There would be time enough after the wedding, when Ron was firmly embedded in his new life with Annabelle and the children, for Beverley to quietly say that she and Andrew had decided they were far happier being friends than lovers.

But there was one thing that was worrying her, which made her wish she had never started this – that kiss. When she had been in Andrew's arms, with his mouth on hers, it had been far, far too easy to let herself believe that this was for real.

And she wished with all her heart that it was.

CHAPTER 17

Andrew wasn't normally a fretter, but after kissing Beverley he had fretted for most of the night. What must she think of him? He had made a right idiot of himself, and he thought he might never be able to look her in the face again.

But however idiotic he felt, he couldn't bring himself to regret it. He could still feel the softness of her as he held her, and every time he thought about it his heart gave a little leap and his tummy turned over.

Ruefully he buttered his toast and gazed at Vivienne's photo. Andrew wondered what his wife would say if she knew how he felt, and what advice she would give him if she could. He suspected she would probably laugh her socks off at his embarrassment, whilst at the same time commiserate with his predicament. She would probably also tell him it was about time he found someone else, and ask him what he was waiting for.

His promise to her not to grieve forever lay heavily on his mind, but how could he not mourn her? She had been his world for so many years. But it seemed he was moving on, whether he was ready to or not.

How on earth had he managed to develop feelings for Beverley? One minute he had been pootling along, minding his own business and wallowing in misery, and the next he was snogging a woman he had only known for a couple of months, and agreeing to be her boyfriend.

The strange thing was, he felt as though he had known her forever. He hadn't realised how drab and colourless his life had become until Beverley had entered it. He just hoped he hadn't spoiled their friendship yesterday.

It was with some trepidation that he headed to the park this morning with Twinkle, hoping that Beverley would be there. He had no idea what he would do if she wasn't. Would he pop round to her house? Or would that freak her out if she was trying to avoid him? He didn't want to come across as a stalker. And if he did pay her a visit, what would he say?

He scanned the park, catching glimpses of walkers through the trees, but none of them were brightly dressed or had a black poodle in tow. His watch said ten-thirty-five and his heart sank.

She wasn't going to show. He had scared her off.

If she hadn't shown her face by quarter-to-eleven, he'd head home and try again tomorrow in the hope that she hadn't come to the park today because she was otherwise engaged, and not because she was avoiding him. Maybe she'd made other plans and had forgotten to tell him.

His relief when he saw her trotting towards him made Andrew wish he could sit down for a minute. He had honestly thought he'd blown it.

'Morning,' he called, when she was within hailing distance.

She waved cheerily. 'Morning to you, too.' She grew closer and squinted. 'You're looking tired. Didn't you sleep well?'

'Meh.' He made a see-sawing motion with his hand.

'Did you try hot milk?'

'I did. And counting sheep.'

She scoffed. 'That never works. Who came up with that load of rubbish? I usually get up and knit for an hour or two. It's better than lying there, thinking of something you wished you'd said to that girl in year four who was nasty to you.'

He chuckled, 'Is that what you think about when you can't sleep?'

'Daft, isn't it? But she was a horrid little thing and she made my life a misery in school for a whole year, until her parents moved away.'

Andrew wished he had thought about those kinds of things last night, instead of replaying the kiss on a loop, then fretting over what Beverley had thought, and worrying about his growing feelings for her. Last night had been one long worry-fest.

'Ron likes you,' Beverley said, changing the subject.

'Good. He seems a nice chap.'

'He is.' She linked arms with him, and he caught a whiff of perfume.

Inhaling appreciatively, he entertained the brief hope that she was wearing it for his benefit, before he told himself not to be so silly.

Her arm through the crook of his elbow felt nice though, both comforting and oddly exciting, and he would have loved to take her in his arms and kiss her again, but he daren't — and not solely because he worried that he might alarm her considering that there was absolutely no need for him to get into character right now. Not unless Ron was lurking behind a tree, spying on them.

The problem was Vivienne. Andrew would never forgive himself if, by giving in to his growing feelings for the woman on his arm, his love for his wife would be diminished. He knew that wasn't possible, but it didn't prevent him from worrying about it.

He had been fretting a lot recently, as his restless night last night had demonstrated, but how could he not be concerned when emotions he hadn't felt for a long time were beginning to rise to the surface and he was scared of the changes they would bring.

'Are we OK?' he asked suddenly.

'Definitely! Why wouldn't we be?'

'Yesterday we… er…'

'Kissed on my doorstep? I remember it well.'

'You do.' His voice was flat.

'I told you I'd enjoyed it,' she said. 'It's been far too long since I was kissed like that.' Her eyes twinkled mischievously before her expression softened. 'Stop beating yourself up over it. It was just a kiss. Don't worry, I know it didn't mean anything. Now, shall we go get a coffee? I'm parched.'

The kiss mightn't have meant anything to Beverley, but it had meant something to him.

It had unleashed a plethora of feelings he had no control over and didn't know how to handle, and now he feared he was falling in love with a woman who would never regard him as anything other than a friend.

***

'Bingo?' This was Beverley's suggestion and she thought it was a perfectly good one, until she saw Andrew grimace.

'Bowls?' That was Andrew's.

They were sitting in their usual café, discussing how best to broaden their horizons, having agreed they needed to get out more. Now that Pepe had decided Twinkle was his best friend ever, Beverley was happy to leave him as long as he had the other dog for company. Not for too long, of course, but long enough to go to the bingo one evening. She had never been, and she wanted to know what all the fuss was about.

'Ballroom dancing?' Andrew suggested when Beverley failed to respond to the bowls one.

'Are we starting at the beginning of the alphabet and working our way through? Because if so, we've left A out.'

'I can't think of anything we could do beginning with A.' Andrew glanced up at the person who appeared at his elbow. 'Thank you, that's very kind.' The waitress popped their drinks on the table, and she had also brought over a bowl of water for the dogs to share.

'Arts and crafts, art gallery, archery,' Beverley began. 'Abseiling, acrobatics...' She was getting into her stride.

'We've already done A,' Andrew said. 'The arcade on the pier? And we've had afternoon tea.' He gestured to the pot of tea in front of him.

'It's not the afternoon,' Beverley retorted, pouring milk into her cup, then dumping three sachets of sugar into it and stirring vigorously. 'It's eleven-thirty, and we're not having sandwiches with the crusts cut off.'

'We are having cake, though,' Andrew argued, then subsided when she shot him a disgusted look. 'Would you like to go out for afternoon tea?' he asked.

'I'd prefer to go abseiling.' The horror on his face made her chortle. 'Just kidding. Archery sounds good, though.'

He made a strangled sound, so she guessed he wasn't keen on that idea, either.

'What do you suggest?' she asked.

'I told you, ballroom dancing.'

Beverley was dubious. She had two left feet and absolutely no sense of rhythm whatsoever.

'Or how about board games?' he suggested.

'Poker?' Beverley's face lit up. She had always thought she had the perfect face for it, despite never having played in her life.

'Poker isn't a board game. It's a card game. It would come under C.'

'C for casino?' She had never been to one of those, either.

'C for being taken to the cleaners and losing money you can't afford to lose, or G for gambling.'

'You're not a gambling man, I take it?'

'Not even remotely.'

'Have you never bet on the Grand National or bought a lottery ticket?'

'That's different.'

'It isn't.' She paused as they ate their cake, thinking they had better fast forward to W so she could join Weight Watchers. She had never eaten this much cake before she'd met Andrew. Thank goodness she had Pepe to force her to take a walk every day. If she carried on in this manner she wouldn't fit into her lovely dress.

'I still think ballroom dancing is a good idea,' he insisted. 'We don't even have to go out in the evening if we don't want to. They do afternoon dances.'

'You don't give up easily, do you?'

'I have been told I can be stubborn.'

'If I agree to ballroom dancing, can I get to choose the next thing?'

Andrew eyed her warily. 'I'm not sure I trust you.'

'Oh, ye of little faith,' she teased. 'I promise I won't ask you to do anything dangerous.'

'And if I hate it, I can say no?'

'Hmph! I can't force you to do anything you don't want to do.'

'I'm a man of my word,' he said. 'If I agree to something I won't go back on it.'

She held her hand out for him to shake. 'Deal?'

He took it. 'Deal.'

Beverley smiled ruefully at the tingle his touch had sent through her fingers.

She had only agreed to go ballroom dancing with him because it would mean he would have to hold her in his arms again. How sad was that?

If she wasn't careful, she might fall for him so hard there would be no getting up from it.

***

'One, two, glide, and then one, two, glide and turn,' the instructor called. 'Now, twirl, dip, and hold it... Good! One, two, glide—'

'I *am* bloody gliding,' Beverley hissed in Andrew's ear.

She was sick of gliding. Her feet, crammed into heels she hadn't worn in an age, were killing her. And God only knows what all this gliding and turning was doing to Andrew's gammy knee. Maybe ballroom dancing wasn't the best activity for someone who needed a knee replacement?

To be fair, he hadn't complained at all. But then again, he wouldn't, because this had been his idea and he had been very insistent, so male pride wouldn't allow him to.

Beverley wanted to complain though. Her memory had been correct: she definitely did have two left feet and she had stumbled more times than she could count, plus she had trodden on his toes enough times to leave bruises. A graceful dancer she wasn't. A hippo on an ice rink was a better description, and this gliding business was starting to get on her nerves.

Being held by Andrew as they dipped and twirled was rather nice though…

'Shall we sit this next one out?' he suggested. 'I expect you could do with a drink.'

More than one, she thought, but she was driving this evening and was sticking with orange juice. Plus, she suspected the break might be more for his benefit than for hers, as a sheen of sweat was glistening on his brow and he was breathing heavier than usual. Pain would cause that, and she guessed his knee was playing up. Her stamping on his toes wouldn't have helped, either.

They went back to their table, buying fresh drinks from the bar on the way, and Beverley studied Andrew as he lowered himself into his chair with a wince. He was also on the soft drinks, she noticed, and guessed the reason.

'Did you bring any painkillers with you?' she asked. She always carried a selection in the bag, along with a first aid kit.

He looked down at the table, not meeting her eyes. 'Yes.'

'May I suggest you take them?'

He removed a blister pack of tablets from his pocket and popped a couple into his mouth, washing them down with a swig of lemonade. 'Don't say it,' he growled.

'I'm not going to say anything,' she protested.

'You're itching to, though. I can sense it.'

'I suppose Go Ape is out of the question for our next date?' she quipped, remembering her visit to Margam Park with the family last summer where there had been a Go Ape Centre. Neither she nor Helen had ventured into the treetops, but the kids had had a brilliant time.

'*Date?*' Andrew was gazing at her, confusion in his eyes, and she realised what she had said and blushed.

'Um… what I mean is, the next time we go out together.' Gosh, is that what she had subconsciously thought this evening was – a date?

'I suppose we have to call it something,' Andrew said.

'A date is as good a word as any,' Beverley agreed, her light tone hiding her embarrassment.

'What have you got lined up?' he asked.

'I'm not sure yet, but whatever it is, I promise you'll love it.'

Andrew's gaze locked onto hers and she couldn't look away as he said, 'I'm sure I will.'

The warmth that surged through her at the intense look had nothing whatsoever to do with the unaccustomed dancing, and everything to do with a sudden urge to take him in her arms and kiss him senseless.

Oh dear, maybe their next 'date' should be taken in separate postcodes.

CHAPTER 18

Andrew was so excited he could hardly keep still. It was a rare event for one of his grandsons to visit him without Judith, and he simply couldn't wait. With Ron and Annabelle's wedding now less than two months away, Beverley had told him that May was getting more and more uptight, and was fretting over the smallest thing, including the photographer. So Andrew had made the suggestion that perhaps Leo should pop down for the weekend to have a chat with Ron and Annabelle. Considering it was a bank holiday this weekend and Leo didn't have any lectures on the Monday, it had been agreed that the lad would come down on Friday, spend the weekend with his grandad, and go back to university on Monday.

Andrew was so looking forward to it. He would get Leo to himself for two whole days. It was unheard of.

He was worried that the boy would be bored out of his mind, but Leo had assured him that he wouldn't be bored at all. He wanted to take lots of atmospheric photos of the pier, especially the structure underneath, and he had a few other things in mind too, and had suggested that his grandad might want to tag along.

Andrew was thrilled to be asked and had spent all of Saturday with his eldest grandchild, watching him work. Leo had even let him take a few snaps with Leo's very expensive camera. Andrew had almost been too scared to touch it in case he broke it, but under Leo's guidance he soon discovered that he could take a half-decent photo and that he enjoyed the experience.

When Andrew had mentioned buying a little camera of his own, Leo had told him gently, 'You do realise you can take photos on your phone, don't you, Grandad?'

Andrew did, and he had taken a few in the past, but they hadn't turned out as well as the snaps he had taken with Leo's posh camera. However, Leo had shown him a few tricks, such as the panoramic view option and using the macro lens, and Andrew had been enthralled. He wasn't interested in taking photos of things though: he wanted to photograph people, like that woman playing on the beach with her children, helping her toddler stack pebbles. The concentration on their faces fascinated him. Then there was the old couple sitting on the bench, not talking but holding hands and staring out to sea. Or the two young women, arms slung around each other's shoulders, laughing into each other's eyes, so clearly in love.

For Andrew photography was more about human interest, than human architecture.

Leo had also spent some of Saturday checking out the bandstand from various different angles, and taking a look at the outside of The Gillespie Rooms.

He hadn't ventured inside, because he was dressed in extremely distressed black jeans, trainers and a very faded T-shirt with the name of some band emblazoned across the front, and Andrew had been fairly sure that Leo wouldn't have been allowed in.

His grandson had been philosophical, saying that it didn't matter because the room probably would look different on the day. But he did take several photos of the outside because it was such a lovely sunny day.

'Just in case it rains on the day of the wedding,' he explained. 'I can tone these down a bit so they don't look quite so bright, but the light is good and it seems a shame to waste it.'

After a delightful day together, they shared a takeaway in the evening. Leo wanted pizza, which was what they ordered, but Andrew would have preferred Indian food. The plan for him and Beverley to maybe share one of an evening hadn't happened yet, but he intended to suggest it soon. It was yet another thing to look forward to.

On the following day, Sunday, Andrew had arranged for Leo to meet Ron and Annabelle at Beverley's house.

She insisted on feeding everyone, which he was pleased about because it meant that he didn't have to cook a meal for Leo. He felt bad enough that they'd had a takeaway last night instead of meat and two veg, and on Friday Andrew had taken Leo to the pub, where his grandson had eaten a posh burger and triple-cooked fries, which hadn't been particularly healthy, either. Telling himself that Leo was an adult and that he probably didn't eat healthily in university, didn't help. He could just hear Judith's voice in his ear bipping on that the boys needed five portions of fruit and vegetables a day, and he felt quite guilty.

But meat and two veg was exactly what Leo was getting at Beverley's house. She was cooking roast chicken with new potatoes, boiled potatoes, Yorkshire puddings, stuffing, cranberry sauce, and four different types of vegetables.

When Andrew and Leo arrived they found Ron, Annabelle and the two children already there, the children playing out in the garden with Pepe, and Ron and Annabelle on the sofa in the living room.

'Beverley's in the kitchen,' Ron said, as Andrew let Twinkle off the lead so she could join in the fun. 'You'd better go and say hello. No kissing, though! I don't want the Yorkshires to burn. Oh, by the way, don't go offering to help, because she won't let you.'

Andrew could feel Leo's eyes boring into him, and when he happened to glance over, his grandson's eyebrows were raised.

'Kissing?' Leo's lips twitched.

Before Andrew could say anything – not that he knew what to say – Ron leapt in with, 'I caught them canoodling on the doorstep the other day.'

'Grandad *canoodling?*' Leo's eyebrows raised another notch, and a grin was starting to spread across his face.

'It wasn't like that,' Andrew protested.

'Yes, it was,' Ron said. 'I was about to suggest you got a room.'

'Grandad?'

Andrew pressed his lips together and, without saying another word, went into the kitchen.

Beverley heard him come in and she turned around with a smile. 'Andrew....'

He moved closer and planted a kiss on her cheek. It was all rather maiden aunt-ish.

She looked beyond him over his shoulder. 'This must be Leo,' she said, extricating herself from his embrace and walking towards Leo with her arms outstretched.

Leo subjected himself to a hug, and Andrew was very conscious of his grandson looking at him, then back to Beverley, and assessing the situation.

Andrew said to Beverley, 'I would offer to help, but I've been told I shouldn't.'

'Good, because I don't need any. Why don't you join the others in the living room? We'll eat first, then Leo, Ron and Annabelle can have a little chat and you can help me wash up. How does that sound?'

It sounded as though he didn't have any choice, so he ushered Leo back into the living room and left Beverley to her cooking. But if he thought the subject of him and Beverley was going to end there, Andrew was very much mistaken.

Leo asked, 'Is Beverley your girlfriend?'

'Um…'

'Not girlfriend, exactly,' Ron interjected, 'because that's a bit teenagerish, isn't it? Shall we say… partner?'

'Go, Grandad! It's about time you got back out there.'

'I'm taking relationship advice from a university student now, am I?' Andrew tried to make light of the comment.

He debated whether to tell Leo the truth later when they were at home, but then he fretted that the boy would let the cat out of the bag. Anyway, it wasn't fair to ask Leo to keep his secret, so it was better all round if Leo was singing off the same hymn sheet as everyone else. No one need know the truth, apart from Andrew and Beverley. It was easier that way.

All throughout the meal, Andrew made sure to send little loving glances Beverley's way and reaching out to grasp her hand now and again. Not that it was a hardship, because he was desperate to hold her, but he was careful not to overdo it.

He could tell Beverley appreciated the gestures, because she positively simpered. Every time he smiled sweetly at her, he noticed Ron and Annabelle exchanging knowing looks, and he guessed he was hitting just the right note.

Everyone had fallen for the image of a lovey-dovey couple that he and Beverley were trying to project, and in a weird kind of way Andrew felt quite proud that he was able to play the part so convincingly. Until he remembered that he wasn't playing a part, because he did like Beverley far more than was wise. And then he realised that he actually meant love, not like.

He *loved* her.

To say that he was surprised to find he had room in his heart for someone besides Vivienne, was an understatement. But later that night, alone in his bedroom and listening to the unfamiliar sounds of someone else in the house as Leo pottered around downstairs, Andrew began to understand that love wasn't a finite commodity to be distributed as parsimoniously as a miser giving alms to the poor. He had plenty of love to go around, and there were lots more where that came from. Falling in love with Beverley didn't mean he no longer loved his wife.

The thought was both shocking and liberating. And also sad, because Beverley didn't love him back, and no amount of handholding and gazing adoringly into her eyes would change that.

Andrew found it hard to believe that in the space of a couple of months he had gone from mourning one woman, to mourning two. Because, although Beverley might be very much alive, he knew she didn't feel the same way about him. His heart was about to be broken for a second time and there wasn't a damned thing he could do about it.

***

May held a silver dress up to her chin and studied herself in the shop's full-length mirror. The material reminded Beverley of the sort of brocade that was used to cover three-piece suites, or that curtains were made out of. It looked stiff and itchy, and she wouldn't like to be the woman to have to wear it all day. She would be scratching and fussing like a chimp with fleas. The colour wasn't the best either, and Beverley would bet her right arm that the silver threads running through the material would far too easily catch and pull. The only thing impressive about this dress was its eye-watering price tag.

'I'm not sure it's you,' Beverley said to her sister, being diplomatic for once in her life.

'Why? What's wrong with it?' May turned from side to side.

'You need a bit more colour.'

'Pish! You *would* say that. Anyway, we're not here to look at mother-of-the-bride outfits, we're on the hunt for bridesmaids' dresses.'

Ah, yes, so they were, but that hadn't prevented May from looking at dresses for herself.

'Why are you fondling that one? I thought you had already bought your outfit,' Beverley said.

'I have, but I like to look, just in case I see something I like better.'

Beverley thought May was fortunate to be well off enough to buy two dresses, because she had barely been able to afford the one. She wasn't rolling in it like May and Terence. They had more cash salted away than a small country. Look at how they had given Annabelle their house and bought a flat near the seafront. Properties there weren't cheap. And May and Terence had also paid for the reception in The Gillespie Rooms. Beverley hadn't enquired as to how much that had cost, but she guessed it would have been a fair bit.

'I still say Annabelle should be with us,' Beverley said, hoping May wasn't going to take it upon herself to buy any bridesmaids' dresses without consulting Annabelle. It would be a silly thing to do anyway, because she had no idea what size Ellis and Portia would need, or what would suit them.

May put the dress back on the rail and reached for another. 'I don't think she's that bothered. If it was up to Annabelle, the only bridesmaid would be Izzie, but that's too much responsibility for such young shoulders.'

'Responsibility?' Beverley had no idea what her sister was on about. Surely all a bridesmaid had to do was to walk down the aisle behind the bride? Or was it supposed to be in front, these days? Beverley couldn't understand how that had become a thing. In her day, the whole point of bridesmaids walking down the aisle behind the bride was to ensure her train didn't get caught up, and also so that the maid-of-honour could hold the bride's bouquet when she reached the alter. It was tradition. This walking in front nonsense baffled her.

'It just is,' May said, without explaining herself in the slightest. 'And one will look odd.'

'What if the bride only knows one person?'

'Don't be so silly.'

'The groom only has one best man. Perhaps he should have a few of them? Best men, they'd be called.'

'He does. They're called *ushers*.'

'Aren't ushers only for church ceremonies?'

May let out a big sigh. 'I don't know, Beverley. And what's more, I don't care, since Annabelle and Ron are getting married on a *bandstand*.' She spat the word out.

'It's a very nice bandstand.'

'Which you booked without consulting anyone.'

'You can talk. You sent invitations to people who Ron and Annabelle didn't even want at their wedding. How did your friends take the news that they were uninvited?'

May scowled, her face thunderous.

'Ladies, can we be of any assistance?' The two women who had greeted Beverley and May with smiles when they had entered their shop, were now eyeing them with caution.

'No, thanks,' Beverley said, at the same time May uttered 'Yes, please.'

'Which is it?' the older of the two sales assistants asked.

'No.' Beverley was adamant.

'Yes.' May was equally as insistent.

Beverley glared at May and May glared back. One of the women gently removed the dress that May was clutching in a white-knuckled grasp, and edged away.

May huffed her displeasure, then realising it would be prudent if she left, she stuck her nose in the air and stalked out of the shop.

'Sorry,' Beverley said to the women. 'Do you know *Copacabana*? The Barry Manilow song?' She pointed at her sister's retreating back and shook her head. 'So sad… so very sad…'

Chuckling to herself at her wit, she dashed outside and caught up with May. 'I don't think we should go back to that shop anytime soon,' she said, but decided it best not to mention that the sales assistants now thought May was a woman who had lost her one true love and had been pining for him ever since. She chuckled again.

'It's no laughing matter,' May said. 'There might have been some nice dresses in there. I'll just have to come back on my own.'

Good luck with that, Beverley thought. Those two probably wouldn't let her through the door.

'Have you asked Annabelle what colour she wants her bridesmaids to be in? And has she bought a dress for herself yet?' Beverley asked.

May shuddered theatrically. 'I don't want to talk about it.' Then she proceeded to do precisely that for the next ten minutes, moaning that Annabelle was digging her heels in about not wanting to wear a traditional dress, and ending with, 'At this rate she'll be turning up in jeans.'

'Don't go buying anything for her,' Beverley warned.

'I'm not that daft,' her sister retorted.

Beverley begged to differ. May was definitely that daft, as today's foray into bridesmaids-dress-land had proved. She'd hoped May would have learnt her lesson after the invitations debacle. Mind you, Beverley wasn't whiter-than-white herself when it came to interfering – she had booked the bandstand without checking with Ron and Annabelle first, but her argument was that she knew they would love it, and that it would bring an end to May's impossible quest for a venue that would host both the ceremony and the reception.

In addition, although Beverley would have hated to lose the deposit, it wasn't so great an amount that it would have made her cry if she'd had to forfeit it; if May had to cancel The Gillespie Rooms, she would lose a small fortune.

'Where next?' she asked, hoping May would say 'home.'

No such luck.

Her sister wanted to trawl around yet more shops that sold bridesmaids dresses, even though it was far too late in the day to order any. Like bridal gowns, they had to be ordered months in advance.

But Beverley stuck with it, especially since May had suggested they have lunch out. Pepe was being looked after by Andrew, so without a valid excuse to rush off, she simply had to grin and bear it.

However, by the end of the marathon shopping session where nothing had been bought apart from a pair of shoes for May and some Marks and Spencer biscuits, Beverley found that she had done a lot of bearing and very little grinning.

She was so looking forward to seeing Ron and Annabelle get married and she knew it was going to be a lovely day, but wedding planning and all the gubbins beforehand was a huge palaver, wasn't it!

CHAPTER 19

'A knitting circle?' Andrew stared at Beverley in disbelief, and she tried not to laugh at the horror on his face. 'Are you for real?' he demanded.

'Look on the bright side,' she said, as she ushered him inside the library and shepherded him towards one of the rooms at the back which were used for things like mother-and-toddler groups. 'There isn't a zip-wire involved.'

'I think I'd prefer the zip wire,' he muttered. 'Can't you leave me here?' He gestured to the main body of the library. 'I'll grab a whodunnit and you can come find me when you're done.'

'This is for your benefit, not mine,' she told him. 'I can already knit.' It would serve him right for strong-arming her into ballroom dancing. She was only getting her own back. And her 'date' would be far less stressful on his knee.

'I thought this was supposed to be something we could do together?' he objected, hanging back so she was forced to grab his hand and almost drag him.

'It is, and we can. We'll be knitting together. But first, I want to show you around the exhibition.'

He immediately brightened. 'Exhibition? I don't mind exhibitions. What is it? Local history? Trains? Ancient artefacts?'

'Knitting.'

'*What?* Like jumpers and stuff?'

'No to the jumpers, yes to the stuff. Have you heard of yarn bombing? It's sometimes called guerrilla knitting?'

'Um… not really.'

Bless him, he looked dazed. But he was in for a treat. If he thought knitting was limited to jumpers, baby blankets and tea cosies, he was about to have his eyes opened, and hopefully his interest piqued. If that young man who was famous for diving could knit and be proud of it, why couldn't Andrew? Knitting and crocheting weren't the confines of little old ladies anymore. Everyone was at it, and as a result the items which were being produced today with yarn and a pair of needles were truly phenomenal.

'Here we go,' she said, pushing open a door and leading him inside. His hand was still in hers, and she felt his grip tighten. He was very much out of his comfort zone, she realised, and she decided that if he did hate the exhibition, she wouldn't hold him to his word and insist he joined the knitting circle. She would take him for afternoon tea instead.

As they stepped inside, the riot of colour took her breath away, and from the noise Andrew made she assumed that he was equally as impressed. This was no under-glass or behind-the-lines jobbie – this exhibition was an in-your-face, touchy-feely explosion of yarns and colours, and outrageously gorgeous imagination. She didn't know where to look first.

'Wow,' Andrew said under his breath.

Wow, indeed. It was simply marvellous.

'I can see why this would appeal to you,' he whispered, dipping his mouth towards her ear. 'This is so you. All these colours—' He broke off.

'Come on, let's look around.'

Still holding hands (she thought he was scared to let go in case he got knitted into one of the exhibits) they walked up to the first one – a full-sized standard lamp. It even had a bulb in it and was fully lit.

Beverley was enthralled by the table of knitted food (the table itself had a covering of wool), the animals (one of them a life-sized emperor penguin), an armchair that was entirely covered in knitted lilac yarn, and the bank of crocheted flowers lining the path that wound through the exhibits.

But what captured Andrew's attention was an array of photos.

'Blimey, that's a bus covered in wool!' he exclaimed. 'It's like it's wearing a huge jumper.'

He let go of her hand to fish his reading glasses out of his pocket and she felt oddly bereft without her palm tucked snugly in his.

She watched him move from photo to photo, smiling at his delighted expression, and when they reached the last one, he slung an arm around her shoulders and pulled her close. His eyes were shining, and his smile was even wider than hers. She had known what to expect though, but this was a brand-new experience for Andrew, and he appeared to be enjoying it.

He said, 'Thank you, that was amazing. Never in a million years would I have thought I'd like this, but it's fantastic.'

'I hoped you would. Which exhibit did you like the best?'

'I don't know. They were all wonderful. The bike, maybe? Or the benches… No! I know what I liked the best – that statue with clothes on it. That made me laugh.'

Beverley had liked that, too. It was a photo of a large stone statue of a naked woman on a horse, and she imagined the fun that the knitters must have had when they dressed it in a full Victorian riding habit. She hoped that whoever had yarn-bombed it would refresh the outfit when the current one had succumbed to the English weather.

'Do you want to try your hand at knitting?' she offered, indicating a door to their left. 'Everyone is welcome.' She had been here once or twice in the past, but not for a while; not since Ron had moved in. Ron had filled a void she hadn't realised had been there.

'Do you mind if I don't? I loved the exhibition, but....'

Beverley took pity on him. 'How about we have a go at home?' she suggested.

He cheered up at that, and they made their way back to his house and two pups who were very pleased to see their owners.

***

Andrew hadn't known what to expect today, but he had thoroughly enjoyed visiting the knitting exhibition. Who knew that so much could be done with a couple of needles and some wool! It had been a real eye-opener, and he had to admire the imagination and the dedication of those unknown knitters.

He didn't want to do any himself, though, despite Beverley getting her knitting out whilst he was making a pot of tea and spreading a selection of mini cakes on a plate.

Seeing her sitting there, needles flying, her eyes on him and not on what her hands were doing, reminded him so much of Vivienne that it brought a lump to his throat, and he had to look away.

'What's wrong?' Beverley asked.

He was hoping she hadn't noticed, but her concerned gaze hadn't missed his sudden anguish.

'It's nothing, honestly.' He bit his lip, willing the tears not to fall. Beverley didn't need to see him upset like this.

He was vaguely aware that she had put her knitting down and got to her feet, and the next thing he knew he was being enveloped in a hug.

Patting his back, she crooned, 'There, there,' as he gulped back sobs.

After several moments of wrestling with his grief, he calmed down enough to pull away and wipe his eyes. 'Sorry,' he croaked.

'What for?'

'Crying.'

'Crying is good for you. You can't keep grief in. It has to come out, and crying is a natural release.' She gazed at him shrewdly.

'Seeing you knitting reminded me of her.'

Beverley cringed. 'Sorry, I didn't think.' She looked mortified, and it was his turn to comfort her.

'It's not your fault. It's not anyone's fault. It happens now and again, and the silliest of things can set me off. You'd have thought I would have gotten over it by now.' He didn't often get this upset, but he had a fair idea what had caused his mini-meltdown today – his growing feelings for Beverley.

It was both a bit too soon and not fast enough. He never thought he would feel this way again, especially having known Beverley for only a couple of months, but he also sensed that time was slipping away, that happiness had to be grasped with both hands *now*, not at some distant point in the future. Because, let's face it, at his age he didn't know how much of a future he had left. And he understood that loving Beverley didn't mean that he loved Vivienne any less. He would always love his wife, but there was room in his heart for two. However, he still wasn't sure how Beverley felt about him, so there was only one thing to do.

He kissed her.

Andrew felt Beverley tense. Her back was rigid, her mouth closed and unyielding, and for a second he thought he had made a horrible mistake. But just as he was about to release her, her arms wound around his neck, her lips parted, and she was kissing him back with such passion and urgency that it took his breath away.

It was several minutes before they came up for air, and he couldn't tell which of them was the most shocked by what had just happened.

'I'm not going to apologise this time,' he warned, in a croaky voice. He was breathing hard, and his body was tingling all over.

'Good. I don't need an apology.'

They gazed at each other for a while, neither of them speaking. Andrew had so much he wanted to say, that he didn't know where to begin. So he remained silent, once again praying that he hadn't messed up a perfectly good friendship.

'Where do we go from here?' he asked eventually, when the silence stretched to such an uncomfortable length he simply had to snap it.

'Where do you want to go?' she countered.

He didn't reply. He didn't need to. Instead, he took her in his arms once more and kissed her.

***

'Tea?' Andrew asked, a little while later.

Beverley licked her lips, thirstily. The thought of what they'd just done made her head spin. Her pulse still raced, and she hoped she wasn't going to have palpitations. It would be worth it though. She hadn't realised that making love could be so… Explosive? Satisfying? Exhilarating?

'Yes, please. Three sugars.' How could they be talking about such mundane things as tea, when her world had been rocked to its core.

'I hadn't forgotten.' He wandered into the kitchen, leaving Beverley in the living room, and she heard him flick the switch on the kettle.

While she waited for her tea, she drifted around the room, examining the photos. When she came to one of Vivienne, she fought the urge to explain to her that she was gone, and Andrew needed to be loved. Beverley hoped Vivienne would understand.

She was sitting primly on the sofa when he returned to the living room with a tray. On it was a teapot, cups and saucers, milk in a little jug and a sugar bowl, along with the plate of cakes they hadn't eaten earlier.

He poured the tea, dumped three spoonfuls of sugar in, gave it a stir and handed her a cup. 'Help yourself to a cake.'

'I'm not hungry, thanks.'

Andrew pressed his lips together. 'Are you OK?'

'I'm grand. How about you?' It might have been Andrew who had initiated their lovemaking, but she prayed he wasn't regretting it. She didn't think she'd be able to cope if he was.

'I'm grand, too.'

Beverley chewed on her lip as Andrew slurped his tea.

'I'm not going to apologise,' he repeated. 'Although I am aware that lovemaking is above and beyond my remit for being your pretend boyfriend.'

'Is that what you were doing? Pretending?'

He turned a shocked face to her. 'No! How could you say that?'

'Just checking.' She had to make sure, even though she thought she knew the answer.

'Were *you*?' he asked.

'Absolutely not.' She sipped her tea. He had made it just the way she liked it. 'You asked me where we go from here?' When he nodded, she continued carefully, 'I can't see us being friends anymore. Not after this. Can you?'

They couldn't go back to the way they had been. It simply wouldn't be possible. How could she treat him as a friend? As she saw it, they had two choices – jump in with both feet or end it now.

She saw his eyes darken and go flat. It was as though all the life had been sucked out of them, and a shiver travelled down her spine. Deciding that she may as well come out with it, she took a breath and blurted, 'I think I love you.'

Then she waited for him to tell her it was over, and that he never wanted to see her again.

Animation seeped back into his features, but she couldn't read his expression. Was he shocked, dismayed, terrified…

His mouth worked, as though he couldn't find the right words, and she braced herself for what she knew was coming.

'I think I love you, too.' His voice was hoarse and hesitant.

If Beverley hadn't been sitting down, she would have fallen, and it took her several heartbeats to comprehend what he had just said. 'You *love* me?'

He raised his eyebrows, as though the news was as much of a surprise to him as it was to her. 'It seems so.'

His hesitancy made her heart melt. Bless him, this couldn't be easy for him. He had so much emotional baggage, whereas she had shed hers years ago. He was going to need a lot of coddling, love and reassurance, and she was more than happy to do it.

'Come here, you silly sod,' she said, putting her cup down and holding her arms open.

He melted into her, and she kissed the top of his head as he buried his face in her neck.

'It'll be all right,' she said. 'As long as I haven't scared you off.'

His voice was muffled. 'You haven't. I thought *I* might have scared *you* off.'

'Fat chance! It takes more than that to scare me.'

'Good, because I want to do it again.' He nibbled the skin below her earlobe, sending flutters of delight through her.

'Behave yourself.'

'Do I have to?'

'No…'

'Well, then…'

When Andrew led her back up the stairs, Beverley realised she had never been so happy. Who would have thought she would find love at her age!

***

Andrew hadn't wanted Beverley to leave. Making love with her had been the best thing that had happened to him since Vivienne had passed away. It was also the scariest.

He knew without a shadow of a doubt that he was in love with her, and he was as sure as he could be that she felt the same way about him. But this was so very new and unexpected, he wasn't sure how he should deal with it.

He felt like shouting it from the rooftops, but he also wanted to hold it close like a secret to be savoured. His mind hadn't stopped whirling, and was filled with questions he didn't have any answers to. The only thing to do, he supposed, was to take it one day at a time.

They had made plans to meet in the park as usual tomorrow, and the routine steadied him somewhat. He liked routine and familiarity, but this was new territory for him and the map was frighteningly bare of landmarks.

'Just go with the flow,' he muttered, as he made his evening meal. Beverley had gone home to cook tea for Ron, but he wished she had stayed. The house felt emptier without her in it. But not as empty as those first few days, weeks, and months after he'd lost his wife. This was a different kind of emptiness and he realised why – Beverley had filled the hole in his heart, and he no longer felt as bereft. He felt hopeful. The emptiness Beverley had left in her wake this evening was an intermission, not the final curtain.

Aside from worrying about his new relationship with Beverley and where that was going, he had some concerns about whether she and Judith would get on. He could see no reason why not. They were quite similar in a way – both of them being forthright and direct, and neither of them suffered fools gladly.

Beverley was more of a bright spark than Judith, who tended to be rather serious, but he supposed that was to be expected – Judith had a career in a tough market and a family to look after. She worked incredibly hard and didn't have a lot of free time.

Beverley, on the other hand, was retired, and had lots of free time: just as he did.

Until recently, Andrew had viewed having so much time on his hands as a burden. Now though, he was beginning to see it as a gift. He wasn't bound by the constraints of nine-to-five and the demands of children – he could see Beverley whenever he wanted.

It was all rather refreshing, and although he couldn't see them doing anything particularly thrilling or exciting (Beverley's mention of a zip wire had made his stomach churn), he found himself looking forward to strolling along the promenade with her, having a picnic on the beach, going to the cinema together or to see a play (he hadn't done anything like that in years), or just enjoying taking the dogs for a walk and popping into the café for a coffee.

It might be mundane in the eyes of other people, but this was what he had missed since Vivienne died – companionship and having a special someone to share the everyday things with.

Hopefully, he might rediscover that with Beverley.

It was only when Twinkle whined and pawed at his leg, that he realised he had been humming – a sound the dog wouldn't have heard for a long time.

CHAPTER 20

Walking hand in hand with Andrew had quickly become one of Beverley's favourite pastimes. They weren't going anywhere in particular today, just strolling around The Open Market, marvelling at the vast array of fresh produce and the stalls selling craft and handmade items, as well as second-hand book stalls, antiques and clothes.

They weren't here to buy anything, they just wanted a change of scenery from the park and the promenade, however, if Beverley saw something she liked she wouldn't hesitate to make a purchase.

They had left the dogs at home today, not wanting to drag them around a busy market with all those people and the risk of having paws trodden on.

Pepe had sulked a little, refusing to look at her and even going as far as turning his back on her, but she had simply chuckled. Although Pepe tried to persuade her that he was hard done by, she had taken him for a nice walk in the park earlier, so he'd had his fair share of the late May sunshine.

'Hang on a sec,' she said to Andrew, as she came to a halt.

'Seen something you like?'

'Not really. I want to take my jacket off. I hope it's as nice as this for the wedding.'

'I hope so, too. It would be a shame to have to move the ceremony inside.'

'It's a concern,' Beverley said, shrugging her lightweight jacket off and folding it over her arm. 'I'm sure the café would look lovely, but I'd like Ron and Annabelle to marry on the bandstand. I can picture it now – ribbons and flowers everywhere, the sea glittering in the background as they say their vows.' She sighed wistfully. 'If I was going to do it all again, that's where I'd like to hold it.'

'Would you consider getting married again?'

Ah… Beverley winced. She hoped Andrew didn't think she was angling for a proposal.

'I haven't thought about it,' she lied. 'How about you?'

'Maybe. I'm not sure.'

'We're all right as we are, aren't we?'

He gave her hand a squeeze. 'Of course we are.' He paused. 'I take it we're not going to go back to being friends after the wedding, like we agreed.'

Beverley blinked. 'I bloody well hope not.'

'Good. I've become quite addicted to a certain part of our relationship, and I'd hate to give it up.'

'What part would that be?' she simpered, gazing up at him coquettishly.

He leant in and nuzzled her neck. 'This part, for starters.'

'Keep going,' she murmured.

'I wish I could, but it's a little too public here for my liking.'

Beverley tapped him playfully on the arm. 'You are so wicked.'

'I try to be.'

She couldn't believe how much Andrew had changed from when she had first met him. Gone was the cloud of desolation and loneliness she had sensed, and in its place was a fun-loving mischievous man who seemed to be enjoying every day. She liked to think she was partly responsible for that, but she was realistic enough to realise that the time had probably been right for him to emerge from mourning and start living again. It was lucky for her that she had been there when it had happened.

'I know you've met Ron and Annabelle,' she said, when they paused by a stall selling second-hand clothes and trinkets. Seeing it had brought her daughter to the forefront of her mind. 'How do you feel about meeting Kate? The kids have got next week off school, and I thought I'd ask if she and Brett wanted to come for a visit. You'll meet them at the wedding anyway, so I thought it might be nice if you weren't total strangers.'

She also wanted to show him off. Kate was dying to meet Andrew: no wonder, considering Beverley didn't stop talking about him whenever she spoke to her daughter.

'Are we at the 'meeting-the-parents' stage?' he joked.

'I think we might be. Unless you're planning on dumping me as soon as the bridal bouquet is thrown?'

'I wouldn't dream of it.'

'Great! I'll ask her. She might have something else on though,' Beverley warned. 'I hope the two of you get along,' she added worriedly.

Andrew slid an arm around her waist. 'I'm sure we will. If she's anything like her mother, I'm going to adore her.'

Adore… Hearing him say that filled her heart with so much joy she thought it might burst. He adored her – and she adored him.

She couldn't wish for anything more.

***

Andrew's heart leapt with pleasure when he saw the number on his phone. 'Leo, my boy! How are you?'

'I've finished my course!' Leo yodelled.

'Woo hoo! That's fantastic news. When do you get your results?'

'Not for another couple of weeks.' Leo became more subdued. 'I hope I've done enough to get a 2:2.'

'I bet you've done enough to get a first,' Andrew said loyally.

'So do I, but right now I'll settle for a lower-second class and be grateful.'

'Have you moved out of your digs yet?' Leo shared a house with three other lads, and from what Judith had told him it was typically messy student accommodation. She hadn't liked it, but Leo had been in his element.

'The letting agreement is until the end of June, so we thought we'd stay on for a while and throw a party. And go to some, too. Everyone we know is celebrating.'

'Don't overdo it,' Andrew warned, and he could almost hear Leo rolling his eyes.

'Of course I will, Grandad. That's what being a student is all about, and as I'm only going to be a

236

student for another month, I intend to make the most of it before I'm officially unemployed.'

'Didn't you say you have a job to go to?'

'I do, but there'll be like a two-month gap or something, which is why I'm grateful for that wedding gig, and I've also got a couple more things lined up to tide me over. But I want to have one last fling before I have to the adulting thing.' He didn't sound as though he was looking forward to being a grown-up and all it entailed.

'As I said, don't overdo it.'

'You're as bad as Mum. Don't worry, I'll be there for the wedding. How is your girlfriend, by the way?'

Andrew sniffed. 'I am nowhere near as bad as your mother. Beverley is fine.'

'Just fine?'

'Concentrate on your own love life.'

'I haven't got one. I can't believe that my grandad has a girlfriend, and I don't!' He sounded so aggrieved Andrew chuckled.

'That's because you like playing the field. There's plenty of time before you should think of settling down.'

'True…' Leo cleared his throat. 'Are you thinking of settling down, Grandad?'

Andrew paused. This was the second time in as many days that he had been asked the very same question. He had asked Beverley first though, so it was only to be expected for her to throw the question back at him. A frisson of disappointment had slithered through him when she had said that she hadn't thought about it – because *he* had.

'I don't know,' he replied.

'You should. You're not getting any younger.'

'Thanks for that,' Andrew said dryly.

'You're not! I mean it, Grandad! You've got to grab life with both hands and wring every last drop out of it!' Leo cried. 'That's what I'm going to do.'

Ah, the certainty and optimism of youth, Andrew thought. When you had the world at your feet and you thought you would live forever, you believed anything was possible.

He hoped his grandson would never find out that life wasn't like that, and sometimes life had a way of grabbing you with both hands and wringing everything out of *you* instead.

But Leo did have a point.

He wasn't getting any younger and life was for living, and with Beverley by his side that was exactly what he was doing. And maybe getting married again might be a possibility.

***

'Try it on for me,' Beverley urged. She wanted to check Andrew's suit situation before the wedding. She was sure the one he had mentioned would be suitable, but she wanted to be certain.

'Why don't you come upstairs, and we can take a look?' he suggested.

Andrew's bedroom was larger than Beverley's, but not by much, and it still had a woman's touch, evident in the matching patterned curtains and bedspread, the plush velvet-covered ottoman and the floral prints on the wall. He began rooting through one of the two fitted wardrobes. It contained a row of neatly hung suits, shirts, jackets and trousers.

'I'm sure it was in here. Perhaps not.'

He opened the other wardrobe, and for one horrible moment Beverley thought she would come face-to-face with Vivienne's clothes.

But all it housed were more of the same… suits and jackets, plus a long woollen coat, and a hefty anorak that she remembered him wearing earlier in the year.

'Here it is.' He took it out, slipped the jacket off the hangar and put it on. 'What do you think?'

Beverley perched her backside on the ottoman at the foot of the bed, and said, 'I can't tell just from the jacket. You need to put the trousers on, with a shirt.'

Andrew did as she suggested and was soon standing before her, neatly suited and booted. But without the boots. He was in his socks.

He looked good, though, very dapper and rather distinguished. She could tell that he felt at home in a suit – he wore it with confidence and aplomb.

'Turn around,' she instructed, for no other reason than she enjoyed ogling his bum. He had a nice bum, quite trim and not at all saggy. Unlike hers.

She wriggled on it, wondering what he thought about her behind, and hoping it wasn't as squidgy as she suspected it might be.

'Looking good,' she told him. 'What about a tie?'

'I've got hundreds of the darned things. Here.' He lifted a tie hanger off the rail and passed it to her to look through.

'No… not this… that won't work.' She stopped at one. 'Flashing reindeer nose?'

'It's a Christmas tie,' he said. 'It's supposed to be festive and tacky. I can wear it to the wedding if you like?'

She raised her eyebrows and his wicked grin subsided. 'You've got loads of nice ties,' she said, 'but none of them are quite the right shade.'

'For what?'

'To match my dress. And I also thought the dogs could wear matching bandanas.'

'You're still planning on taking the dogs with us?'

'Absolutely! And if I can talk Ron into it, I think it would be great fun if they carried the rings down the aisle.'

Andrew said faintly, 'Is that such a good idea?'

'I think it's brilliant.' Pepe was as much a part of the family as she was, and now Twinkle was fast becoming part of it too.

And Andrew.

Beverley had been having a think about what he had said the other day when they were at The Open Market, and she had come to the conclusion that she would like to be married again. There was nothing she would like more.

She would get Ron and Annabelle's wedding out of the way first – because she didn't want to spoil their thunder – then she would ask him to marry her.

Beverley might be old-fashioned in some respects but when it came to getting what she wanted she could be as modern as the next woman.

She would propose, and if he said yes it would make her the happiest person in the world.

Ron would walk her down the aisle, all the granddaughters would be bridesmaids, Kate would be her maid-of-honour, and the grandsons (Andrew's included) would be ushers. She might even consider booking the bandstand, too.

But there was no way she would be inviting blasted Helen to *her* special day!

***

Andrew decided that Kate was lovely three seconds after he met her. She had swept him into her arms, had given him a smacker of a kiss on the cheek, and had told him he was as handsome as Beverley had said he was.

It had made his day!

Brett was a decent chap, too, and had welcomed him with open arms – although the open arms was more figurative than literal, as the two of them had shaken hands instead of sharing a hug. And Beverley's grandchildren were smart, polite kids. Kid was the wrong word for the girls – they were young ladies and both of them were stunning. Sam, her grandson, was funny and sunny, and at the moment was all knobbly knees and sharp elbows as he approached his teenage years.

Ron, Annabelle, Jake and Izzie had joined them for a picnic on Hove's shingle beach, and the family had chosen a spot near enough to the lagoon for Ron and Brett to take the boys and Izzie for a sailing taster session.

Ellis and Portia seemed happy enough to sprawl out on their towels, soak up the sun's rays and do some people watching, whilst simultaneously playing with their phones. Ellis had taken some snaps of the pretty beach huts to post on Instagram, and both girls had taken so many selfies that Andrew had lost count. They appeared to have adopted the dogs, who lay between the girls and snoozed happily in the sun, keeping one eye open for any goings on.

Andrew would suggest a stroll across the beach soon, to stretch his legs and those of the dogs, but right now he was too comfortable.

Ron had thoughtfully packed a couple of deckchairs for Andrew and Beverley to sit on, and Andrew slumped into his with a contented sigh that was tinged with only the slightest hint of envy: he wished he could do something similar with Judith, Duncan and the boys. Judith wasn't keen on British beaches, even though she had grown up in Brighton. She preferred Caribbean or Mediterranean ones, and he bet she wished that was where she was right now, instead of jollying Mark along as he prepared for his A-level exams which were just around the corner. He was glad he wasn't in her shoes, as he remembered only too well the fun and games he and Vivienne had when Judith was sitting hers. She had been awful – stressed and diva-ish, and nothing either of them had said or done had made it better.

Leo hadn't been half as bad, but Mark was more highly strung, like his mother.

Idly Andrew wondered how Kate was coping. Ellis was coming to the end of her first year at university, and Portia was sitting her GCSEs. Apparently, she had brought some revision with her, and he wondered whether she was doing any. Kate was far more laid back as a parent than Judith – but maybe she didn't have to be as naggy, and she trusted Portia to get on with what her daughter needed to get on with.

Kate and Annabelle were sitting side-by-side on a towel, chatting away whilst rummaging through the assorted bags of food and drink they had brought, and Andrew's stomach growled.

'Hungry?' Beverley asked.

He patted his polo-shirt clad stomach. It wasn't quite warm enough for him to take it off, but that might change as the day wore on and the temperature rose. 'I'm always hungry lately,' he admitted.

Over the past couple of months, he had noticed he was starting to put on weight around his middle, and he blamed Beverley for that. She insisted on cooking him proper meals and ensuring he ate regularly, and along with their frequent coffee-and-cake stops, he was chunkier now than he had been for a while.

'Looking healthy' Beverley called it, and he must admit that he felt really well. Happy, too. It was unbelievable considering that at the start of the year he didn't think he would ever feel happy again.

He left it until after lunch (and after a snooze in the deckchair) to suggest a walk.

Ron, Brett and the three younger children had returned from their sailing lesson and were now splashing around in the sea, and Ellis and Portia had decided to join them, with a considering amount of shrieking and squealing.

Andrew had been tempted to take his socks and deck shoes off and go for a paddle, but the water looked too cold for his liking, so he decided on a stroll instead. It would do him good to walk off some of the huge lunch he'd packed away.

He hauled a grumbling Beverley out of her chair, and they set off across the beach, the dogs racing ahead, tails wagging furiously as they darted here and there, sniffing for all they were worth.

It was a delight to see them play together, chasing each other to the sea and back, leaping and splashing through the waves. Twinkle was behaving like a pup again, and it made Andrew's heart sing.

'Thank you for inviting me,' he said, taking Beverley's hand in his. 'It's been lovely.'

'It was my pleasure. I wanted you and Kate to meet.' She stopped and he turned to face her. 'You both mean such a lot to me, and I would hate it if you didn't get on.'

'I can't imagine anyone not getting on with Kate,' he replied. 'She's lovely.'

'She is.' Beverley beamed with pride.

'And Brett is a top bloke.'

'He's not too bad,' Beverley conceded, but she was still smiling. 'He would be even better if it wasn't for that mother of his. He told me over breakfast that she was 'so looking forward to the wedding and for everyone to meet Carlton'. Reading between the lines, I reckon she can't wait to show him off. Well, I can't wait to show *you* off, either.'

'I had better be on my best behaviour,' he teased, lowering his head to hers and capturing her mouth.

Whatever she intended to reply was lost as she kissed him back, not caring who might be watching, and the promise of more to come made his head spin.

God, how he loved this woman!

When the wedding was out of the way, he might suggest they have a wedding of their own. All he hoped was that she would say yes.

CHAPTER 21

'Dad? I'm coming to Brighton.' Judith's tone didn't brook any argument and Andrew wondered what had got his daughter all fired up.

He soon found out.

'Leo has told me all about you and that wom— er, Beverley,' Judith snapped.

Cross that his daughter had almost said *that woman*, his only response was, 'I see.' To be honest, he had assumed she knew – or had at least realised that he and Beverley had become more than friends, because he mentioned Beverley quite often when they spoke. Mind you, he didn't speak to Judith more than once a week, and—

'When were you going to tell me you had another woman?' she demanded.

Taken aback, Andrew said, 'You sound as though I'm having an affair.'

'What would *you* call it?'

'Not an affair. That implies one or the other of us is married.'

Silence hung heavily between them.

Eventually Judith spoke. 'I can't help it if I feel you still are.' Her voice was devoid of emotion, as though she was scared to let any show.

'I'll never stop loving your mother,' he assured her.

'But that didn't stop you making eyes at Beverley. Leo told me you were all over her when he came to see you last month. I want to meet her.'

'Right.' He blew out his cheeks. 'OK. When?' It was probably a good idea that she did, considering he had met Beverley's family more than once.

And considering he was planning on asking her to marry him.

He supposed it was only natural Judith would want to meet her. Since Vivienne passed away, he'd not so much as looked at another woman, and his daughter was bound to be feeling strange at the thought of him dating again.

'As soon as possible, don't you think?' she said sharply.

He guessed so, but he would have preferred to have left it until after the wedding. Beverley had enough on her plate at the moment what with May and Annabelle at loggerheads over one thing or another, but when Judith was like this there was no stopping her. She had always been a Bessy-Bossy-Boots and he wondered how Duncan put up with it. Mind you, Judith's mother had been the same, and Andrew had put up with it just fine. Most of the time. There had been occasions when he had flatly refused to be bossed around, but they had been few and far between. Anything for an easy life, eh?

He may as well get this over with and let Judith meet Beverley. It would be fine. He suspected that they wouldn't get on like a house on fire because they were different kinds of people, but as long as they got on well enough that was all that mattered.

***

Now Beverley knew how Andrew must have felt when he had met Ron for the first time, she thought, as she walked briskly along the pavement, Pepe trotting happily by her side. Andrew had suggested they meet at that nice pub in The Lanes, rather than him trying to cook a meal for the three of them. A café would have done just fine as far as Beverley was concerned, but she understood that he wanted to make an effort.

She hoped she and Judith would get on, because if Andrew accepted her marriage proposal it would make life more difficult if Judith didn't like her.

Andrew hadn't said a great deal about Judith's reaction to him having a girlfriend, but Beverley had read between the lines and guessed that his daughter wasn't pleased about it. He had mentioned something along the lines of this being a new situation for her, and that she may need some time to adjust. Beverley had interpreted that information as Judith being scared that another woman was about to take her mother's place in her father's affections.

It was an understandable reaction – for a *teenager*. Not for a woman in her late forties. And it wasn't as though Vivienne had only recently passed: Andrew's wife had been gone nearly four years. Didn't his daughter *want* him to be happy?

Another thing – Beverley had been surprised that Andrew hadn't told Judith about her before now. But she supposed he knew his daughter better than

247

anyone, and how best to handle the situation. She was just relieved that they were going to meet at last, and it was preferable they met now, before she proposed, rather than afterwards. Assuming he agreed to marry her, that is. Despite him telling her on a daily basis that he loved her, she wasn't convinced he would want to formalise their relationship.

Andrew and Judith were already seated at a table when Beverley entered the pub. She was pleased to see that it wasn't the same one as the last time, but she was dismayed when she realised Andrew hadn't brought Twinkle with him. She could have sworn she had told him she was bringing Pepe.

It took Pepe a few minutes to settle down, because he kept sniffing around under the table as though he expected Twinkle to miraculously appear. And once or twice he peered up at Andrew and whined pitifully, wanting to know where his little friend was.

From the expression on Judith's face, the woman wasn't particularly amused. She had an 'I've been eating lemons' look about her and sighed a couple of times.

Andrew was very apologetic, saying, 'I'm sorry, I didn't realise you would be bringing Pepe.' He leant across the table to give Beverley a belated kiss, and Beverley was conscious of Judith's eyes boring into her.

'It's my fault,' Beverley said contritely. 'I assumed that by coming here, you would be bringing Twinkle.'

He said, 'Never mind, Pepe can see her later.' Then he caught his daughter's eye. 'Or tomorrow, in the park,' he amended, and Beverley wondered what Judith thought their relationship was, as he said, 'I'm being remiss; Beverley, this is my daughter Judith; Judith, this is my…' he hesitated.

'Girlfriend?' Beverley supplied. 'I don't think partner sounds right, does it? I'm so pleased to meet you,' she said. 'Andrew talks about you all the time.' Beverley reached across the table and put her hand on top of Andrew's.

Judith's eyes widened. 'He doesn't talk about *you*. In fact, it was quite a surprise when Leo informed me that my father had a girlfriend,' she said frostily. 'Shall we order?'

'Good idea,' Andrew said, and Beverley heard the relief in his voice at the change of subject.

Beverley waited until Judith's attention was on her menu, then she caught his eye and mouthed, 'Sorry.' She hadn't meant to land him in it, and she trusted him to deal with Judith in his own way and his own time.

Vowing to be on her best behaviour, Beverley studied the menu, and after they had ordered, she began a charm offensive. 'Andrew tells me you're something big in crisps,' she began.

Judith scowled. 'That's not quite how I would describe my job,' she said, 'but yes, I suppose I am. What did you used to do before you retired?'

'I was a nurse.'

Judith's eyebrows rose a notch. 'Which department?'

'All kinds,' Beverley told her. 'I've worked on gynae wards, obstetrics, casualty – before it changed to A and E – children's wards… you name it and I've probably worked on it.'

'Have you ever been married?'

Beverley heard Andrew's intake of breath, but the question didn't bother her. 'Yes, I have. He left me.'

'Oh, so you're not a widow?'

'Not unless he's dead,' Beverley quipped, and noticed Andrew slowly close his eyes before opening them again, so she reined herself in and said, 'No, we got divorced. I'm a divorcee.'

'Dad tells me you have a daughter,' Judith said.

'That's right, Kate. She's about your age. Lives in Pershore.'

'And what does she do?'

Blimey! Was this the Spanish Inquisition? 'She works for a charity.'

'Is she married?'

'You really *haven't* told Judith anything about me, have you?' Beverley said to Andrew, who pulled a face.

'No, he hasn't,' Judith retorted sharply. 'Nothing meaningful anyway. I had to rely on my son for that.'

Beverley decided not to respond to that comment. 'She's married to a chap called Brett. They've got three children: the oldest is eighteen and the youngest is twelve. Two girls and a boy. He's a golf course manager.'

Judith brightened. 'I do like a game of golf.'

She would, Beverley thought. She seemed the type. The *Helen* type. Beverley could honestly say she wasn't warming to Andrew's daughter – but hopefully things would improve.

'Do you play?' Judith asked.

'Not golf, poker.' Beverley heard Andrew groan, and once again remembered her vow to behave herself. 'Just kidding,' she added hastily, but couldn't resist asking, 'Who was it who said golf spoiled a good walk?'

'Someone who didn't own a dog probably,' Andrew chipped in. His expression was pained. 'Twinkle loves finding golf balls.'

'Pepe doesn't. He thinks chasing after balls is a waste of time, don't you, my darling?'

Pepe lifted his head listlessly, gave her a disgruntled glare, then dropped back down with a sigh. It looked like her dog was having as little fun as she was.

She would make it up to him after lunch, with a walk along the beach. She had a pair of old trainers in her bag for this very purpose.

Their meals arrived and the three of them concentrated on their food, although why Judith had bothered to order anything was beyond Beverley's comprehension. The salad looked nice enough, but Judith only picked at it, and spent most of the time pushing unidentifiable green leaves around her plate.

Beverley, on the other hand, tucked into her meal with enthusiasm. She loved food. It was one of the great joys in life as far as she was concerned, and she had never worried much about her figure. Which was the reason she was plump – but at her age that was to be expected and, as the only person whose opinion mattered was Andrew's and he assured her he loved her just the way she was, she had no intention of starving herself.

'I understand that Ron is not actually your son,' Judith said, putting her fork down and steepling her fingers.

'He's not,' Beverley replied, 'but he might as well be. He feels like a son to me. I took him in nearly eighteen months ago.

'So he's your lodger, then?'

'I suppose you could say that.' Although Beverley didn't view him as such.

'And he's marrying your niece?'

'That's right. She moved back to the UK from Australia about a year ago. They met on holiday last summer.'

'A short engagement,' Judith observed.

'Why wait? When you know it's right, you know it's right.' She couldn't help glancing at Andrew, and Judith's eyes narrowed.

'Dad said you met whilst out walking in the park?' Judith said.

'Yes.' Beverley smiled fondly at Andrew. 'He literally knocked me off my feet.'

'I think you'll find it was the other way round,' Andrew said lightly. 'Pepe's lead got tangled in Twinkle's and we both ended up on the ground.'

'You could have broken a hip,' Judith huffed. 'Honestly, Dad!'

'No one got hurt,' he said. He didn't sound as though she was getting to him, but Beverley noticed how savagely he speared a floret of broccoli.

'I take it you don't live far from my father?' Judith continued.

'The other side of the park and a few streets away. Staley Avenue.'

Judith nodded. 'I remember those houses. Victorian terraces are quite deceptive. Do you own it or do you rent?

Beverley sucked in a sharp breath. That wasn't the kind of question you asked someone you've only just met, she thought, and out of the corner of her eye she saw Andrew's mouth drop open. Feeling sorry for him for having such a rude person for a daughter, Beverley decided to answer Judith civilly, rather than telling her to mind her own business.

'No, I don't—' she began, but just as she was about to explain that she had signed her house over to Kate and the reason why, Pepe spotted another dog coming through the door and he made a lunge for it, yanking Beverley's chair and nearly causing her to topple off it.

'Pepe!' she cried. 'Naughty boy.'

She planted her feet firmly on the floor, reached down and grabbed hold of the lead. She had wound it around the chair leg as usual, and every other time she had done so he had been perfectly behaved. Trust him to show his naughty side today.

Pepe let off a volley of barks, not pleased at being restrained, and Beverley spent several minutes trying to shush him and get him to settle down again. The other dog, a golden retriever, didn't take the slightest notice of Pepe's antics, and sat quietly at his owner's feet whilst the man leant on the bar drinking his pint.

'Why can't you behave like that other dog?' Beverley chided, wagging her finger at Pepe, who glared back at her balefully. 'Just because Twinkle isn't here, doesn't mean you can play me up. You wait until I tell Ron how naughty you've been. Everyone is looking at you,' she added, as though the dog understood her.

Actually, she wouldn't be surprised if Pepe did. She had spent so much time talking to him over the years, that he had probably picked up quite a lot. The dog certainly knew he had misbehaved, but he didn't seem bothered by it. In fact, he appeared to be quite defiant. Maybe she should think about making a move in a minute: her poodle had clearly run out of patience. And so had she, if she was honest. Judith's questioning was intrusive and unrelenting, and Beverley was beginning to find it rather annoying. She felt like she was being interviewed for a job.

Having already eaten the last chip and without appearing to be too hasty, she finished her drink then made her excuses.

She didn't imagine the look of relief on Andrew's face, and she gathered that he also thought the lunch hadn't gone as well as he would have liked.

Which was a shame. She had hoped Judith would like her and that they would get on.

Never mind, they could try again after the wedding, and when Judith learnt that her dad was getting married again, they would have to make more of an effort to be friends.

If Andrew consented to be her husband, that is…

***

'Why the glum face?' were the first words out of Ron's mouth when he arrived home from work later that afternoon. He crouched down to fuss Pepe, but his worried gaze remained on her.

'I met Judith today. She doesn't like me.'

Ron straightened up. 'Of course she does. Everyone likes you.'

'Judith doesn't. She made it very clear. But I'm not sure whether it's *me* she doesn't like, or the fact that her father has a girlfriend.'

Ron gave her a squeeze. 'It's probably the girlfriend bit, not you. Some people struggle when they lose a parent and that parent falls in love again. She'll come around.'

'I wish I could be as certain as you.' Beverley sighed. 'It was like being questioned by the Gestapo. She wanted to know everything. I'm surprised she didn't ask me my bra size.'

'It's only natural she wants to get to know the woman her father has fallen in love with.'

Beverley scoffed, 'I don't believe he has shared that snippet of information with her. She barely knew I existed until a couple of days ago. Leo told her when he went home at the end of term. Judith had no idea that her father was seeing someone, and I'm fairly sure she doesn't know how he feels about me.'

'I expect she does. You only have to look at his face to see that he's head-over-heels.'

'I suppose.'

'Come on, cheer up. It's not like you to be so down in the dumps. Everything will be fine. I promise.'

Ron was probably right, Beverley sighed. It would be fine. *Wouldn't it?*

CHAPTER 22

This would be the last time they would all be together before the wedding, Beverley realised, glancing around the table.

It had been Annabelle's suggestion that the two sides of the family go out together for a meal this evening, in lieu of neither the bride nor the groom having had a stag or hen do.

Beverley knew that May was quite relieved, because her sister wasn't a party kind of animal, and the thought of trundling around Brighton dipping in and out of pubs whilst wearing wobbling plastic penises on her head, wouldn't have appealed. Beverley wouldn't have been too keen on that, either. She was too old for a pub crawl.

It was strange to think that in a week's time Ron would have a wife and he would no longer be living under Beverley's roof. It had been decided that he would move in with Annabelle, rather than Annabelle sell her house and the two of them buy a new one together. Beverley knew that May was torn: on the one hand her sister was happy that the home where Annabelle had grown up wouldn't be sold, but on the other hand she was a bit aggrieved that Ron was going to live in it. May might have accepted Ron into the family, but that didn't mean she was over the moon about it. She no longer had the reservations she once had, but Beverley knew that first impressions could linger. Which was why she couldn't get Judith's reaction out of her head, despite Andrew's assurances that Judith didn't hate her and that it would just take his daughter some time to come around to the idea that her father was romantically involved with another woman.

'I'm sure we've forgotten to do something,' May said, a frown creasing her brow.

'Like what?' Terence asked.

'I don't know, do I? If I knew, then I wouldn't have forgotten.'

'Now, now, don't be so tetchy. I'm sure if it was that important you wouldn't have forgotten in the first place,' her husband said.

May didn't look convinced.

Beverley tried to reassure her. 'The ceremony is booked, the registrar knows where to turn up and when, canapes and drinks are organised, the reception is sorted, we've even arranged transport. You've got your dress, Annabelle has got hers, and Ron has bought a suit.'

'The flowers?' May looked panicked.

'Ordered,' Annabelle said. Her expression was glum; she didn't look in the least bit like a bride on the brink of her wedding day, and Beverley narrowed her eyes. Annabelle clearly wasn't happy about something.

'The cake? Who is doing the cake?' May began to flap.

'Mum, we've had this conversation. I told you, no one is doing the cake. We don't want a cake.'

'You've got to have a cake,' May insisted. She turned to Terence. 'She's left it far too late. I doubt if we can get anyone to make a cake by Friday.'

Her husband blew out his cheeks. 'If Annabelle doesn't want a cake, we can't force her,' he said.

Beverley guessed he was using the term *we* in a rather tongue-in-cheek manner. There was no *we* – May was doing all the organising and flapping. Terence hadn't been allowed to make a single contribution.

'But—' May began and Annabelle smacked her palms down on the table, making the glasses tinkle.

'Can we talk about something else, *please*?' Annabelle demanded. 'I'm sick to death of it.'

May said, 'Don't be silly! Of course you aren't! It's just pre-wedding nerves.'

Annabelle ground her teeth. 'I am *not* suffering from pre-wedding nerves. I am suffering from my mother-is-getting-on-my-nerves nerves.'

May's face tightened. 'That's a fine thing to say!' she spluttered. 'After everything I've done to help.'

Beverley thought it prudent to intervene. 'I'm sure Annabelle didn't mean it,' she soothed. 'Let's change the subject: whatever it is you think you might have forgotten, it's too late to do anything about now. As far as I can see everything is on track and we're going to have a lovely day.' She glared at her sister. 'Aren't we?'

May nodded then picked up her wine glass and took a hefty gulp.

But Beverley might have known May wasn't going to let the subject drop, because when she nipped off to the loo, her sister was hot on her heels.

As soon as the door to the ladies swung shut behind them, May began complaining.

'I can't believe Annabelle is being so ungrateful,' her sister grizzled. 'It's all been such a mad rush, and she hasn't heeded a word of advice. I do wish she had waited another year. I don't know why she insisted on getting married so soon. Anyone would think she is pregnant.' There was a pause, then May gasped and held a hand to her throat. 'You don't think she is, do you?'

'Would it be a problem if she was?'

May was too shocked to speak for a moment, but when she did all she could say was, 'You would have thought she'd be more careful at her age. And Ron is no spring chicken.'

'Lots of people have babies in their forties,' Beverley pointed out.

'If you ask me, it's too old,' May said.

'It's lucky they're not asking you then, isn't it?'

'So you *do* think she might be pregnant!'

'Actually, I don't. They decided on the date back in February. So if she is pregnant, she's hiding it extremely well.'

May subsided, relief easing her scowl. 'I still think she should have waited. If they had got married next year, we wouldn't have had the fiasco with the bandstand, and she would have had time to get a proper wedding dress.'

Beverley drew herself up to her full height and crossed her arms. 'There was no fiasco with the bandstand,' she retorted. 'If there was any fiasco, it was of your own making. Fancy sending out the invitations without consulting Ron and Annabelle.'

'If I had left it up to them, the invitations wouldn't have been sent at all.'

'They didn't need to be,' Beverley retorted. 'Everyone who is coming already knew the date.'

'You know perfectly well that's not how it's done. And I can't believe she's wearing blue to her own wedding.'

Beverley barked out a laugh. 'You do realise that white is supposed to signify purity and virginity, don't you?'

'That doesn't matter anymore.' May stuck her nose in the air.

'And neither does sending out invitations,' Beverley countered, then decided to leave the matter there, whilst she had the upper hand.

Quickly washing her hands, she hurried out of the ladies' loo and back to the table.

As she sat down, Andrew whispered, 'Is everything all right?'

'Don't ask. May just went off on one. She's got a bee in a bonnet about this sodding wedding.'

'I remember Judith and her mother being at loggerheads on the run-up to Judith's wedding. I think there's too much pressure put on brides these days.'

'It's all their own making,' Beverley said, then amended, 'Although not in this instance. This is all May's making. Annabelle and Ron were quite happy to have a registry office ceremony and a little get-together for a meal afterwards. My sister has blown this out of all proportion.' She didn't mention that she had also wanted them to have a nice reception…

'I'm sure it will be lovely, though,' Andrew said.

'What will be lovely?' Ron asked.

Beverley leapt in. 'The wedding, of course. I can't wait to see you married. Annabelle will make a lovely bride and you are going to look so smart in your new suit.' She ignored May's expression as her sister plopped herself back into her seat.

Ron looked fondly at his fiancée. 'She always looks beautiful regardless of what she's wearing,' he said. 'She could turn up in jeans for all I care. I just want to marry her.'

'Aw, that's so sweet.' Beverley could feel tears threatening, and she began to worry: if she was like this at the thought of them getting married, what was she going to be like on the actual day? She must remember to shove a couple of packets of tissues into her bag.

Sniffing loudly, she dabbed her eyes, and Andrew put his arm around her and pulled her close, planting a kiss on her temple.

Ron turned his attention back to Beverley. 'Look at the two of you,' he said. 'I reckon you're going to be next.'

Annabelle chirped, 'Do us all a favour, Beverley, and elope to Gretna Green. I don't think I can go through this again.'

Ron muttered, 'I wish *we* had done that. It would have saved a lot of hassle.'

Annabelle perked up. 'Is it too late? Can we still do that?' She looked at her groom hopefully.

Izzie asked, 'What does elope mean?'

'Run away,' Ron said. 'Gretna Green is the place that people who want to get married run away to.'

'Why would you want to run away to get married?' Jake asked.

'To stop people like your grandmother interfering in their wedding plans,' Annabelle said grimly, and Jake's eyes widened.

'Yes, it is too late,' May piped up. 'And even if it wasn't, you wouldn't dare. Not after all the trouble I've gone to – and Beverley too, of course – to make this a special day for you.'

Looking at Ron and Annabelle's faces, Beverley wasn't too sure that they wouldn't, if they could. She had a feeling that if they were given the opportunity that was exactly what they would do. But May was right – it was too late. Ron and Annabelle's marriage was going to take place on the bandstand in Brighton on the 26th of June, whether they would have preferred to have run away to Gretna Green or not.

***

Andrew climbed stiffly out of Ron's car and turned to Beverley who had also clambered out. She was waiting until he had brought Pepe out and handed the dog over before demanding a kiss, which Andrew duly obliged.

'Can you two get a move on?' Ron called through the open window. 'Some of us want to get to bed.'

Beverley sniggered. 'So do I,' she hissed in Andrew's ear.

'Behave yourself,' he said, stroking her cheek. 'I'll see you tomorrow.' They couldn't spend *every* night together, otherwise they may as well just live together. Besides, he was tired and he'd had one drink too many this evening.

He waved goodbye to her, standing on the path until Ron's estate was out of sight, then he turned and went inside.

He couldn't help mulling over what Ron had said about he and Beverley being next.

Was it so obvious that he was planning on asking her to marry him? The thought of proposing made his stomach turn over; he hoped she would say yes, but he wasn't certain.

He let Twinkle out into the garden for a wee, and whilst he waited for her to have a sniff around, he decided to make himself a cup of cocoa.

He was just getting the milk out of the fridge when his mobile phone vibrated. He had left it at home this evening, thinking that he wouldn't need it, but maybe he shouldn't have, he realised, when he saw that he'd had several missed calls from his daughter.

He checked his messages, but she hadn't left one and he began to worry. Going over to the landline in the hall, he picked up the handset, hoping she might have left a message on that. She had called, but once again had failed to leave a message.

His heart churning and his mouth suddenly dry, he was just about to phone her back when his mobile rang, frightening him to death.

Letting out a muted yell of surprise, he hurriedly answered it. 'What's wrong?' he cried. 'Are you OK? Is it Duncan? The boys?'

'Dad, why should there be anything wrong? Everything is fine.'

'I've had several missed calls. What do you expect me to think?'

She ignored his comment. 'Where have you been? I've been trying to call you all evening.'

'Out to dinner. Why, what's wrong?'

'I just told you, nothing. But I have been thinking—' She broke off.

Andrew groaned. The phrase 'I've been thinking' was one that must strike dread into the heart of many a man. Where Vivienne had been concerned, it usually meant she had wanted a room redecorated, or French doors put in, or some other kind of DIY nonsense.

'What about?' he asked. 'Couldn't it have waited until tomorrow?'

'I did ring you earlier,' she said, 'but when I didn't get any answer, I started to get a bit worried.'

'I told you, I was out to dinner.'

'Why didn't you take your phone?'

'I didn't think I'd need it.'

'Dad, that's what mobiles are for.' He heard her sigh. 'Were you with Beverley?' she asked.

'Yes.'

'I thought as much.'

'Is that a problem?'

'It might be.'

'How so?' He had no idea what she was about to say, but he had an unsettling feeling he didn't want to hear her say it.

'I know you think the world of her, and I know she's your girlfriend, but don't you think it's all a little peculiar?'

'In what way?' Andrew was baffled.

'The way she suddenly attached herself to you.'

'What if I tell you that it was *me* who attached myself to *her*?' He wasn't sure where this was going.

'I just think it's all a bit suspicious. A widower like you could be regarded as fair game.'

'Fair game for what?'

'For a con man. Or should I say, a con *woman*.'

'You think Beverley is trying to con me? I haven't got anything worth conning.' Andrew was struggling not to laugh. His daughter was being ridiculous.

'You've got your house, your pension and your savings,' Judith pointed out.

'Do you think I'm stupid? I wasn't born yesterday. I wouldn't simply hand over my money and my house simply because someone asks for it. I'm aware of the scams out there.'

'I didn't say you were stupid, Dad. I just mean that you're a good catch.'

'Have you been reading too much Jane Austen?'

Judith huffed. 'The way I look at it, you're quite a desirable prospect. As I said, you have your own house, you have your savings, and you have a pension, and more importantly, you don't have a wife or partner. You are ripe for being exploited.'

'No one is exploiting anyone,' he said. This would be laughable, if Judith wasn't so serious.

'I don't think you're seeing the wood for the trees,' she argued. 'I bet you any money that if you asked her to move in with you, she would be there like a shot.'

'Is that what you're worried about? That Beverley and I might move in together?'

'I'm worried she might con you into marrying her, and if that happens, she'll make you change your will and leave everything to her because she would be your wife.'

'Woah, lady, where did this come from?' He was astonished that Judith would think such a thing.

'She told me herself that she doesn't own her own house.'

'And you believe she's after mine?'

'It wouldn't be unheard of, and can you categorically say she isn't?'

'No, but—'

'I rest my case. I'm worried about you, Dad, and I don't think you should see her anymore. I know you like her – actually I think it's more than like on your part – but I believe she's only after you for your money. I'm going to stick my neck out and go as far as to say that if you carry on seeing her, I'll never speak to you again.'

'*Pardon?*' Andrew thought he must have misheard.

'I said, if you carry on seeing Beverley, I won't speak to you again. I'll not have my mother's house ending up in the hands of that grasping woman. I can't bear to think of her sleeping in my mum's bed and sitting at my mother's table. I don't care how much you think you like her, Dad, this has got to stop.'

'You're asking me to stop seeing the woman I love?'

He heard Judith gasp. '*You love her?* Dad, how could you? She really has done a number on you, hasn't she? That's it! You're definitely going to have to choose – *me* or *her.* Which is it to be?'

CHAPTER 23

Beverley jerked awake at the sound of the phone ringing, her heart thudding. Feeling groggy but scared, she threw back the bedclothes, staggered out of bed and flew down the stairs. The phone rested on a side table in the living room, and she snatched it up.

It was May and she was awfully upset. Beverley's sister didn't cry very often and at first Beverley thought something dreadful had happened. But when she found out that May's distress was caused by a falling out with Annabelle, Beverley felt nothing but relief.

'You got me out of bed to tell me that?' she grumbled.

'I thought you would be up by now.'

'What time is it?'

'Half-past nine.'

Blast. She liked to be up before Ron to make him breakfast – even if he didn't take her up on the offer very often – but it appeared he had already left.

Telling May that she would be there as soon as she'd had her breakfast and got dressed, Beverley ended the call and stomped into the kitchen. She needed a cuppa before she dealt with her sister.

May had calmed down by the time Beverley arrived, but she was still snuffly and her eyes were red. She had buzzed Beverley in the main entrance downstairs and had left the front door of the flat ajar, purely so May could be found sprawled dramatically on the sofa with her arm draped across her eyes, like some weepy heroine in a Victorian drama.

'Go on, tell me what's happened,' Beverley said, after making them a cup of tea and taking it into the living room, because May was pretending to be too distraught to perform such a simple task as making a brew. Pepe, as usual, was consigned to the kitchen, much to his disgust.

All the windows were open, and sound from the road below drifted through them. The flat was already warm and Beverley shrugged her cardigan off and made herself comfy.

'Annabelle hates the wedding favours I bought,' May sniffed.

Beverley sank back into the cushions. 'Is that all?'

'Trust you to take her side.'

'I'm not taking anyone's side. From the way you were acting I thought it was something serious.'

'It is serious!'

Beverley sipped her tea and tried not to scoff. Serious, indeed. May wouldn't know serious if it bit her on the arse.

'What didn't she like about them?' she asked.

'Everything,' May wailed. 'She doesn't want favours at all. She doesn't see the point. And she hates the ones I bought.'

'There will only be a few of us,' Beverley pointed out. 'I'm sure no one will even notice if there aren't any favours. What were they like anyway?'

May went into the kitchen to fetch one.

She handed Beverley a small spiky cactus wrapped in a parcel of white paper, with a piece of card tied around the pot with silver ribbon. The card said, 'Thank you.'

'*Cactus?*' Beverley examined the plant and tried to work out what had been going through her sister's head when she had bought it. Not a lot, she assumed.

'It was supposed to be an aloe vera – a succulent is meant to represent that the couple's love will keep growing.'

'It does?' That was news to her, and she wondered whether any of the other wedding guests would have understood the significance. Still, a plant was better than those nasty sugared almond thingies.

May nodded. 'But they didn't have enough, so I got the cactus instead.'

Bloody hell, you couldn't write this stuff, Beverley thought. Cactus? Un-sodding-believable. No wonder Annabelle didn't like them. They didn't exactly exude wedding bliss and marital harmony.

'Come on, May. What did you expect?'

'She might have been a bit more appreciative.'

'I wouldn't have been.'

'That just about sums you up. You have been no use whatsoever.'

'I beg to differ. I sorted out the bandstand, and the wedding cars and charabanc, and the ring-bearers.'

'The *what?*'

Oops. Beverley hadn't meant to let that slip. She was planning for the two dogs to each carry a pouch in their mouths, which would contain the wedding rings. It was supposed to be a surprise for Ron and Annabelle.

'Ring-bearers,' Beverley said in a small voice.

'My daughter is having *two* pageboys but only *one* bridesmaid?' May threw her hands in the air. 'I give up. Is this your doing? I bet Jake isn't happy. He told me he didn't want to be a pageboy, but I can understand *him* being one what with Izzie being a bridesmaid, but you just had to drag Sam into it.'

'I haven't dragged Sam into anything. He's not a pageboy.'

'Who, then?' May demanded. 'There isn't anyone else.'

'PepeandTwinkle,' Beverley muttered, running the names together into one word in the hope that it would sound more palatable.

May froze and Beverley watched the play of emotions move across her sister's face – confusion, understanding, disbelief, and finally anger.

'Please tell me this is a joke.' May's voice was calm, and all the more scary because of it.

Beverley caught her bottom lip between her teeth and shook her head.

This wasn't meant to happen. Beverley had been hoping that the first May would know of it was when Pepe and Twinkle were trotting down the aisle, when it was too late to object.

'Ron will love it,' Beverley said, hoping she was right. She should have run it past him first. Maybe having Twinkle was overkill – perhaps it would be better with just Pepe on his own? It seemed a shame to waste one of those lovely velvet pouches though:

she had bought two, in the very same colours as her dress, Andrew's tie and the doggy bandanas.

'He would,' May said bitterly.

'What do you mean by that?' Beverley asked, indignation rushing through her. Her sister grasped any opportunity she could to run him down.

May didn't enlighten her. Instead, she drew in a breath, her eyes flashing with fury. 'If you insist on going ahead with this stupid, ridiculous idea, I'll never speak to you again.'

'Don't be silly. You've got to speak to me – I'm your sister.'

'I'll disown you.'

'You can't do that!'

'Watch me. And what's more, I don't want you or your dog at my daughter's wedding.'

'May!' Beverley was shocked. 'It's not up to you.'

'In that case, I'll refuse to go to the wedding.'

Beverley was about to tell May to stop being so dramatic, when a loud crash coming from the direction of the bedrooms made them both jump. It was immediately followed by another, and accompanied by a volley of excited barks.

Shit! *Pepe!*

Beverley leapt to her feet and saw that the door to the kitchen was ajar. The little sod had managed to slip out and was doing goodness knows what in the bedroom. Destroying the place, by the sound of it.

May was hot on Beverley's heels as she bowled into the room, and blundered into her when Beverley stopped dead.

Oh, hell…

'How did *that* get in here?' May cried, shoving Beverley towards the creature she was referring to.

That was a ginger and white cat, and it was being chased at speed around the room by a hysterical poodle. The crash appeared to have been caused by a chest of drawers which had toppled over, spilling drawers and their contents onto the floor.

The cat made a bid for safety and shot up one of May's brocade curtains and clawed its way to the top, where it peered balefully down at Pepe and hissed furiously.

'Get it down!' May yelled. 'Those curtains cost a fortune.'

Even from here, Beverley could see the scags that the cat's claws had made in the fabric. And then she noticed what Pepe was dancing around in and smearing all over May's new cream carpets, and her heart sank to her boots – bronzing powder.

Half of it was on Pepe, who was now a strange shade of glittery tan colour, and the rest of it was being ground into the shagpile by his paws as he bounced around, uttering high-pitched yips of frustration at his inability to get at the cat.

'Look what he's done!' May shrieked. 'My carpet, my lovely cream carpet!'

Beverley lunged towards her hyped-up pooch, and it took her a couple of goes before she was able to grab him and haul him away. His paws scrabbled on the carpet as he tried to hold his ground, but he had to admit defeat when she scooped him up and wrapped her arms firmly around him in case he wriggled free.

She left the cat where it was. May could sort that out.

Beverley had no idea who it belonged to (her sister would never entertain the idea of having a cat) but she could guess that it had got in through the door May had left open for her earlier. May had also failed to close the kitchen door properly, so it was her fault that Pepe had got out.

Unfortunately, May didn't see it that way. As far as she was concerned, Beverley was entirely to blame.

'Argh!' May screamed and stamped her foot. 'Get out and take your dog with you. I never want to see you or that horrid thing again. Do you hear me? Never!' May accompanied the final word with another stamp of her foot, and then promptly burst into tears.

'May, I'm sorry, I—'

'*Get out!*

'At least let me help you—'

'I don't need your help. Haven't you done enough?'

Beverley thought it wise to do what May wanted, and give her sister time to calm down and gain some perspective. She would apologise later, even though this wasn't totally her fault.

But as she retrieved her bag and her cardi, all she heard was May's anguished wails as her sister viewed the full extent of the damage. Beverley just hoped May would be able to bring herself to forgive her before Saturday – because there was no way Beverley was going to miss Ron's wedding.

***

Beverley was surprised and relieved to see Ron's car parked on the pavement outside the house when she got back from May's.

She was so upset it had been hard to hold back the tears as she walked home, a totally unrepentant poodle at her heels. He was no longer leaving little bronze paw prints on the pavement, but she could still see it glistening in his fur and she assumed that the tub of powder must have fallen on him before it hit the carpet.

Oh, God, May's bedroom carpet would never be the same again.

Despite it not being wholly Beverley's fault (who could have anticipated a cat wandering into the apartment?) she would offer to pay for the carpet to be cleaned, and the curtains to be replaced if necessary.

She hoped May had managed to shoo the cat outside, and the poor creature hadn't been too traumatised. However, she thought May might never get over the shock.

Mindful that as well as the dog, Beverley herself was coated in a fair amount of bronze powder, as soon as she opened the front door she picked Pepe up and took him straight through the house, careful not to touch anything in case the powder rubbed off on her own soft furnishings, and deposited him in the garden. The naughty dog could stay there for a while, until she had changed her clothes and washed her orange-palmed hands. As soon as she had done that, she would give him a bath. He wouldn't like it, but it would serve him right.

Ron had been standing in the living room as she hurried down the hall and into the kitchen, and she called, 'I didn't expect you to be home, but I'm glad you are. I've had an awful morning.'

She closed the back door (ignoring the dog's pitiful expression), washed her hands in the sink, and as she dried them, she glanced down at herself to find orange streaks all over her top and cardi. She hoped they would come out in the wash.

Ron came into the kitchen. He didn't look happy: he looked downright cross in fact, and she hoped his morning hadn't been as bad as hers.

'You won't believe what has just happened—' she began.

Ron leapt in. His voice was grim. 'Oh, I would. I've spoken to Annabelle.'

'It's worse than wedding favours,' Beverley said, 'although why my sister thought a cactus was a good idea, beggars belief. Pepe has—'

'I know what Pepe did.'

'It wasn't his fault. There was this cat and—'

'I agree, it wasn't his fault. It was yours. And May's. None of this would have happened if you and May had kept your noses out and left Annabelle and me to sort our own wedding out. *Our* wedding. Not yours. Not May's. We told you that we didn't want a fuss. You know we wanted a simple wedding, yet between the two of you, you and May have managed to turn it into a three-ring circus. I thought weddings were supposed to be joyful occasions, but this has been nothing but hassle from the start. I wish we'd never told anyone we were getting married. I wish we'd just gone ahead and done it. Believe me when I say that eloping to Gretna Green sounds like a damn good idea right now. I've a good mind to uninvite everyone!'

Ron was furious. Beverley had never seen him lose his temper, and she was dismayed and horrified to think that she and May were the cause of his distress.

He snapped, 'Annabelle is incredibly upset. It'll be a miracle if she turns up on the day at this rate. I'm going to her house now to see if I can sort it out. I'm not sure when I'll be back – if I come back at all.'

Before Beverley could say another word, he turned on his heel and strode down the hall.

She watched him yank the front door open and winced when it slammed shut behind him. Then she promptly burst into tears.

***

For once, Beverley didn't take Pepe with her when she went to Andrew's house. She left him at home, even though she knew Twinkle would wonder where her friend was. Beverley wasn't mad at her dog: she was mad at herself. If only she had kept her nose out of Ron and Annabelle's business...

After having sobbed until her eyes were sore, Beverley had tidied herself up, bathed a reluctant dog, then phoned Andrew. She was desperate to hear a friendly voice; he would know what to do and what to say, and even if he didn't, she would feel better simply by being in his arms.

He hadn't answered, despite her calling his mobile and his landline, and she hoped he wasn't still waiting for her in the park. It was way past the time they usually met, and she prayed nothing was wrong: she didn't think she could take any more today. Worried, she put her jacket on, stuffed her feet into her walking shoes and hurried out of the door.

Her relief when she neared Andrew's house and saw Twinkle in the window looking out into the street, was palpable. But it soon changed to concern and her own problems were pushed to the back of her mind when Andrew opened the door.

His face was grey, and he looked as though he had been crying.

'You'd better come in,' he said, standing to the side to let her pass. She expected a kiss at the very least, but when she moved towards him, he shrank back.

Fear raced along her veins and lodged in her heart. 'What's happened?'

'It's Judith—'

'Oh, God, is she all right?'

'She's fine.' He held up a hand, as though warding her off.

They were still in the hall, and he hadn't closed the door. He was standing there as though she had popped in to read the electricity meter and would soon be on her way again. She also realised he was wearing the same clothes that he'd had on last night when they'd gone out to dinner, and she knew that whatever this was, it was serious.

'Let me say my piece,' he said, swallowing hard. 'You and me… it's over. I don't— I

can't—' He swallowed again. 'I can't do this anymore.'

Beverley's blood turned to ice and the shards pierced her heart. She prayed she hadn't heard him right, but she was terrified she had.

'Why?' was all she was able to force out.

'I… just can't.'

She searched his face for some sort of clue. What had happened? How could he have fallen out of love with her between last night and this morning?

'Don't you love me anymore?' Her voice was small, and to her own ears she sounded broken.

'Please, Beverley, don't make this any harder than it already is.' He opened the door wider, his intention clear. He wanted her to leave.

'But, why?' she asked again, her voice catching in her throat, thick with tears.

He refused to look at her. His gaze was on the floor, and all he did was shake his head.

Blindly, Beverley blundered past him and out onto the street. Her mind was numb, but her heart was breaking, and as her tummy clenched, she felt she might be sick. With tears pouring down her cheeks and legs barely able to hold her up, she stumbled home.

And when she got there, she took herself off to bed and cried until she could cry no more.

***

'It's done.' Andrew sounded as bitter as he felt. He hoped Judith was pleased with herself.

'Good. I know it was hard for you, Dad, but it's for the best.'

Who's best, he wondered. He hadn't even given Beverley a reason. He'd just told her it was over and asked her to leave. The look on her face would stay with him for the rest of his life, which, right now, he hoped wouldn't be too long. He felt worse than when Vivienne died, and that was something he couldn't have believed possible.

Yet here he was, his heart so full of pain that he feared it would break.

Damn Judith and damn her ultimatum.

How could his daughter do this to him, even if she did have his best interests at heart? Perhaps he should have sat Beverley down and explained that Judith thought she was only with him for what she could get out of him, but he had ended it cleanly, no long, drawn-out discussion. Just a swift fatal blow.

However, that the fatal blow had been to his own heart as well as to their relationship, because he didn't know how he was ever going to recover from this.

And the awful thing was… Judith didn't even appreciate what she had done or the pain he was in, as she said, 'Gotto go, Dad. I'm late for a meeting. Bye.'

Her cheery, unconcerned voice was like a knife to his stomach, and he wished with all his heart that he had never set eyes on Beverley Collins.

CHAPTER 24

Pariah, wasn't that what an outcast was? Beverley thought she might as well have a bell around her neck and shout 'Unclean' at anyone who came too close. But that was the problem – no one had come close at all since yesterday. Ron had briefly popped in to grab some clothes and check that she was still upright and breathing – which was nice of him – but he hadn't stayed long. Certainly not long enough to notice that her heart was in pieces. And she didn't go out of her way to tell him.

She hadn't heard a peep from Andrew – not that she had expected to, considering he had made it perfectly clear that he wanted nothing more to do with her – and she had made a point of avoiding the park and any other places he might be. Instead, she had put Pepe in the car and had driven a couple of miles away to take the dog for a walk this morning.

And as for her sister… God knows what was happening there, because Beverley didn't. The sound of her phone not ringing was deafening. The only person she had spoken to was Kate.

She'd told her daughter everything, and Kate had wanted to hop in the car and drive straight down, but Beverley had told her not to be so silly, adding that she was fine and would see her on Friday, as planned. However… the wedding was only four days away, and Beverley didn't even know if she was still invited. Or whether anyone else was, for that matter. It might not even be going ahead.

Bugger it! She couldn't sit here and fret. She had to know what was going on, so she picked up the phone and dialled Ron's number.

It rang and rang, and she was about to hang up, when a voice from behind said, 'You called?'

Beverley uttered a squeak and dropped the phone.

She had been so engrossed in what she was going to say to him, that she hadn't heard him come in. He was standing in the doorway to the living room, wearing a serious expression. Pepe wriggled in his arms and tried to lick his face, but he wasn't paying the dog much attention.

She swallowed nervously. 'Are you and Annabelle still getting married?'

Ron jerked in surprise. He put Pepe down, ignoring the dog when he scrabbled at his legs. 'Of course we are. Whatever gave you that idea?'

'You did.'

He sighed. 'I might have mentioned something like that, but I didn't mean it.'

'Am I still invited?'

'That's what I'm here to talk to you about.'

Beverley's chin wobbled. It had been doing that on and off since yesterday, usually accompanied by copious amounts of tears.

'Aw, don't cry,' he said, moving closer and gathering her to him. But as she felt his arms go around her, she promptly burst into loud sobs.

'It's OK,' he crooned. 'It'll all be sorted: you see if it won't. May's not going to stay mad at you forever, and I'm here to make sure the two of you kiss and make up before the wedding. Annabelle is doing the same with May.'

'That's good,' she bawled, and cried even harder.

It was quite some time before she had calmed down enough for Ron to release her, and when he did and saw that his T-shirt had a large damp patch on the front, she began to cry all over again.

'I've made a mess of your T-shirt,' she wailed.

'It's no biggie. It'll come out in the wash.'

And that made her think of May's cream carpet and the state it must be in, and it started her off all over again.

Eventually though, her tears subsided into hiccupping snuffles, and she allowed Ron to make her a cup of tea.

'This isn't like you,' he said. 'I'm so sorry. I never wanted to hurt you – you're like a mother to me. But I saw red when I realised how upset Annabelle was, and I lashed out. It was unforgivable.'

'You have every right to be mad,' Beverley sniffed. 'May and I were well out of order. We knew what you and Annabelle wanted, yet we ignored your wishes and did the exact opposite.'

Ron smiled. 'You did go a little overboard,' he said. 'Now, dry your eyes. Things aren't as bad as they seem.'

Oh, yes, they are, she thought, fresh tears beginning to trickle down her face. And when Ron asked what was wrong, she told him everything.

'You were actually going to propose?' he said, after she'd finished relating her sad little tale. 'You love Andrew that much?'

'I do.' She blew her nose noisily and cleared her throat.

'Do you think he might have guessed what you were going to do and got cold feet?'

'I dunno. He didn't give me a reason. That's what I find so hard to take. Did I mean so little to him?'

I don't believe that for one minute. I saw the way he looked at you. If he isn't a man in love, I don't know what is.'

'If he did love me once, he doesn't anymore.'

'You don't just stop loving someone for no reason. He seemed fine on Sunday.'

'I know.' She gulped down some tea, her throat sore from all the crying she had done.

'I've got a mind to go round there and ask him what he's playing at,' Ron said.

'Please, don't. What's done is done, and knowing won't make any difference.'

'It might give you closure.'

'And it might not,' she argued. She did want to know, but at the same time she didn't want to appear as though she was trying to win him back. Her heart might be in bits, but her dignity was intact, and she wanted to keep it that way.

'Do you know what's really daft?' she said, with a bitter laugh. 'I think I was subconsciously planning the wedding I would have wanted when I was interfering in yours. The bandstand is what I would have chosen for myself, and the charabanc. Not so sure about The Gillespie Rooms, because they are hideously expensive, and I would have liked to have a wedding cake and have Pepe as the ring-bearer.'

Ron bit his lip. 'I think it was that, as much as the mess on her carpets, which sent May over the edge,' he said. 'I wouldn't have minded, and neither would Annabelle – as long as the little sod behaved himself and not run off with them. I can see him now, tearing off across the beach with the rings in his mouth and everyone chasing after him.'

Unfortunately, so could Beverley.

'How is May's carpet?' she asked.

'She's having it professionally cleaned. The chap who came to take a look was hopeful he could get the marks out.'

'Good. And the curtains?'

'They didn't fare quite as well. The cat took some persuading before it would come down, and from what I can gather, when she finally got it down it landed on the matching bedspread and scagged that, too. She's taken the whole lot to a charity shop and is hunting for some new ones. A different colour, apparently, because she wasn't sure she liked the other one. So I suppose you could say you did her a favour, because she now has an excuse to buy new without Terence telling her off for spending more money.'

'I don't think she'll see it that way,' Beverley said.

'Probably not.' Ron got to his feet. 'Let's get a hot meal into you, because I bet you haven't eaten anything much since yesterday.'

He was right, she hadn't, and she felt herself begin to relax as she let him fuss over her. She was determined to make the most of it, because after Saturday she would be on her own in the house again, and she wasn't looking forward to it in the slightest. Not without Andrew in her life.

And she was filled with such sadness that it took every bit of willpower she had, to not break down again. There would be time enough to cry after the wedding.

***

'Grandad? Open up, it's me, Leo.'

Andrew had heard someone knocking but he had ignored it. He hadn't been expecting anyone and even if he had been, he didn't want to talk to them.

Leo was a different matter.

Stiffly Andrew got to his feet, his gammy knee aching more than usual. He guessed the reason was because he hadn't moved out of his armchair for over twenty-four hours, apart from to let Twinkle out. He had fed her too, at some point, but he hadn't bothered feeding himself – he had been too depressed to think of food. Anyway, he didn't have much of an appetite.

'Leo? What are you doing here?' he asked as he let his grandson in.

'I've come for the wedding.'

'But that isn't until Saturday. I thought you were arriving on Friday?'

'I was, but...' Leo hesitated. 'I was worried about you. And I was right to be.'

'There's no need to worry about me,' Andrew said, as he shuffled into the kitchen to put the kettle on.

Leo was studying him. 'I think there is. Grandad, you look awful.'

'It's just a bug. I'll be fine in a bit.'

'Mum told me that you and Beverley have split up.'

'Did she tell you why?'

'Kind of. She said Beverley was a gold-digger and only after your money.'

'Hmm.'

'I didn't think she was like that.'

Andrew heaved a sigh. 'Neither did I, but your mother seems to think I'm a good catch.'

'You what?'

'An attractive prospect, financially.'

'You're hardly rolling in it.'

'I know, but…'

'She told me something else – that she gave you an ultimatum. Her or Beverley. She shouldn't have done that.'

'Maybe she shouldn't have,' Andrew agreed. 'But she was trying to make me see sense.'

'What did Beverley say when you told her?'

'Not a lot. I just told her it was over and that was that.'

'That's harsh.'

'Yes…'

'I'd hate it if someone dumped me like that. No explanation or nothing.'

'What could I say? That my daughter thinks you're a gold-digger because you don't own your own house?'

'I see your point. I'm guessing you're not going to the wedding.'

'Hardly.'

'Does Ron and Annabelle still want me to take the photos?'

'I don't know. Have you asked them?'

'Do you think I should?'

Andrew nodded. 'You'd better check.'

Leo eased his mobile out of the pocket of his jeans, and Andrew watched the lad's thumbs tap at the screen. He couldn't even summon up the energy to feel envious of the boy's dexterity.

'Done. I'll just have to wait for Ron to get back to me. Where's Twinkle?'

Andrew gazed around. 'Um… I'm not sure. Twinkle? Twinkle!'

There was a faint bark from outside, and he remembered that he had let her out for a wee a few hours ago and had forgotten to let her back in.

As soon as Leo opened the back door, the dog shot to her water bowl and lapped at it thirstily.

Andrew collapsed against the fridge, remorse washing over him. The poor little thing had been outside all day, and he hadn't given her a second thought. No wonder she was thirsty. He should be ashamed of himself. And he was – thoroughly, utterly ashamed.

Suddenly his head was in his hands and tears were pouring down his face.

He was aware of Leo steering him into the sitting room and lowering him into a chair, and he was aware of his grandson's muted voice conducting a heated conversation with someone, but that was it. He was too consumed by his own misery to pay attention to anything else, apart from Twinkle – who evoked a renewed flood of tears when she crawled into his lap and tried to comfort him with doggy kisses.

When he eventually stopped crying and his tears had dried to a trickle, Andrew said, 'I'm sorry, I don't know what came over me.'

'I do,' Leo said grimly, 'and I've told mum she should be ashamed of herself. She's on her way.'

'Tell her not to come,' Andrew said, beginning to fret. 'She's busy. I'll be all right.'

'I don't care if she's busy or not. She needs to take responsibility for what she's done and apologise for her behaviour.'

'She's just looking out for me.'

Leo knelt by his feet. 'You are perfectly capable of looking after yourself. You don't need Mum to do it for you.'

'But what about Beverley and the gold—'

'Grandad! Do you honestly think Beverley is like that? And even if she is, you should be able to decide for yourself how you want to deal with it. Mum making you choose between her and Beverley is despicable.'

'I did think it was rather extreme,' Andrew admitted, 'but she's my daughter.'

'She's out of line,' Leo retorted. 'Even if she is right, she went about it in entirely the wrong way. Do you think she's right?'

Andrew closed his eyes. Then slowly opened them again. 'No, Leo, I don't.'

'Didn't think so. OK, we need to get you and Beverley back together because, let's be honest Grandad, you're a mess without her.'

'You're right, I am. I haven't been able to think straight since Sunday night. I was going to ask her to marry me.'

Leo's face lit up. 'You were? Sweet.'

'Yes, I think it might have been. But she'll never have me back now, not after the way I've treated her.'

'Don't give up yet, Grandad, I've got a plan.'

CHAPTER 25

'How do I look?' Beverley did a wobbly twirl. Her heels were rather higher than she was used to, and she felt as though she was on stilts.

'Like a million dollars.'

She beamed at Ron. It wasn't a full-watt beam, but it was the best she could manage. Hopefully it was enough, because she didn't want her misery to put a dampener on his wedding day.

Nervously he tugged at his tie, and she reached up to slap his hand away.

'Stop messing with it, you'll make it grubby.' It was the same shade of blue as Annabelle's dress, and the same shade of blue as the sash on his soon-to-be stepdaughter's bridesmaid's dress.

Beverley ignored the insidious thought that Andrew's tie had been the same colour as her own outfit, and she tried to forget that she would never get to see him wear it.

Pepe was wearing his bandana, though. Despite May's protestations and obvious disapproval, the dog was coming to the wedding. Annabelle and Ron had insisted on it, although they had drawn the line at the poodle trotting down the aisle with the precious wedding rings in his mouth. Beverley thought it was a wise decision on their part. Pepe was not to be trusted.

But that hadn't prevented Beverley from being a tiny bit wistful when she had put the pouch back in the drawer – he would have looked so cute… But Ron was right, Pepe had a mind of his own and he could have caused ructions.

'What time is the charabanc arriving?' Ron asked for the fourth time that morning.

'Don't panic, we've got an hour yet.'

She heard a car pull up outside and glanced out of the window. 'Here is your best man. Aw, doesn't Brett scrub up well? Kate looks gorgeous, too.'

Her daughter was wearing a blush pink dress with a matching hat.

'Charity shop,' Kate hissed when Beverley complimented her on it. Giving Beverley a hug, she added, 'and the hat. £35 in total!'

'I would never have guessed if you hadn't told me.'

'I know, fab, isn't it? I told Helen I paid £500 for it. She nearly had a fit. Her outfit was only £375. Talk of the devil.' Kate nudged Beverley and jerked her chin.

Another car had pulled up behind Brett's, a flashy black number with lots of gleaming chrome.

Beverley could see Helen sitting in the passenger seat, and she continued to sit there until a man, who Beverley assumed to be Carlton, got out of the driver's side, walked around the front of the car and opened Helen's door.

'Bloody hell, look at Lady Muck,' Beverley muttered.

'Now, now, play nice,' Kate warned.

As Helen got out of the car, Beverley tried a smile on for size. It felt odd, so she allowed her face to fall into its usual expression.

Kate sent her a concerned look. 'Are you OK?'

'Not really. But I will be, I just want to get today out of the way without bursting into tears.'

'If you do cry, we'll say it's because everyone cries at weddings.' Kate turned to the door and smiled as her mother-in-law stalked in. 'Helen, you look lovely. Hi, Carlton, it's good to see you again. Are you well?'

Beverley sighed, plastered another smile on her face, and stepped forward. 'Helen.' She nodded at her arch-enemy.

'Beverley.' Helen nodded back. 'Meet Carlton. I've told him all about you.'

I bet you have, Beverley fumed, eyeing the chap who thought he was brave enough to take Helen on. She estimated him to be in his mid-70's and he clearly looked after himself. He had an upright stance, a trim figure and was well-manicured. Beverley begrudgingly admitted that he and Helen looked good together.

With the niceties taken care of and Helen having kissed her son, greeted her grandchildren and wished Ron some slightly frosty congratulations, Helen glanced around the living room.

'Aren't you going to introduce me to your gentleman friend?'

The term set Beverley's teeth on edge. 'I would, but unfortunately he can't make it today.'

'How unfortunate.' Helen smirked, giving Beverley the distinct impression that she hadn't believed Beverley had ever intended to bring a plus-one. 'Andrew, wasn't it?'

'That's right.' Beverley pressed her lips together.

'Such a shame. You'll be all on your own.'

'I'm sure I can cuddle up with you two.'

'Any particular reason why he can't attend?' Helen's smile was saccharine sweet.

'Yes. A personal one. But his grandson, Leo, is the photographer, so I suppose you could say that he will be here by proxy.'

'Oh?' Helen raised perfectly sculpted and pencilled-in eyebrows.

Beverley wished she had got hers done, but the thought hadn't crossed her mind.

'His grandson? That's nice.' The faintly sour expression on Helen's face gave away the fact that Helen hadn't actually believed Andrew existed. 'Are we waiting for anyone else?' she enquired.

'May and Jake. Izzie is going in the car with her mum and Terence.'

'Only the *one* car?' Helen looked down her nose.

Beverley, cross that Helen, who was taller than her anyway and was still taller than her despite the new heels she was wearing, drew herself up to her full height and said, 'There didn't seem much point in having a second. We can all fit in the bus.'

And she took great satisfaction in seeing Helen's face fall.

'A *bus?*' Helen glanced at Kate, as though to check she had heard correctly.

'It's an old charabanc,' Kate informed her. 'Not the Number 47 to Seaford.'

Helen placed a hand on her chest. 'Thank goodness for that. You had me worried for a minute.' Her tinkling laugh made Beverley wince.

If she had to put up with this all day, she thought she might scream. Although, there was one good thing to be said for Helen's annoying presence – it was helping to take Beverley's mind off Andrew.

***

Beverley kept a close eye on Helen as everyone piled into the charabanc, and she was pleased to see that the woman seemed to be impressed with the old bus.

Painted a pale cream and navy, the vintage vehicle was around a hundred years old and was very stylish. It was a real head-turner, and as it travelled genteelly from her house to the seafront, people stopped to watch it go by. Beverley felt like royalty and was tempted to give passers-by a queenly wave.

Her gaze kept coming back to the groom and the best man, who were sitting in the front seats. Bless him, Ron looked terrified, and once again she felt guilty for putting him through all this, knowing that he hated being the centre of attention and he hated this fuss. But she also hoped he would look back on today and think what a fabulous wedding they'd had.

As would Beverley herself.

It was going to be perfect. She just wished she didn't feel so desperately sad. Her heart was broken and there was nothing that could be done to make it whole again, and she felt the lack of Andrew by her side keenly. She was trying to put a brave face on it, but she missed him so much and the pain wasn't just confined to her heart; every bit of her ached for him and she didn't think it would ever stop. Not at her age. This would be with her for the rest of her life.

She was jolted out of her misery (for the time being, at least) by the sight of the bandstand, and she gasped in delight.

The ornate structure, beautiful as it was in its natural state, was now bedecked with white flowers and tumbling greenery which was threaded along the top of the balustrades flanking the walkway leading from the promenade, and more blooms were wound around the pillars.

White-clad seats had been arranged on either side of the bandstand, facing out to sea, and there was a beautifully decorated table where Ron and Annabelle would say their vows.

It was understated, elegant and very tasteful, and it brought tears to Beverley's eyes. Her instincts had been right: this was the perfect location.

Carefully, because she was unused to wearing heels, Beverley picked up Pepe and descended the steps of the vintage bus and onto the promenade, where she paused for a moment to gather herself.

The air was warm and filled with the clean tang of the sea and the scent of flowers. The sun shone overhead and sparkled off the water, and Beverley's spirits lifted. She knew it wouldn't last, but she would take what she could get. This was Ron's day and she owed it to him to be as happy as she could possibly be. And she *was* happy for him. She was overjoyed that he had found someone he wanted to spend the rest of his life with.

May was fussing around, making sure everyone was in their allocated seats: although with the guests amounting to less than twenty people, Beverley didn't think it mattered where they sat. But May wanted everything to be perfect, so she flitted around, telling people where to sit.

Beverley guessed that May was also fussing because she would have preferred to be with

Annabelle in the bridal car, so she had to be seen to be doing her bit elsewhere.

Even with this small number of guests there was some milling around and chatting, and as soon as one person was seated, another got up to go to talk to someone else. It was clearly driving May batty, as she tried to get everyone to sit down.

Beverley sat obediently, not wanting to upset her sister more than she already had this week. It had been a surprise when Ron had asked her to go with him to Annabelle's house, to find May already there when she arrived. But both Ron and Annabelle had threatened that if the sisters didn't kiss and make up, there wouldn't be a wedding for them to squabble over.

The truce was tentative, but at least she and May were speaking, and Beverley thought that their relationship had been helped along by her offer to pay for the new curtains and bedspread. May hadn't accepted, saying that it wasn't the money but the offer that was important, and so the two of them were now on speaking terms again.

A flurry of exclamations at the arrival of the bridal car soon had everyone rushing to their allotted seats, and Beverley felt a tug on her heartstrings when she saw that the chair next to hers was empty. It had been meant for Andrew, but in all the excitement of the past couple of days it must have slipped May's mind, and she had forgotten to take Andrew out of the equation.

Still, she supposed Pepe could sit on it: he might like that. After all, he was as much a part of this family as anyone. It was only right he had a seat of his own.

Beverley twisted around and craned her neck to catch her first glimpse of the bride, but she also kept one eye on Ron, who was shuffling from foot to foot and looking as though he was about to be sick.

But when he froze and his eyes widened, Beverley knew he had seen his bride, and she turned her attention to Annabelle.

The pale blue floaty dress Annabelle wore was perfect. It brought out the golden highlights in her hair and reflected the blue of her eyes. She was carrying a bouquet of white roses, and white rosebuds were woven through her tumbling locks. She also wore the widest smile Beverley had ever seen. Joy radiated from her, and Beverley's eyes filled with tears.

Annabelle looked stunning – beautiful, happy, and radiant – everything a bride should be, and when Annabelle met the gaze of her groom, her tinkling laugh rang out.

Terence walked her slowly towards Ron, Izzie following solemnly behind, but when she caught Ron's eye a huge grin appeared on her little face.

As soon as Annabelle reached Ron, Beverley heard him say, 'You are beautiful,' and she began to well up.

Giggling, Annabelle wrinkled her nose at him, then handed her bouquet to Izzie for safekeeping.

The registrar waved for silence as the bride and groom turned to face her, but a small kerfuffle from the back made her glance up. Ron turned around to see what was going on, and nudged Annabelle.

Annabelle clapped her hands, and to Beverley's surprise she waved.

Wondering what was going on, Beverley also turned to look, but Pepe whined and began tugging at his lead, so she transferred her attention to her dog, hoping he wouldn't make her regret bringing him.

'Behave, 'she hissed. 'Don't be naughty.'

He didn't calm down though, and the tugging grew more insistent until she looked up to see why he was getting in such a tizzy – and froze.

Andrew was trying to tiptoe down the side of the bandstand, avoiding the aisle and going for the scenic route of dodging around the chairs.

He was heading straight for her!

Beverley had just enough time to register that he was wearing his suit and that he had Twinkle with him who was dressed in her bandana finery, when he reached her side and lowered himself onto the chair next to her with a grunt.

The two dogs were delighted to see each other, and a sniff-fest was accompanied by little yips of happiness.

Beverley was mortified and she bared her teeth in a grimace, realising everyone was staring at them. Strangely though, they were all smiling. Even May. Her sister was nodding, and when May gave her a double thumbs-up, Beverley wondered whether this was a dream, and she would find herself naked and doing the cha-cha before she woke in a cold sweat.

When the registrar once more called for silence and Beverley was still fully clothed, she knew this was real.

'What are you doing here?' she whispered, barely able to get the words out because her throat was so dry. Her heart was thumping so hard she thought she might pass out, and her hands were clammy. Oh, God, she was going to faint…

'Later, 'Andrew said, out of the side of his mouth.

She stared at him blankly, ignoring the registrar who had just launched into her spiel. 'But—'

'Shh. I love you.'

Huh? 'Did you say you love me?'

'Yes, shh, Ron and Annabelle are about to be married.'

Beverley raised her unruly, unplucked eyebrows. 'Is that so? I hadn't realised.'

'Shh!'

***

The canapes looked delicious, but Beverley was too het up to eat any. She did polish off a glass of champagne though. And then another.

'Well?' she demanded.

Andrew hadn't left her side, except for when her presence had been required for a photo, and this was the first chance she'd had to ask him what was going on. She was pleased to see him, but she was also wary – what had changed for him to turn up today? She had been persona non grata on Monday, their relationship at an end. Yet he had rocked up today as though she hadn't spent the last five days breaking her heart over him.

He owed her an explanation. And an apology.

She mightn't accept it though… Once bitten, twice shy, and all that.

But she couldn't deny that she was still madly in love with him, or that he looked bloody gorgeous in that suit.

Andrew picked up a glass of bubbly and downed it in one. 'I'm sorry.'

'So you should be! I loved you.'

'*Loved?*' He gazed at her with a stricken expression and seemed to collapse in on himself.

'Excuse me, can I just get to the…?' Aunt Madge's carer eased between them to grab a couple of canapes.

Beverley took hold of Andrew's elbow and pulled him to the side. 'OK, *love*. I still love you. But believe me when I say I wish I didn't.'

'Please don't say that.'

'It's true.' She refused to look at him and instead she fixed her eyes on Ron and Annabelle who were having a series of arty shots taken on the beach.

'I've hurt you badly, haven't I?'

'Duh!'

'If it's any consolation, I was hurting just as much.'

'Good, I'm glad. But I sincerely doubt you were.' She jabbed herself in the chest. 'Dumpee,' then pointed to him, 'Dumper.'

'I didn't want to break up with you.'

'So why did you?'

'Judith made me.'

Beverley had just taken a slurp of the very moreish champagne, and almost spat it out. Fishing a hankie out of her bag, she dabbed at her mouth. 'I've heard it all now,' she said in disbelief.

'It's true. She gave me an ultimatum – you or her.'

Beverley was flabbergasted. 'She *didn't!* I did get the impression she wasn't keen on me, but to say *that?* Bloody hell.'

'She seemed to think you were after my money.'

Beverley barked out a laugh so loud it made the dogs jump. 'She's not all there. Why would I want your money? I didn't know you had any, for a start. Are you a secret millionaire?'

'I wish.' He sighed. 'I've got some savings put by, and a decent pension, and then there's the house…'

'I've got my own savings, and pension, and I've got my own house. Kind of.'

'You told her that you didn't own the house you are living in, and she thought…' He trailed off, before finishing in a rush, 'That you were a gold-digger.'

'I've been called some names in my time, but never a gold-digger,' she said. 'You can tell your daughter that the only reason I don't own my own house is because I signed it over to Kate so the government doesn't get its greedy paws on it if I have to go into a care home. But until that happens, and touch wood it never does—' she tapped her head '—I can live in it as long as I like. So there.' She stuck her tongue out, as cross as hell that Judith would say such a thing.

'I know,' he said, gently.

'Is that why you turned up today? Because you no longer believe I'm a gold digger and you want us to get back together? Hmph. That's not going to happen. Who told you anyway?'

'Ron. He came to see me.'

'He did? When?'

'Thursday. He wasn't happy. Leo told him what Judith had done.'

'*Leo?*' Was everyone in cahoots and going behind her back?

'Leo came to Brighton early because he was worried about me. Judith had told him about her ultimation, and that you and I were no longer together.'

'And whose fault is that?' Beverley interrupted.

'Mine. All mine. I know she's my daughter and I was terrified of losing her, but I should have trusted my instincts. I should never have let her dictate what I can and can't do. Anyway, back to my story: Leo spoke to Ron and told him what was going on. He also told him that he thought I was having a breakdown because I was so upset. He said that I love you, and that the only reason I broke up with you was because I didn't want to lose my daughter. Ron told me how badly you had taken it, and I felt awful. I had already decided I couldn't live without you, but I wasn't sure if you would want me back after what I had put you through. I didn't care whether you were a gold digger or not.'

'I'm not! I thought we had established that.'

'Ron told me about your house, but that had no bearing on my decision to try to win you back. I don't care about material things – all I care about is you.'

Beverley's heart melted, even though she had been trying not to feel any hope, because how could she trust a man who would do that to her, and one who had caused her this much heartache?

But she also understood. Judith was his daughter, and like any parent he would lay down his life for his child, no matter how much pain it caused him.

'We can't get back together,' she said, her heart breaking all over again. 'I can't let you choose me over your daughter. You'll regret it if you do. It's bad enough that you don't see her very often; imagine how you would feel if she cut off all contact with you? I can't let that happen.'

'You don't have to. Judith has seen the error of her ways. To be honest, her concern was more to do with the fear that her mother was being replaced.'

'I could never replace Vivienne,' Beverley said softly.

'No, you can't, but you can sit beside her in my heart. It's big enough for both of you. If you can forgive me, that is.'

'I think I can manage that,' Beverley said. 'You can kiss me if you want.'

'I most definitely want,' Andrew replied, and he put his hands on her shoulders and was just about to lower his head to hers, when the cheery voice of his grandson cried, 'Say cheese!'

***

Andrew watched Beverley ease her shoes off and rub her toes.

'I should never have worn heels,' she groaned. 'My feet are killing me.'

'I'm surprised you can feel them at all after the amount of wine you've drunk,' he teased. 'Never mind, the reception is almost over and you can go home and change into your pyjamas and slippers.'

'I am looking forward to my bed,' she admitted. 'I'm absolutely shattered. It's been a lovely day though, hasn't it?'

'It certainly has,' Andrew agreed.

He had started off the day as a bag of nerves as he'd got dressed in his wedding finery and wondering whether he would be welcome, or whether Beverley would send him away with a flea in his ear. And now here he was, with the reception winding down, his arm around the woman he loved and feeling on top of the world.

His face ached from all the smiling he had done, and his lips tingled from all the kissing, but he was so happy he could weep.

He and Beverley hadn't been the only ones to be all lovey-dovey. It seemed that attending a wedding brought out the romance in people. Kate and Brett had been sharing kisses all day, and May and Terence had been spotted gazing into each other's eyes and whispering sweet nothings. Even Helen and her fella had shared a brief kiss, and Ron and Annabelle had been so loved up it had been a delight to see.

Then there was his grandson. In between taking hundreds of photos, Leo had managed to catch the eye of Beverley's eldest granddaughter.

Andrew hadn't been surprised, because Leo was a very good-looking young man and he oozed confidence. He and Ellis, being of the same age, had gravitated towards each other, and Andrew had to admit they made a striking looking pair. Ellis was extremely pretty and she had an ethereal quality about her that was very attractive. Portia was more like her maternal grandmother, slightly left of centre and quite outspoken. She would be a force to be reckoned with when she was older, just like Beverley.

He squeezed Beverley tighter, happiness surging through him and threatening to spill over, and he wanted to shout it from the rooftops. However, this was Ron and Annabelle's day, and although they had been very kind in allowing him to come to the wedding and hiding it from Beverley until it had been too late for her to object, he didn't want to intrude any more than he had done already.

'Ron and Annabelle are staying here tonight,' Beverley announced, sending him a sideways look. 'May and Terence are babysitting. You know what that means, don't you?'

Andrew shook his head. He didn't dare hope…

'It means that I've got an empty house.' She raised her eyebrows suggestively.

'Is that so?'

'Uh, huh.'

'And?' Andrew knew full well what she was getting at, but he was enjoying teasing her.

'*And*,' she said, elbowing him in the ribs, 'you come back to mine this evening.'

'I haven't got any pyjamas,' he said.

'Don't worry – you're not going to need them!'

CHAPTER 26

Beverley wrinkled her nose. 'I thought we could have a lazy day, slobbing around and watching TV.' She was exhausted after the excitement of yesterday – both from the wonderful wedding and from her reconciliation with Andrew – and couldn't think of anything better than cuddling on the sofa.

'We can do that later. The dogs need a walk, and I don't know about you, but I'm starving.'

'I can pop a couple of pieces of bread in the toaster,' she offered. Andrew was right though, the dogs did need a walk. It wasn't fair to keep them cooped up all day just because she didn't feel like going out.

'It's nearer lunch than breakfast,' Andrew pointed out.

'OK, I'll make us a sandwich.'

'Let's go out to brunch. We could have an all-day breakfast.'

Beverley's tummy rumbled. An all-day breakfast sounded just the ticket – crispy bacon, grilled tomatoes, beans, a fried egg… Yum. And the bonus was that she didn't have to cook it herself or do the washing up.

'Does the café we usually go to do all-day breakfasts?' she asked. 'I can't remember.' She only ever looked in the cabinet where the cakes were displayed.

'I don't think so.' He clapped his hands. 'I know! Let's go to the bandstand café.'

'Now? We were only there yesterday.'

'I hadn't forgotten, but we had such a lovely time, it'll be nice to go back and have a sit-down meal. The dogs can play on the beach afterwards.' He glanced out of the window. 'Come on,' he urged. 'It's such a lovely morning, we'll only regret not making the most of it.'

He had a point.

'Let me get changed.' She was still in her pyjamas.

Andrew was wearing a pair of Ron's jogging bottoms and an old T-shirt with Def Leppard on the front. 'I'm not going out like this,' he said. 'I don't even like Def Leppard.'

'Do you want to go home and get changed?' she asked.

'Nah, I'll wear my suit, but without the tie. I can always take the jacket off if I get too warm.'

'In that case, I'd better wear something nice,' Beverley said. She didn't want to look like a bag lady if he was all dressed up.

'Great. How about we treat ourselves and get a taxi? I'll pay.'

'So you should, considering I only want you for your money.'

Andrew tutted at her, and she went upstairs to find something nice to wear, love and contentment filling her. Last night had been magical. It was as though the upset they had suffered this past week had brought them even closer together.

As she rooted around in her wardrobe, asking herself what May would wear (the bright orange and yellow top that she had just picked up probably wouldn't be May's first choice – or even her fiftieth) Beverley brimmed with happiness. It was too soon to think about asking Andrew to marry her, but she would do it at some point, now that Ron and Annabelle's wedding was out of the way. She'd give it a couple of weeks, though.

'The taxi is here,' Andrew called, and Beverley grabbed her bag and trotted down the stairs. Pepe and Twinkle already had their leads on and were waiting in the hall, tails wagging.

Beverley ushered everyone out, locked up, then took a step back in shock.

On the pavement, its engine idling, was a limousine.

'Sorry,' Andrew said, as the driver got out and hurried to the back of the car. 'This was all they had. They asked if I minded, because it was supposed to be on another job but it was cancelled.'

'I don't mind at all,' Beverley said, letting the driver open the door for her and climbing in. 'Can we have you on the way back?' she asked him.

'You're—' the chap began, but Andrew interrupted him.

'I highly doubt it, Bev. It's not every day you get sent a limo instead of a black cab.'

'Pity, I could get used to this.'

'Do you think I'm made of money?' he joked, and they shared a knowing look.

Beverley settled back to enjoy the short ride to the seafront, glad that Andrew had talked her into it. She couldn't wait to tell May all about it – her sister would be well jealous.

The sea came into view, the bandstand a distant blob on the horizon, and Beverley wound the window down to let Pepe have a sniff of salty air. By the time the limo pulled into the curb he was scrabbling to get out.

Pepe adored the beach and loved the sea: it was a shame he hadn't been allowed near it yesterday. But she would rectify that today. He could play in the waves for as long as he wanted. There was no rush to go anywhere or do anything – she and Andrew could please themselves.

Brunch first though: she was starving.

The car had pulled up directly in front of the bandstand, and when Beverley alighted she began to walk the short distance along the promenade to the steps leading to the café underneath, but Andrew caught hold of her elbow.

'This way,' he said, and guided her towards the bandstand itself.

'You can't get to the café from there,' she reminded him. 'We need to go down those steps.'

'We're not going to the café.'

'But I thought you said—'

'We are eating there.' He pointed to the exact spot where Ron and Annabelle had exchanged vows, and Beverley was surprised to see a table and two chairs in what should have been an empty space.

The table sported a pristine white cloth, sparkling glassware and was laid for two.

'I don't understand.' She blinked owlishly, trying to work out what was going on.

'This is my way of saying sorry. I hope you don't mind?' Andrew looked so anxious that Beverley's heart went out to him.

'This is so incredibly thoughtful! I love it. Thank you.' She pressed her lips against his. 'Can I still have a cooked breakfast?'

Andrew chuckled. 'You can have whatever you like, my love.'

My love... Oh, that sounded so sweet.

They sat down as a waitress stood by to take their order, and whilst they waited for their food to arrive, Beverley reached across the table to hold Andrew's hand. 'Have I told you how much I love you?'

'Once or twice. I love you, too.'

She uttered a contented sigh. What a perfectly romantic thing to do. Andrew was definitely a keeper and she intended to hang on to him. She couldn't think of a time when she had been as happy as she was now, and she didn't want this moment to end.

The food was delicious (you can't go wrong with a cooked breakfast, she said to herself) and Andrew had talked her into having a Buck's Fizz to go with it. The waitress had even brought out a couple of pork and beef sausages for the dogs, as well as a bowl of water for them. Andrew had thought of everything.

'There is one more thing,' he said. 'I've ordered a bottle of champagne. Would you like some?'

'Are you trying to get me drunk so you can have your wicked way with me?' she joked, feeling slightly lightheaded already from the Buck's Fizz. Or was that because she was so deliriously happy and in love with the most wonderful man? Accepting a flute of pale bubbly liquid, she took a delighted sip.

Andrew smiled. 'Absolutely. I'd do anything to get you into bed. Including this.' He pulled a smoke-grey velvet pouch out of his pocket and placed it on the table.

Beverley stared at it in confusion. It looked remarkably similar to the pouch she had bought for Pepe to carry Ron and Annabelle's wedding rings down the aisle. If she wasn't mistaken, it *was* the same pouch.

Gingerly she picked it up and turned it over in her hands. There was something inside.

'Open it,' he urged. 'Carefully.'

Bewildered, she undid the drawstring and tipped the pouch up.

A ring tumbled into her hand: a ring made of white metal with a glittering lilac stone in the middle, surrounded by smaller equally glittery white stones.

Andrew slid off his chair with a grunt and knelt beside her.

'What—?' she began.

'Will you marry me? I love you, Beverley, and I can't imagine my life without you in it. Actually, I can, and I don't like it one little bit, so please say yes.'

Beverley swallowed. Her pulse was racing and her heart was going like the clappers. 'Marry you?'

'Yes.'

'But—' she began again.

He blurted, 'At least say you'll think about it?'

'You didn't let me finish. *I* was going to ask *you* to marry *me*.'

'Today?'

Well… no… not today exactly. But soon.'

'You were?' His eyes shone. 'Is that a yes?'

'Yes, it's a yes!'

'Give that here,' he said, reaching for the ring and sliding it onto the third finger of her left hand. It was a perfect fit. 'It's platinum with a lilac amethyst surrounded by diamonds.'

'It's beautiful. Oh, Andrew, I'm so happy.' She held her hand out to admire the sparkle.

'So am I.' He scrambled awkwardly to his feet. 'And so are they,' he added cryptically, then leant over the balustrade and shouted, 'She said yes!'

A cheer went up from below, and amongst the clapping and whooping Beverley could have sworn she heard Ron yell, 'Thank God for that!'

'Andrew…?' Beverley turned to her brand-new fiancé, a question on her lips, but before she could ask it she saw a stream of people hurrying towards the steps.

Ron, Annabelle, Kate, Brett, the kids, May… Judith.

Judith?

'Isn't that your daughter?' Beverley asked.

'Yes, it is!'

'But—'

'No more buts. She knows how much you mean to me, and she's given us her blessing. She'll apologise later. Oh, and you might want to say thanks to Ron and Leo for giving me a kick up the bum, to Annabelle for helping me choose the ring, and to May for organising all this in less than a day. Your sister is a force to be reckoned with.'

'I'll thank them now,' Beverley said, but Andrew pulled her into his arms.

'Oh, no, you won't. There's something else you have to do first.'

'What?'

'Kiss me.'

This time neither of them heard Leo when he shouted 'Cheese!' but both of them felt the boop of dog's noses on their legs… just in case their owners had forgotten they were there.

THE END...
APART FROM...

Beverley and Andrew were married the following September. The ceremony took place in glorious autumn sunshine on Brighton's bandstand. The bride wore white, but she did have purple hair. The groom wore grey. His tie matched the bride's hair colour.

She had three bridesmaids but didn't insist on a page boy. Unfortunately, Pepe didn't fulfil his dream of being a ring bearer, but he and Twinkle were given a nice chew each to keep them quiet during the ceremony.

The reception wasn't held in The Gillespie Rooms. It was held at the funfair on the pier. The wedding invitations advised everyone to wear flat shoes.

Helen was invited – she brought a different plus one. He didn't propose to her the next day, but she's still hopeful. After all, if Beverley can bag a husband at her age and with her fashion sense, then surely Helen can...?

If you enjoyed this book, you might want to take a look at the other books in the series

A Typical Family Christmas
A Typical Family Summer

About the Author

Liz Davies writes feel-good, light-hearted stories with a hefty dose of romance, a smattering of humour, and a great deal of love.

She's married to her best friend, has one grown-up daughter, and when she isn't scribbling away in the notepad she carries with her everywhere (just in case inspiration strikes), you'll find her searching for that perfect pair of shoes. She loves to cook but isn't very good at it, and loves to eat - she's much better at that! Liz also enjoys walking (preferably on the flat), cycling (also on the flat), and lots of sitting around in the garden on warm, sunny days.

She currently lives with her family in Wales, but would ideally love to buy a camper van and travel the world in it.

www.ingramcontent.com/pod-product-compliance
Lightning Source LLC
Chambersburg PA
CBHW050752190726
48285CB00005B/1628